HIDDEN BEHIND THE
MIST OF ARROW LAKES

SO DEEP ARE THE SINISTER SECRETS
THAT HIDE IN PLAIN SIGHT.

HIDDEN BEHIND THE MIST OF ARROW LAKES

A NOVEL INSPIRED BY REAL EVENTS

Lucia Mann

Aperion Books

AGOURA HILLS, CALIFORNIA

Aperion Books™
Agoura Hills, California

Copyright © 2023 by Lucia Mann
www.LuciaMann.com

The story and persons in this book are based on historical events. However, some of the events have been dramatized and certain identifying details have been changed to protect the privacy of individuals.

10 9 8 7 6 5 4 3 2 1
First Edition 2023
Printed in the United States of America

ISBN: 978-0-9856039-7-7
Library of Congress Control Number: 2023915929

Cover & book design by Dynamic Book Design
www.DynamicBookDesign.com

Disclaimer

HIDDEN AMONG THE MISTS OF ARROW LAKES is grounded in historical facts that have been uncovered through thorough, extensive research, interviews, and publicly available information. The story incorporates real-life historical figures as a contextual backdrop for some additional characters. Certain names and scenes have been fabricated to enhance the dramatic effect, and some of the supporting characters might be composites or entirely fictional.

Regardless of your personal belief in the authenticity of these events, it is crucial to consider the existing historical evidence when shaping your perspectives.

Dedication

I FIRMLY BELIEVE THAT NO ONE can definitively know the number of Jewish men, women, children, and babies murdered during the Holocaust, also known as *Shoah*, from 1941 to 1945. (The word *Holocaust* is derived from the Greek word *holokaiston*, which means "*sacrifice by fire*.")

This book is dedicated to all the countless souls who perished in Adolf Hitler's killing operations that stretched across German-occupied Europe and Russia during World War II. And dedicated to the courageous, who risked their own lives to save the persecuted, and to the millions of Jewish families, whose lives were ripped apart, never to see the assemblage of normality ever again.

I also dedicate this book to the survivors, those whose lives are forever damaged, and to those who sank into madness.

This moving quote by Elie Wiesel, himself a survivor, brought tears to my eyes:

Never shall I forget the little faces of the children whose bodies turn into wreaths of smoke under a silent blue sky.

Last but not least, this writing is primarily dedicated to Maria, my mother, who survived a notorious death camp in Poland.

Acknowledgments

My deepest gratitude goes to all who have assisted me in this writing journey of insuperable tragedy. It has been the most challenging of all my writings.

I'm grateful to Israeli Intelligence—Mossad, the Simon Wiesenthal Center in Los Angeles, and to the British and Canadian Intelligence. Without their kind help, this book could not have been authentically written.

Table of Contents

PART ONE

The Romanovs

PART TWO

The Past and the Present
›‹◊◊›‹

PART THREE

The Atrocities
›‹◊◊›‹

Table of Contents

PART FOUR
Arrow Lakes Valley Connections

EPILOGUE
Crimes Against Humanity

Author's Preface
There is nothing as
powerful as truth!

I HAVE NO DESIRE TO CHANGE innumerous inaccurate facts uncovered during my exhaustive research of German, Russian, and other historical documentation. Nobody knows exactly how many innocent Jewish people were put to death or survived World War II. Despite the conflicting history, I did my best to present what I believe to be the most perceptible.

What drove me to pen this story? I've never thought of myself as a controversial writer, but just a writer whose truth has forever been my fight, goal, and oxygen.

Even though generations have passed, the remembrance of the cold-blooded slaughter of humans in the Holocaust *must* never be lost to the marching of time. After ground breaking work of historical investigation, I now present my version of the history of the Holocaust.

World War II began on September 1, 1939, with Nazi Germany's invasion of Poland and ended with the signed admission of defeat by the Germans on May 8, 1945. After the war, millions of German citizens, who'd accepted every word spewed from Hitler's mouth without doubt, enabled his rise and stay in power. The German population was unaware that they were manipulated by a mentally unbalanced mind.

Even though many years have passed, Germans who accepted Hitler's every word as being truth resumed their everyday lives as if crimes never happened. It's the oldest story: "Honestly, I didn't know what was going on!"

These unconscionable liars took the homes and possessions of their missing Jewish neighbors. Survivors lost their clothes, jewelry, musical instruments, artwork, furs, and their bank accounts to their neighbors. Dispassion is an unforgivable attitude toward Holocaust survivors who tried to reclaim what was rightfully theirs, from their unscrupulous neighbors.

And what about the offspring of these human snakes? Did they inherit their parents' ill-gotten gains? Beyond a shadow of a doubt!

Close to my home in British Columbia, the Arrow Lakes region, I discovered "Nazi-tainted" children and relatives born during and after the war who have embraced new identities by changing one or two letters of their last or birth names to avoid recognition. They live a carefree existence with no worries about money or need to work. They own opulent homes, drive luxury vehicles, and keep only fellow compatriots' company.

Research informs me that 26,973 persons have been honored as "Righteous among Nations" —those who risked their lives to save Jews from extermination.

Among Arrow Lakes' residents is a brave woman whom I interviewed. She risked her own life to shelter two orphaned sisters during the war. The sisters now live in the United States and remain in contact with the woman who saved them. This woman, who I will call "Sabine," has my admiration and respect.

However, I had to point out to her that Jews are not a race, as Adolf Hitler branded, "It is *faith,* just like Christian and Muslim beliefs!"

Although seventy-eight years have passed, infamous Nazi camp guards, collaborators, and Brown Shirts (Hitler Youth recruitment) remain unexposed here in Arrow Lakes.

The crossing of "fated" paths inspired this controversial story! I will now bring this storytelling to life because that's what I do for living—find things out!

On a summer's day in July 2017, I stopped at a farmers' market in Arrow Park, BC, and an elderly woman came up to me and introduced herself, "Hi, I'm Betty Beals. I'm told that you are Lucia Mann, an investigative journalist. Is this correct?"

"I *was,* but now I'm happily retired writing books." I could never have guessed that our meeting would begin a long journey into the sinister secrets hidden behind the mist of Arrow Lakes.

Blue-tinted circles around octogenarian irises met mine, "Maybe what I *know* will entice you to come out of retirement."

My *trained* mind sparked. Neurons fired with immediate intrigue—*tell me more.*

You may wonder why I have emphasized: *trained*. I will tell you.

Up to now, I have not disclosed my former profession as a board-certified expert in body language, the science of nonverbal signals such as gestures, facial expressions, and eye gaze movements; therefore, I *know* when a person is truthful or deceitful! In the past, when I was handed an assignment from Behavior-analytic Services (a service which helps to decrease inappropriate behaviors and teaches individuals functional skills), I stayed on it come rain or shine!

Though I am long retired, my "Intel credibility privileges" still allow me "a foot in the door" to access information that's unavailable to the public.

With a lovely summer breeze cooling the high temperatures, Betty smiled like a naughty child. *For goodness sake, spit it out!*

"I'd like to invite you to tea," she offered. "Is tomorrow afternoon, okay?"

"I would love to visit," I eagerly replied. "See you tomorrow."

Armed with her address, I arrived at her farmhouse on Walnut Grove (British Columbia) a little before 2:00 p.m. with my notepad. The chat began with her background setting.

Betty, I learned, was born in Chester County, Pennsylvania, and kept me spellbound with colorful stories, primarily about being raised solely by females. Her grandmother, mother, and two aunts were Protestant Christians known as Quakers, Betty informed me. (Quaker is a religious movement that originated in Great Britain during the seventeenth century by George Fox and Margaret Fells.)

Betty revealed that her relatives were also abolitionists. "My great-grandmother participated in the Underground Railroad," she proudly announced. (The Underground Railroad is a network of secret routes and safe houses established in the United States early-to-mid-nineteenth century to provide shelter to enslaved Africans.)

One of her stories and her body language, however, didn't ring true. She said that, as a small child, she had traveled with her mother and aunts in a wagon pulled by oxen along the Oregon Trail to obtain free land. I'm well-read on the Oregon Trail. It was developed in 1812 as a wagon-safe passage over the Continental Divide at South Pass into present-day Wyoming. In 1836, the first migrant train traversed the trail. Betty is eighty-seven years old, which does not fit the time line. You can do the math! Her reasoning for this far-fetched tale remains answered.

I wanted to know the reason behind my invitation but got distracted. "Betty, how did you end up here in Lower Arrow Lakes?"

My background in reading people did not prime me for her disclosure. "Well, my dear, I was raised to believe that *all* men are demons of lust, and that I'd be in great peril if I even spoke to a man. That fear changed in the spring of 1948. I was at the basin stand, washing dishes and saw a dark-haired young man exiting one of our hay barns. I had never seen a male on our farm."

Her voice faded to thoughts that had occupied my mind: *Why was her household comprised solely of women? Was it merely exercis-*

ing power through feminism or a deep-seated contempt for the op-posite sex?

A grin crossed my lips. When my children asked *why* I retorted, "Because WHY is a letter you can't make straight!"

With ears back into focus, I paid attention to Betty's elucidation. "My mother told me that he was a tractor mechanic from the city, come to fix our broken harvester. The next day, while they tended to the animals and soybean fields, I saw his vehicle parked outside the barn. I just had to see for myself. 'How ya doing, pretty girl?' he said in a buttery Southern drawl. His gleaming white teeth, coffee-brown eyes, fringed with thick lashes, and long hair, braided like an Indian made my heart flutter. To cut a long story short, two days later, we eloped and headed for the Canadian border in his Ford pickup. I think we traveled about three hundred miles before arriv-ing in Ontario."

"We stopped there for a while, and then we drove across Cana-dian Provinces, stopping at farms to work for food, gas, and a place to sleep. It was in Saskatoon, Saskatchewan, that our nomad lives improved. Lucas spotted a poster pinned to a store wall: *Sharecrop-pers urgently needed in the Arrow Lakes Valley.*"

Betty paused to sip tea. "Lucas and I began work for Bill Oakes, an elderly dairy farmer in Arrow Lakes. He gave us a small, rustic timber cabin without running water or electricity."

Betty shut her eyes, inhaled sharply, and then continued, "Three-hundred and sixty-five days, year after year, we worked our fingers to the bone to save up enough money to buy this parcel of land. Enough of my past. I want to mention your well-written books. I've read every one of them. I must say that you are a good writer."

"I'm humbled and honored. Thank you, Betty."

"Your penmanship is *the voice of the voiceless*, which brings me to why I invited you here." *At last,* my small voice rejoiced.

"Check out why Germans came in droves to this valley. I don't think it's a coincidence." Betty made eye contact. "You know what I think? I bet they are hiding terrible Nazi pasts."

My thoughts scrambled: *Was there credible evidence to support this? Or was it just another of her colorful stories?* I'm not a fan of gossip, so I probed, "Please explain, dear lady."

Betty's, *I got you thinking,* smirk penetrated through me. "In the early fifties, sixties, and seventies, many Germans arrived here in Arrow Lakes Valley, buying up large acreage lots, lakefront properties, living a life of extravagant luxury." Betty ran her fingers through her thinning white hair, waiting for a memory door to open.

"Ah," she smiled. "I must tell you about the man who appeared in my garden in the spring of 1960, who I believe is *also* hiding his past."

"I was looking out my kitchen window, and there in my apple orchard was a skinny, black horse and its rider as naked as the day he was born! I rushed outside. 'This is private property!' The fellow inched his emaciated horse forward toward me. '*Krowa* has gone,' he said. I had no clue what a '*krowa*' was. 'You are trespassing on my property. Please leave.' His steely blue eyes ran right through me. He turned the horse, repeatedly bellowing, '*Krowa, Krowa!*'"

"I telephoned my closest neighbor, Thomas Funkle, who informed me the stranger in my garden was my new neighbor. I didn't even know Thomas had his property up for sale. There were 'For Sale' signs outside the driveway. Thomas told me the buyer had paid over his asking price in wads of American dollars. When I asked who my new neighbors were, Thomas revealed that the buyers signed, Count Andrew and Princess Anna Polanski, country of birth, Russia."

Betty's voice became inaudible. *Are you kidding me?*

Like a crafty chess master, two steps ahead, my thoughts maneuvered into position. *Why did a purported nobleman and his royal wife select Thomas's property? The small cabin sat on six acres and was in shambles. It had no plumbing. This cabin with an outhouse toilet was undeniably no home fit for a royal! Why were they living off the grid? And Polanski is not a Russian last name, but one hundred percent Polish!*

Sounds a bit shady, right? I made a mental note to check into their backgrounds.

Betty wasn't finished sending my brain into hyperactivity. "Do you know they hold parties in their homes on *Kristallnacht*? Do you know what that is?"

"Yes, Betty, I'm much acquainted with the *Night of Broken Glass*."

The "Night of Broken Glass" was named for the unmatched sadistic attacks on Jewish properties before World War II. It foreshadowed Adolf Hitler's Final Solution blueprint to exterminate all European Jewry.

The violence was fueled by the murder of a German government official in the French Embassy in Paris! On November 9th, 1938, Herschel Grynzspan, a seventeen-year-old Polish Jew refugee in Paris, learned that his parents had been sent to a German labor camp and ultimately died from hunger.

Herschel snuck into the Embassy and shot Ernst von Rath, the third secretary in the German delegation, dead.

In retaliation for Ernst's death, Gestapo Chief Heinrich Müller dispatched telegrams to every *Bundespolizei* (federal police) across Germany:

IMMEDIATE ACTIONS AGAINST
THE JEWS, ESPECIALLY
THEIR SYNAGOGUES, WILL TAKE PLACE
THROUGHOUT GERMANY TONIGHT. YOU
HAVE MY BLESSING TO ARREST ANYONE
WHO DARES TO INTERFERE.

The anti-Semitic assaults commenced at midnight on November 10, when arsonists torched synagogues. Fire chiefs instructed the fire fighters, "Only intervene if the fire threatens adjacent Aryan properties."

Over two days, thousands of synagogues, some with worshipers locked inside, burned to the ground. While pyromania remained vigorously active, police officers, firefighters, and thugs smashed storefront windows.

Residences, hospitals, and schools were also vandalized, and tombstones were defaced with swastikas. Hate-fueled marauders raped Jewish women and girls, despite severe penalties regarding sexual relations between Jews and German citizens. Their actions would have no consequences because the rape victims were shot or strangled to death. Those who didn't perish in the fires or by murder were arrested, flung into trucks, and transported to one of the first of one thousand labor camps built—Dachau.

Countless defenseless souls in death camps across Germany and Poland perished from malnutrition, worked to death, or succumbed to virulent diseases such as tuberculosis, typhoid, meningitis, dysentery, malaria, and from physical injuries that resulted from brutal beatings, whiplashing, and the dreaded, "Sic'em," commands by the dog handlers to attack prisoners. Also, interned in these "deathtraps" were artists, intellectuals, the physically and mentally disabled, and homosexuals, who were immediately castrated. Anyone who Hitler saw unfit for his *new* Germany were sent to death camps.

But only Jewish men, women, and children were subjected to human experimentation. Medical research was crucial to curtailing the malaria epidemic raging across Germany. Jewish "guinea pigs" were subjected to burning injections of extracts from mucus glands of female mosquitoes. Many succumbed to agonizing deaths.

According to entomologists, mosquitoes are the *deadliest* creatures on Earth. Over one million people worldwide die from mosquito-borne disease each year.

Before the unthinkable Kristallnacht events, the Nazi government coerced Jews to migrate to other nations. Only affluent Jews could meet those terms. For those who did not have the means or have relatives to go to foreign countries, the Führer had an evil scheme to rid Germany of its remaining Jews—*Genocide*.

I take issue with Holocaust disbelievers.

The mass murder of Jewish people is *not* fiction.

Following the attacks on Jewish-owned properties, synagogues, hospitals, and schools, the destruction amounted to millions of Reichsmarks. Jewish communities across Germany were fined two million Reichsmarks for dirtying the streets with rubble. Unbelievably, the victims of anti-Semitism, elected as *enemies* of the State, were ordered by the Reich Minister of Finance to hand over life insurance coverages, property policies, and Swiss bank accounts, not only of the living, but of the deceased as well.

Another outrageous order mandated that the cleanup was to be carried out by Jewish laborers only. Hefty fines awaited non-Jewish citizens who only wanted to aid their neighbors. Believe me, I'm not making this up!

There are two or more sides to any story, right? Angry thoughts of neighbors profiting from the dead and the living Jews swallowed up my slumber for many a night.

It's hard to believe anything when one hasn't slept for three days. But I couldn't stop envisioning the jaws of pliers ripping out gold teeth from Jewish mouths to be melted into ingots. Gold wedding bands were yanked from fingers, some cut off swollen fingers. Beautiful long, black hair removed from their roots to be knitted into socks for German soldiers. Soft flesh tattooed with ink intentionally made from pig's blood. I visualized roaring flames into enormous gas chambers and smelt burning flesh.

Mountains of corpses, children's heads beaten against walls, some thrown alive into ovens...these images filled my disturbed mind with mixed emotions of rage, anger, sadness, and the "Y" one can't make straight.

In the quiet of the night in my office, I reached out to a retired Mossad contact of mine via email:

 Aharon, I need your help.

I received a response ten hours later.

Shalom, my dear friend. It's been a while since we last communicated, actually many years. How are you? And how can I be of assistance?

I inundated the Israeli intelligence agent and World War II expert.

Question: What became of the extracted gold fillings of concentration camp victims?

Fillings smelted into gold bars to pay for the war lined the pockets of Hitler's inner circle for their lavish lifestyles. How do you think they paid for expensive mink coats for their wives and mistresses? Hugo Blaschke, a dentist in Auschwitz, left ten kilograms of dental gold to his wife and four children. His wife died shortly after the war. One of his children lives in Canada. My Israeli contact bracketed: *I will send you more details and check into the German names you have provided.*

Shockingly, a verified fact ended that email:

The largest commercial bank in Germany is still holding thirteen hundred twenty pounds of gold nuggets from extractions.

Purportedly, a few Germans commemorate *Kristallnacht* behind closed doors. How could my contact know this? Ah, I have long learned *never* to doubt intelligence sources!

Aharon's revelation provoked musings: *What else do these hiding-in-the-valley patriots celebrate—Hitler's birthday with a Nazi salute?*

I imagined their smug attitude: *Du blöder Hillbilly* (dumb hillbillies) *will never know.* I'm not here to judge, but in my opinion "bad" Germans represent everything rotten in Germany.

I contacted the Immigration Canada head office. "Why weren't background checks done on the tidal wave of non-Jewish German immigrants and other foreigners entering Canada after the war?"

"We were understaffed!" I found that response to be very disconcerting.

So, I tried again, "How many Nazi criminals snuck through the 'Welcome to Canada' doors?"

"Not sure what you mean."

WHAT?!

It was a brazen attempt to get out of telling the truth!

Maybe having shown proof of substantial bank accounts answers the failed system!

"Do you have a 'Wanted List' for Nazis here in Canada?"

"I can't answer that!" the irate voice said at the other end of the line.

Although four summers turned the corner, I never gave up the opportunity to do what I do best, which is to find truthful facts. The time had come to pen what had kept me awake for many nights. I rummaged through umpteen storage boxes looking for the notebook I'd carried to Walnut Grove.

Scrawled across the notepad's first page in stenography, I'd drafted:

The perfect hiding place is the one that's in plain sight. Followed by, *In the remoteness of chosen rural areas, they did not have to look over their shoulders!*

Spying is an itch that does not go away.

Finding the truth has been emotionally and mentally challenging.

Conclusively, I discovered that evil snakes *do* exist!

Do Nazi blood relatives have monsters inside them? Some do!

I set into motion my professional training, and, after viewing an old German photograph, I confronted an elderly German man on the main village street. The Nazi certainly did not suspect a blond, green-eyed person as Jewish.

"Guten nachmittag, mein Herr. Does *Kinder Sicherer Hafen* ring a bell?" (Children Safe Haven was an underground organization set up after World War II to protect the children and relatives of Nazis who had received their family's ill-gotten gains).

Ah, you just never know who is living beside you with no moral compass!

On that afternoon, our eyes locked. Edmund's face turned ashen, then his smooth and slick tongue went into verbal defense mode, "Never heard of it!" he growled like a rabid creature. "Stay away from me *or else!*" he ended in a snarly threatening tone.

I felt the tingling of goosebumps but then realized threats can be a guilty reaction.

I did not bite, but oh boy, I so wanted to! The Nazi did not realize verbalizing a threat is against the law!

A clueless, innocent retort would be spontaneous: "What the F are you talking about?"

These Nazi-blemished individuals who think they can remain veiled in the boondocks, and no one will know—think again!

For obvious reasons, I've masked the living and the dead, who heritably *are* connected to a vile, malevolent era in history.

Why they have not been shamed beats me! Do I want to find a dead creature hanging from my porch, or worse? Even though I walk a tightrope in this narration, do I regret embarking on this journey to uncover the truth? Not for one second! However, I admit there was hesitation: *Ummm, don't go there!*

Regardless, I will not live this life with hate in my heart, not on prejudice or judgment or feelings, but the writing of *Hidden Behind the Mist of Arrow Lakes* is deeply personal.

Why? Because I am the daughter of a Holocaust survivor! I owe it to my mother and to my relatives that perished in the Holocaust! And so, I have worked tirelessly to bring this story to life, combining my family history of these events and my emotional knowledge. The written word can have the ability to change history. So here we go. *Bring it on!*

Dirty looks, hate mail, or even a dead cat swinging from my porch is not going to stop me from revealing the truth about the most evil race in the twentieth century!

Introduction

Today I will once more be a prophet: if international finance Jewry in and outside Europe should succeed in plunging the nations once more into a world war, then the result will not be the Bolshevization of the earth, and thus the victory of Jewry, but the annihilation of the Jewish race in Europe.
    —ADOLF HITLER, REICHSTAG, JANUARY 30, 1939

HE *WAS* THE MONSTER under the bed everyone feared because this "banality of all evil" nearly succeeded in bringing the whole world to its knees. No one could have imagined what he could do until it was too late. However, Hitler's defeat in World War II put his ideology proclamation of "A Thousand-year Reich," down the toilet!

Why were the majority of Germans hypnotically attracted to Nazism following the World War I defeat?

Was it the product of social anxiety caused by millions of people being out of work after the first war?

In all likelihood!

Historians have documented that the outcome of World War I

became a national shame and humiliation of not just losing the war but being blamed for its inception.

The icing on the cake came when other European countries delivered punishment in the form of crushing debt repayment—financial restitution of 132 billion gold marks, approximately 33 billion USD today, enforced upon Germany under Article 231 of the Treaty of Versailles, signed in 1919.

The Treaty of Versailles was a peace agreement drafted in Paris, France, ending the Great War.

Germany was shut out of any deal-making while the Allies debated and could not agree. France wanted to remove the German threat. Great Britain wanted to preserve its status. The United States of America wanted a peaceful world with the establishment of the League of Nations, and Italy wished to take over the territories promised to them in 1915.

On May 7, the Treaty was presented to Germany. Predictably, they declined to sign. A month later, the Allies gave Germany an ultimatum, *sign or have the war resume!*

The four representatives of Allied powers were Clémenceau for France, Wilson for the United States of America, Lloyd George for Great Britain, and Orlando for Italy, the German Minister for Foreign Affairs, Müller, and a German jurist and politician from the Centre Party, Doctor Johannes Bell, who briefly served as Minister of Colonial Affairs and as Minister of Transport.

They accepted the *diktat* (peace) on June 17, 1919, ending the five-year conflict. This solemn occasion was undoubtedly not celebrated with decorum by die-hard Germans. This shameful occasion sowed an "even the score" mentality that sparked World War II.

There have been many power-hungry fools throughout history, but not as the origin of all evil, like a twisted iron rod associated with the most infamous name in history—*Adolf Hitler.*

Henceforth, a political fool emerges, a twisted human with an exaggerated sense of importance who believes he has divine super-human powers!

What made Hitler, the twentieth century's most hated person? His dysfunctional background has the answers.

At 6:30 p.m., Saturday, April 20, 1889, in the village of Braunau Am Inn, population 15,500, on the south bank of the Inn River, which separates Austria from Germany, a "bad seed," as I see it, indeed landed on Earth.

It's commonly argued that there is no such thing as a bad child. Why is it arguable? Clinical studies have revealed that psychopathic hereditary traits, maternal and paternal, *are* passed along through family ancestry, especially offspring of incest. But is there sufficient scientific evidence to prove abusive parenting leads to killer instincts? Or perhaps the "despise" of your own ancestral blood may contribute to homicidal instincts?

According to the studies conducted by Belgian researchers, Adolf Hitler had Jewish and African ancestral blood. My doubtful mind wants proof of this finding. Without DNA evidence, we don't know for certain the man who instigated the Holocaust was either Jewish, African, or a combination of both.

These findings solicit further explanation. Was Adolf Hitler told of his Jewish origins by a parent or a relative at a very young age? Could the potential of having Jewish blood triggered Hitler's anti-Semitism? It's possible because he had an obsessive hatred for Jews!

Sometimes there is a puzzle you cannot solve.

Hitler's psychological aberration worked because he mesmerized German citizens into believing the Jews were responsible for the country's economic crisis. The German race mocked the whole world. Why did other nations sit back and not step up sooner? Hadn't the maniacal Adolf provided clues in a beer hall speech in 1922?

Once I am in power, my first and foremost task will be annihilating the Jews. As soon as I have the power to do so, I will have gallows built in rows—at the Marienplatz in Munich, for example—as many as traffic allows. Then the Jews will be hanged indiscriminately, and they will remain hanging until they stink; they will hang there as long as the principles of hygiene permit. As soon as they have been untied, the next batch will be strung up, and so on down the line, until the last Jew in Munich has been exterminated. Other cities will follow suit, precisely in this fashion, until all of Germany has been thoroughly cleansed of Jews.
—ADOLF HITLER, OCTOBER 1922

After Paul von Hindenburg, who led the Imperial General Army during World War I, passed away from lung cancer on August 2, 1934, Adolf Hitler, with the help of his mentor Dietrich Eckert, an anti-Semitic, the founder of the Workers Party, and father of four young sons, was instrumental in creating the alter ego Adolf Hitler, who was immediately appointed Chancellor of Germany.

The Nazi Party was born. With supreme powers as Führer (Leader), he and his Nazi units considered the idea of mass deportation as a method of ridding Europe of the hated Jews. This summary, written by Timothy Snyder, a Yale historian, tries to pinpoint when Hitler chose murder as a means of removal.

It cannot be stressed enough that the Nazis did not know how to eradicate the Jews when they began the war against the Soviet Union in the summer of 1941. They could not be confident that SS men would shoot women and children in large numbers.

Hogwash! The Nazis *were* confident!

On December 18, 1940, Hitler issued *Führer Directive 21*, an order to invade the Soviet Union. He plotted to bring the Soviet population and its economic potential, natural resources such as oil and natural gas under German control with Operation Barbarossa (named after the Medieval Holy Roman conqueror, Emperor Frederick I, and the code name for the Nazi Germany invasion of the Soviet Union).

Hitler launched the Russian invasion on June 22, 1941. The mass murder of people commenced at the hand of the *"Einsatzgrüppen,"* aka Mobile Killing Units, which Heinrich Himmler (SS) established in 1939. It was assembled earlier by Otto Ohlendorf—the "Nazi Demon of Death" who allegedly has a close blood-relative in Arrow Lakes Valley, British Columbia, Canada.

So, who was Otto Ohlendorf? He was born into an impoverished family in February 1907 in northwest Germany and was a teenager when Germany suffered defeat in World War I. Otto ascended the educational ladder with a doctorate in jurisprudence (the philosophy of law), which secured him the position as director of World Economy and Maritime Transport in Kiel. Ohlendorf's ultra-reactionary ideas of National Socialism came to the attention of Reinhard Heydrich, who then appointed Ohlendorf as leader of the Einsatzgrüppen in 1936. The paramilitary death squads, thousands of wannabe teenage soldiers, and misfits, were individually chosen for their passionate belief in Nazi ideology and loyalty to Hitler.

The Einsatzgrüppen, who were unconscionable humans, did not need official commands. Their hate-filled hearts killed humans without a flick of an eyelid. Nazi Germany's state secret was "Record nothing." Hitler's evil puppets carried out the mass murders of men, women, children, babies, senior citizens, and disabled persons as if it was an everyday chore.

The Einsatzgrüppen's presence was a death sentence for the entire Russian Jewish population. They are responsible for killing around ninety thousand Soviet Jews, thirty thousand Roma, and twenty thousand communists.

Are these statistics accurate?

Hardly!

Charred bones of murdered humans are *still* being discovered across Russian soil today. There can be no rational justification for this!

Philipp Bouhler, the high-ranking Nazi official responsible for the euthanasia program that killed more than seventy thousand disabled people, stated, "Eagerly, he (Hitler) took the solution to the

Jewish problem to its furthest extremes."

The pivotal moment for the decision to exterminate came on December 12, 1941, at a secretive meeting with fifty of Hitler's Nazi officials, including Joseph Goebbels, the Nazi Minister of Propaganda, and Hans Frank, Governor of occupied Poland. Though no documentation of this particular meeting survives, Goebbels did write in his journal found after the war:

Regarding the Jewish question, the Fuehrer is determined to clean the table. He prophesized that should the Jews once again bring about a world war, they would be annihilated. These were no empty words. The world war has come; therefore, the annihilation of the Jews has to be its inevitable consequence. The question has to be examined without any sentimentality. We are not here to pity Jews, but to have pity for our own German people. If the German people have sacrificed about 160,000 dead in the battles in the east, the instigators of this bloody conflict will have to pay for it with their lives.
—PAUL JOSEPH GOEBBELS, DECEMBER 13, 1941

German diplomat Otto Brautigam also penned on December 18, 1941:

As for the Jewish question, oral discussions have taken place and have brought about clarification.

Philipp Bouhler, the killer of handicapped people, stated in his journal:

Everything is going as intended.

A year later, in 1942, the Wannsee Conference was held. It was at this event where top government officials of Nazi Germany planned the deportation and extermination of Jews as a priority agenda.

Was Hitler solely responsible for the genocide?

How complicit were lower-level Nazis and members of the Order Police? "I was just following orders" doesn't cut it. After the fall of the Soviet Union, a surfeit of wartime bureaucratic records became available, proving just how much leeway Nazi officials had. Numerous Nazis involved in enacting the Final Solution were much more significant than previously believed.

Hitler's loathing of Jews, exterminating them like unwanted rodents, was loud and clear in public speeches. One of his proclamations took on a more precise sinister tone:

The wholesale slaughter of all Jews, including German Jews and Western European Jews, must be carried out systematically by gas chambers and concentration camps.

After this hate-filled proclamation, SS Chief Heinrich Himmler implemented *Endlösung* (Final Solution), ordering the first mass transport of Jews to extermination camps. That day sealed death sentences for all Europe's Jewry with a single signature.

Before World War II, approximately ten million Jewish people lived in Europe in 1933. The Nazi regime murdered six million European Jews and at least five million prisoners of war in concentration camps, pogroms, or ghettos, and mass executions, referred to as the Holocaust.

What became of these evil-minded Germans and their collaborators who participated in the slaughtering of innocent people?

Thousands escaped prosecution, fleeing to non-European countries such as Tasmania, Australia, Canada, South America, Central America, and privately owned islands. Governments and other refugees had no qualms about giving these maggots safe havens.

Why? Because most could bring to the table "pilfered" monetary assets. Then and now, countless human "vultures" profit from the dead.

Former Nazis, their offspring, and relatives, have prospered from the plunder of Jews, assets confiscated by their parents or relatives during World War II and after the war ended. These unconscionable folk now hide in plain sight.

PROLOGUE
The Koptyaki Boreal Forest, Russia
- Wednesday, July 18, 1918 -

They shared a doom against which
human morality had no defense.
—LUCIA MANN

AS THE CRIMSON ROBES OF A SUMMER SUN began to set, shrinking daylight to the ancient old growth Koptyaki forest with antediluvian trees towering well over one hundred feet tall, two orbs of intense light pierced through the dimming sunlight of the forest canopy layers. The rear-mounted, dark green Garford-Putilov armored truck traversed through bushwhacked terrain, tracking the white ribbon markers placed on trees for guidance. The forti- fied vehicle decelerated and, in a squeak of brakes, came to a high- pitched grating halt. Three heavyset, bushy-bearded uniformed men, displaying bright-red collar jacket tabs, dirty army footwear, and caps atop tousled hair, staggered out of the transportation.

Heavily intoxicated from copious shots of vodka, the older Bolshevik, with a leathery elongated face and sunken steel-blue eyes, staggered to the truck rear and began wrestling the rusty metal tailgate handle, declining to open. The forty-nine-year-old Commissioner Yakov Yurovsky's frustration boiled over. "Дерьо (Shit)," he cussed in slurred, inebriated speech. Many foul words followed, and finally, the impaired former watchmaker unlatched the corroded tailgate latch. Unsteady on his feet, he climbed in and dragged a lifeless body of a naked man, about five-foot-six, to the tail ledge. The Bolshevik's hardened, gristly face distorted as gloved hands clasped nose and mouth. Vomit threatening to expel the contents of his stomach, Yurovsky bellowed to his comrades taking a smoke break, "It stinks of piss, shit, and rotten eggs. Get here *now* and give me a hand to get them out before I puke."

His internal dialogue said something different. *What the hell have I gotten myself into?*

Yurovsky reflected on the unsettling telephone conversation that rerouted his arrangement to spend time with his wife, Ester, who complained, "I hardly see you, husband, and I can't take it anymore!"

"I promise I will make it up to you," he returned. Part of him wished he hadn't picked up the telephone receiver.

"Comrade Yurovsky, rumors are spreading fast," Commander Alexander Bogdanov's said. "People are demanding answers to where the bodies are. You *must* drive to "Four Brothers Mine" and retrieve them. Load them, and drive to Koptyaki. The gravediggers have placed white markers on a forest trail for you to locate the new burial site." The Bolshevik commander's voice increased in demanding intensity, "Make haste, Comrade. Time is crucial!"

Commissioner Yurovsky, who had long distanced himself from his Jewish roots, hadn't the nerve to examine this higher-ranking superior's order. But perplexed musings had struck a curious mind: *Why on earth move them? That mine has been closed for eighty years. No one goes there! Hadn't Benzene been poured through the nine-foot shaft coalface in an attempt to collapse the rock structure? What if—*

The uncomfortable thought of retrieving decomposing humans had made Yurovsky's skin crawl with millions of invisible creepy crawlies. The soldier had little choice but to get his shit together, or he could end up with the bodies.

Insubordination was a death sentence!

Shortly before noon, Yurovsky and his two comrades, Kirill and Artyom, arrived at Four Brothers Mine, an abandoned coalmine fifteen kilometers from Yekaterinburg, to carry out their macabre assignment. Yurovsky's helpers descended the vertical ninety-degree incline without nose and mouth coverings using a rope ladder. The possibility of toxic Benzene fumes lingering, eighty-year-old hazardous silica dust, or unstable rock face collapsing on them had not been brought up by their superior.

In restricted ventilation, Kirill and Artyom wrapped rope ties around the stiff necks of the eleven deceased strewn around the coal slag, who had lain there since the predawn hours of the previous day, July 17. Kirill hoisted the last body and unwittingly rehashed Yurovsky's earlier musings, "I don't see the point of removing them, do you?" Kirill contended. "No one is *ever* going to find them."

Artyom nodded, agreeing. "Orders are orders, Comrade. But I have an idea."

Kirill frowned angrily. "Yeah, and what is that?"

"Before we drag *them* out, let's take off their clothes. My wife would love that lace dress." Artyom gestured to the older woman's outfit. "What a perfect birthday gift to replace my wife's sack-cloth dress. I think the boy is about my son's age. He will *love* the fine clothes—"

Kirill interrupted his partner-in-crime's intentions. "Are you blind?" he scolded. "Take another look, idiot! The clothing is badly stained with dried blood and shredded with gunshot holes, bayonet slashes, and coal dust. No one could wash or sew these clothes to make them wearable!"

The deceased's outer garments remained undisturbed, but he was unaware that her underwear was gone. They had been violated.

Who committed necrophiliac acts? The answer would come many years later when one of the rapists drunkenly blabbed his mouth off to a monarchy sympathizer, "I knew the bitches *well*, especially the girls!" An amused smirk pursued his mouth. The digger ended, "I had *fun* with them before they were carted off."

One of their rapists hung from a beam in his home twenty-four hours later. Was it suicide or homicide? The latter is the most likely!

If the "tomb robbers" had only *known* that a fortune of royal gems was sewn into their corsets, what a life-altering discovery that may have been for those whose task was to rebury the dead!

In the fast-fading light, the dead were hurled into an eight-foot grave. Shoving index fingers up nostrils, Yurovsky grumbled, "Let's go. I can't stand the rotten stench anymore."

"It's going to get a lot worse if the hole is not quickly filled in," Kirill said.

Artyom laughed, "That's their job to bury stinky people, and they are fucking late!"

Halfway back to the truck, Yurovsky signed. "Hang on, I nearly forgot." He removed the 1914 hand grenade (known as a *bottle grenade* for its shape) from his belt trouser clip, walked over to the dugout, pulled the pin on the explosive device, and flung it into the dugout. Three men galloped like racehorses to safety behind the military vehicle.

BOOM! The detonation was thunderous, sending emerging night creatures, mammals, and reptiles scattering to hiding places.

Could anyone have survived the blast? Greater forces had the short answer—yes, but against impossible odds.

Under the pyramid pile of incinerated human flesh, a faint heartbeat pulsed through the breastbone of a petite, five-foot-one girl with cherubic features that had been compared to one of "Botticelli's Angels," by Sandro Botticelli, a Florentine Renaissance Italian artist.

Miraculously spared suffocation from being buried alive, the teenager's lungs sprung open, gulping the cooling night air hungrily. A good dose of life-saving oxygen flowed throughout her body as scorched eyelid flesh stretched sorely upward into the starry night sky. In unbearable discomfort from burned eyelids, third-degree burns to lips, missing upper front teeth blasted out by detonation, a gun wound, and a stab gash, the teenager was lucky to be alive!

Along with the terrible injuries, amnesia swallowed memories. The injured girl was unaware of the brutal reality—that her father, mother, three sisters, only brother, and three other loved ones laid dead underneath her.

Emotional torment had a way of twisting the brain, bypassing remembrance. A sea of tears flowed through coal-dust-encrusted cheeks. *"O, Bozhe* (Dear God), help me!" a faint voice implored. Had HE heard her plea, giving the injured girl the drive to survive? Long fingernails dug into hardened earth, inching the way out of the pit.

Out in the open, cornflower blue irises checked out her surroundings. Without knowledge of where she was, how she got there, or who she was, the girl moved at a snail's pace towards a cluster of stunted trees, copious vines, and bushy ferns. Plant life adapted to the permanent shade of a canopy, permitting no light to pass through.

Under a bush, on dry moss, she drew her knees to her chest. Cognitive function waning like her dying heart, death laid its icy talons on the victim of an unspeakable crime. But fate loves the fearless, finding ways to influence the firm resolve of an unwavering soul with survival in her blood.

Hadn't this young survivor of such an evil, cold-blooded murder attempt beaten the odds? She was now in the mighty hands of fate! This seventeen-year-old girl's disappearance will be shrouded in mystery for many years until…

PART ONE
The Romanovs

"Happy voices, smiling faces, golden memories of
a summer afternoon, of a world that could still
laugh and talk of war as something far away."
From the book, *The Romanov Sisters: The Lost Lives
of the Daughters of Nicholas and Alexandra*
—Helen Rappaport

CHAPTER ONE
The Ipatiev House, Yekaterinburg, Russia
- April 1918 -

Please take me away from all the Death.

—BRAM STOKER

IN THE EARLY HOURS OF THE SLUSHY SPRING month of April, thunderous hammering jolted homeowners Nikolai Ipatiev and his wife, Maria Feodorovna, upright from peaceful slumber.

"Who could that be at four in the morning?" forty-five-year-old Maria asked in a hushed tone, then hastily pulled the bedcovers over her head. Nikolai spoke soothingly, "Do not fuss, wife. I will go and see who it is."

He put on a long-sleeved mohair-woven housecoat and leather slippers. Tightening the housecoat's cord around his waist, he began making his way to the stairwell.

The insistent pounding continued.

"Hold your horses! I'm *coming*," Nikolai shouted, stress lines tightening his forehead.

He hurriedly unlocked the large, two-panel hand-crafted entry door and flicked a switch to power the external electric-mounted light fixtures, which only the wealthy could afford.

Nikolai glared at the heavy-set pock-faced man that could put scarecrows to shame. "What's the meaning of this at this time of the morning?" Nikolai shouted, vexed.

The Bolshevik government representative, attired in civilian clothes, did not introduce himself. In place of good manners, the self-inflated, socially positioned agent made hostile eye contact. "Nikolai Nikolaevich Ipatiev," he said. "You are being served with an eviction notice." He handed Nikolai a document. "You are ordered to vacate Ipatiev House immediately. Your home has been *claimed* for the needs of the Council. You are further ordered to clean the entire home. You have two days to do so."

The half-awake Nikolai's brows creased. *Was this just a dream?*

Alexander Zhilinsky, a high-ranking Social-Democratic Worker's Party member with a generous pot belly, continued an intimidating glare at the six-foot-two-inch, blonde homeowner, nervously fingering his handlebar mustache. Nikolai knew better than to ruffle the feathers of this ill-mannered, beardless Bolshevik. Still, he couldn't refrain from asking, "Can you guarantee our possessions left behind won't be damaged by whoever occupies my family home? Can you please tell me how long the tenancy will last?"

The Bolshevik snapped, "You will take only your personal belongings, like clothing, from the house. That's a *direct* order."

"Forgive me. I misspoke," Nikolai returned passively.

Did the homeowner have any choice but compliance?

Not by any means. Because the Revolution, brought about by

Vladimir Lenin, had stripped them of their rights!
Who was this formidable man?

CHAPTER TWO

Simbirsk, Russia
- 1870 to 1917 -

As an ultimate objective, "peace"
means communist world control.
—VLADIMIR LENIN, 1917

THE CREATOR OF THE SOVIET UNION was born Vladimir Ilich Ulyanov in Simbirsk, located on the Volga River, on April 22, 1870. Thirty years later, he adopted the pseudonym "Lenin" while doing underground communist party work. What made him change his birth name remains a mystery!

Lenin was the third of six children; his whole family were intellectuals, and he was very close to his parents in an unhealthy way.

Education was fundamental in Lenin's childhood. His father invoked education fever in all his children, especially Lenin, who finished first in his high school class. The promising student had a given gift for Latin and Greek. But not all was easygoing for the bright, young scholar. Several traumatic events shaped his life. The first was the scandal of his father, an Inspector of Schools, who was threatened with early retirement by an Imperial government official that was agitated about the influence public school had on Russian society. Lenin's father died suddenly from a brain aneurysm, which left the impressionable young Lenin inconsolable.

It was just the beginning of loss in the bonded family.

In early 1886, Lenin's older brother Aleksandr Ulyanov, a virtuoso biology student who transformed from an ascetic student to a terrorist, was arrested. Aleksandr had allied with several politically troubled students in St. Petersburg University square.

They plotted to kill Tsar Nicholas II, but the plot failed when someone in the group revealed the plan to authorities. Aleksandr and the coconspirators were hanged without trial.

This incident became a catalyst for Lenin, a vendetta driven by the death of his brother.

The irony is that Aleksandr's fate subsequently catapulted Lenin into a political and economic ideology advocating for the making of a classless society in which properties and wealth are owned communally instead of individually.

As expected, Tsar Nicholas II, who owned many opulent palaces and otherworldly riches, would be targeted for elimination. Lenin believed that, so long as the Romanovs existed, royalism counter-revolution was predictable.

After the death of Lenin's beloved father and older brother, the short, stubby head-strong male with a receding hairline became the man of the family. A year later, he was expelled from Kazan University for participating in a politically motivated student demonstration.

Exiled to his grandfather's domain in the village of Kokushkino, a rural community in Tatarstan, Lenin stayed with his sister Anna, whom the *militsiya* (police) had also ousted to this remote village, a dire consequence of her dubious activities.

In hiding, Lenin immersed himself in a plethora of radical literature, including the 1863 novel by the Russian philosopher, journalist, and literary critic, Nikolai Chernyshevsky, who wrote, *What Is to Be Done*. Chernyshevsky's principal character is Rakhmetov, who was devoted to revolutionary politics.

Lenin also delved into the writings of Karl Marx, the German philosopher whose famous book, *Das Kapital*, was Lenin's favored reading matter. It impacted Lenin's belief in recognizing and accepting nationalism among oppressed peoples.

In January 1889, Lenin declared himself a Marxist, an ideological figurehead behind Marxism–Leninism, and a champion of socialism for the working class. (Marxism is the left-wing to far-left practice of socioeconomic analysis, which uses the material interpretation of historical development, better known as materialism, describing the class relations and social conflict dialectical perspective to view social transformation.)

Lenin obtained his law degree in 1892 and relocated to Samara City, an inland port in a southeastern part of Russia. His clients were mainly Russian peasants. Their ongoing struggles in a class-biased legal system reinforced Lenin's Marxist beliefs. In time, he focused more of his energy on revolutionary politics.

Lenin left Samara mid-1890s to start a new life in St. Petersburg.

The young man connected with other like-minded Marxists and participated in their underground activities.

His coup did not go unnoticed!

In December 1895, Lenin and his coconspirators were arrested and sentenced to three years in Yakutia, the coldest region where the average winter temperature is minus 58 degrees, in subzero conditions.

Only fourteen prisoners survived.

After his release, Lenin traveled to Munich, Germany, where he co-founded *ISKRA,* a periodical, to grow Marxist support for his considered leadership to overthrow Imperialism.

He attended the Second Congress of the Russian Social Democratic Labor Party in 1903, and Lenin argued for up-to-date party leadership, which involved a network of lower-party organizations and their workers.

The larger-than-life Lenin demanded, "Give us an organization of revolutionaries, and we *will* overthrow Russian Imperialism!"

Lenin's outcry for change wasn't taken seriously. His domain dispute was not a walkover, as assumed!

A year later, the Imperial Japanese government was apprehensive about the encroachment of their Asian land. Japan offered to recognize Russian dominance in Manchuria in exchange for recognition of the Korean Empire being within the Japanese sphere of influence. Tsar Nicholas's obstinacy, as expected, staved off the offer, demanding the establishment of a neutral buffer zone between them and Japan in Korea, north of the 39th parallel.

Japan declared war and attacked Russia!

Tsar Nicholas's overconfidence in effortlessly winning this war was, to say the least, unmatched for ancient-minded Japanese Kamikaze military fighters, who were trained to fight till death.

The border dispute resulted in over ninety thousand casualties, including many civilians. Twenty thousand soldiers and umpteen civilians were wounded. Forty-two thousand were captured, and many more were unaccounted for.

In the wake of this botched fight, Russian farmers were angry. They had been overtaxed to raise money for the war, now putting an undue strain on food prices, fuel prices, and other essential resources. In the post-war period of high bread and additional food costs, poor people vocalized discontent over the country's political and economic structure, demanding reform.

When food shortages were at their peak, a rising insurgency was inevitable! A tired, hungry, and war-weary Russia became more restless than usual.

Lenin, seeing a path forward to seize power, openly condemned the newly formed Provisional government, which bourgeois liberal parties secretively assembled. That didn't go well, but the headstrong Lenin wasn't giving up. His desire to have a government ruled by armed forces, peasants, and workers was foremost. Lenin was finally elected the Soviet leader after the October Revolution, a *coup d'état*—the forcible overthrow of a ruler or government.

Lenin's wishes had come true.

Three years of bloody civil war followed. The Lenin-led Soviet government faced phenomenal odds. The anti-Soviet forces, headed by tsarists, generals, and admirals, fought desperately to overthrow Lenin's Red Army.

Funding to overthrow Marxism wasn't an issue. World War I

Allies—the British Empire and France—supplied the anti-Soviet forces with money and well-trained troops. The resolute Soviet leader, Lenin, ruthless in his push to secure power, launched the "Red Terror," a campaign to eliminate the opposition.

Once more, Lenin's power-hungry persona did not go unobserved. In August 1918, he narrowly escaped an assassination attempt by political opponent Pavel Axelrod, a Swedish leader of the Menshevik Party, which opposed the Bolsheviks from outside Russia. However, Lenin's speedy recovery from four gunshot wounds fortified his presence amongst his compatriots. Although his health was debatable, his defeat of the left-wing opposition that kept Russia tethered to capitalism had ushered in an international retreat for the Lenin-led government.

As Lenin saw it, Russia would be void of class conflict and the global wars it fostered. However, the Russia he led was reeling from the bloody civil war he had helped promote. Famine and poverty now shaped most of society.

By 1921, Lenin faced the same kind of peasant uprising upon which he had risen to power. Widespread strikes in cities and rural sections of the country broke out, intimidating the stability of his government. Lenin strategically introduced the "New Economic Policy" to ease the tension, allowing workers to sell their grain on the open market. However, the continuing stress of governing an unstable nation took its toll when he suffered a massive stroke in May 1922, followed by a second one in December of the same year.

With his health in apparent decline, the bedridden Lenin turned his thoughts to how the newly formed USSR—Union of Soviet Socialist Republics—would likely be governed after he was gone. He imagined a government straying far from its primary revolutionary goals. Demonstrating his belief, he released his "Testament," an anecdote in which he expressed remorse for being unable to bring about a positive outcome for Russia. Disenchantment toward his probable successor Joseph Stalin, the General Secretary of the Communist Party who had begun to amass greater power, was strongly mentioned in his writings.

The Testament would be Lenin's last chronicled document. On March 10, 1923, Lenin suffered a third stroke that robbed him of speech. Ten months later, he slipped into a coma from neurological complications and never regained consciousness.

Lenin died in Gorki, an urban locality on the outskirts of Moscow, on January 21, 1924, at the age of fifty-three. The official cause of his death was a brain hemorrhage due to an incurable disease of the blood vessels.

Something is *questionable* about that! Lenin didn't smoke and never let smokers near him. Though he was a heavy drinker, his lungs, kidneys, and liver were in remarkable condition. He was not overweight, had no elevated cholesterol or diabetes, no genetic predisposition to hardening of the arteries, and no syphilis, as was rumored. The hospital record indicated that Lenin was active, capable of speech, and hyper-talkative a few hours before his death.

One thing is for certain—Lenin had lots of enemies, particularly Josef Stalin. Was Stalin's megalomaniac rise to rule Russia the cause of Lenin's demise?

It seems Josef Stalin's method of enemy elimination was *poisoning* anyone who stood in his way of becoming the new leader of the Soviet Union. Some of the readily available poisons included:

Cyanide, extracted from the seeds of apples, cherries, almonds, and apricots; Ricin, extracted from castor oil seeds; Amatox, extracted from wild mushrooms; Rodenticedes, rat poison; and Sarin, a deadly nerve gas.

Why a toxicological investigation hadn't been performed at his autopsy is baffling!

It makes my suspicious mind ponder: was Vladimir Lenin killed by one of the listed poisons? It seems a plausible cause.

In tribute to Lenin's robust standing in Russian society, his corpse was embalmed after the autopsy to prevent natural decomposition. For four days, he lay in an open casket at Union House in the center of Moscow. Fifty thousand people passed through the hall to see him. Later, he was placed in a mausoleum in Moscow's Red Square, where he remains.

CHAPTER THREE
No Entry Under the
Penalty of Death

*You cannot ever know the dark
motives lurking in others!*
—LUCIA MANN

TORRENTIAL SPRING RAIN POUNDING THE DRIVEWAY, Nikolai Nikolayevich Ipatiev watched the pock-faced Bolshevik climb into the Rolls-Royce Silver Ghost. This luxury vehicle had been confiscated from someone very wealthy, Nikolai assumed.

Nikolai relocked the door to the home built on an elevated hillside behind him.

The two-story manor was commissioned by Ivan Redikortsev, an official in the mining industry, who sold it to Nikolai. He named his new home: Ipatiev House.

The reception area, lounge, main bedroom, and several guest rooms were richly decorated with figurines, stucco moldings, high ceilings artistically brushed in classic Italian style, and modern amenities such as electricity, sewerage, wood-fueled water heaters, and even telephones.

He and his wife lived on the upper floor, with friends and colleague's downstairs in Nikolai's thriving business quarters.

A worried Nikolai entered his spacious office, passing a sideboard with numerous framed family photographs and other memorabilia along the way to the ebony cabinet containing valuable books, gold coins, and heirloom jewelry. He locked it, put the cabinet key in his robe pocket, and headed upstairs.

Nikolai touched his wife, Maria, shaming sleep. "Hurry, get dressed," he instructed. He had heard footsteps behind him on the stairwell and felt her presence at the back of a post. She'd undoubtedly overheard the conversation but hadn't let on.

"Lock up our silverware," Nikolai urged. "And don't forget our gold dinner service."

Maria exhaled noisily. "Very well," she replied.

Maria, attired in a modest white dress with long sleeves and Nikolai, in casual trousers and a wool jacket, began packing valuables. The homeowners carried their crammed suitcases to the court adjacent to the ground-floor entrance and entered a cellar.

This part of the building would embrace the worst of all night terrors. They placed valuable belongings in the fifty cubic foot cellar with thick, double-wood doors with upper and lower locks.

Nikolai locked the basement, putting the two keys in his trouser pocket. He looked at his pale-faced wife to reassure her, "Of all the rooms in our home, Maria, this one is the most impenetrable. A thief must have a powerful ax to hack through fortress-like doors."

Maria looked at her husband, hoping he wasn't just trying to ease her apparent concerns about looting.

With help from the gardeners, the couple moved chests containing luxurious linen to the carriage house opposite the basement. Later that day, Nikolai hired two local cleaners.

Twenty-four hours later, Ipatiev House was spotless and ready for inspection. The stress of the rushed hard work, plus not knowing *who* would occupy their home, broke Maria. "What will become of us if the Bolsheviks take away our home for good?" she wailed. "Our children were born in this house, Nikolai! It has such happy memories."

Nikolai hugged her tightly. He could feel her trembling under his embrace. "Do not worry, my dear," he comforted. "We will soon be back in our home."

The couple had led a quiet and peaceful life until that day in spring 1918. They had no idea who would occupy their home and couldn't even begin to imagine the horrendous history that was about to unfold seventy-eight days later.

A couple of days after Nikolai was handed the eviction notice, Commissioner Avdeev arrived at Ipatiev House at 7:00 a.m. With the owner at his side, the stern Bolshevik began placing red Soviet Security Seals across the doors that read, NO ENTRY UNDER PENALTY OF DEATH.

Nikolai protested, "What if I need to get something?"

Avdeev glared at Nikolai, snorted like a bull, and roared, "The seals will remain in place until the house becomes empty!"

"And when do you think that will be?"

"When we *tell* you!" was the curt response.

Before vacating Ipatiev House, Nikolai called his cousin Yevgenia Poppel, who lived not far away. "Keep an eye on my home and send me a telegram when the tenants vacate the house, okay?"

A telegram reached Nikolai's temporary home in Moscow on Monday, July 22, 1918. Four capitalized words said, THE OCCUPANTS HAVE LEFT.

Nikolai immediately made a telephone call. "*Cheka*," a male voice answered. "How may I assist you?" (The Bolsheviks created *Cheka* (Secret Service), made up of released political prisoners and murderers who had no moral qualms with killing on command.)

"I am Nikolai Ipatiev," he said, introducing himself to the Ekaterinburg security police dispatcher. "I'm the property owner of Ipatiev House on Voznesenskaya Street. My neighbor tells me the guards have left, and my house stands empty. I want to get my house keys."

"Wait a moment," the dispatcher said, "I must speak with my superior."

Left dangling on the line, Nikolai was apprehensive. He had not received an official notice to reenter his home, but calling the police was his best shot.

"Hello, you still there?" the dispatcher asked.

"Yes."

"You can possess your house, but Commissioner Zhilinsky doesn't know where the keys are. They are probably still in the house."

"Thank you," Nikolai ended. He was happy not to face the pock-faced man again.

The next day, July 23rd, the happy homeowners drove to Ekaterinburg, eager to return to their home, only breaking the journey to purchase a local newspaper at a kiosk. Nikolai's eyes stuck onto the front-page headlines.

THE BLOOD-DRINKING TSAR AND HIS FAMILY ARE DEAD, EXECUTED IN YEKATERINBURG

Nikolai didn't know what to make of it. The devoted Tsar supporter did not know who took occupancy of his home and was unaware that the Bolsheviks had removed eleven cot beds, bedding, clothing, and other items used by the occupants.

Zhilinsky's instructions to the house cleaners of: "*Leave no trace of any evidence,*" backfired.

Maria's loud earsplitting, "Dear God in Heaven!" brought her husband flying to her side.

Nikolai entered the cellar with an unidentified foul odor. Brow's furrowing, he gaped at three of their stylish velvet-padded dining set chairs toppled over and smeared in dried reddish-brown stains. His gaze averted to the greyish-blue wallpaper decorating the back wall.

Maria clasped her hand over her mouth.

Uneasiness ran through his veins as Nikolai inspected the wall. "If I'm not mistaken, this is dried blood, and the holes in the plasterboard are rifle bullet indentations."

Maria gasped loudly. "Something really evil has happened here, but..." Almost unimaginable was the bloody handprint of a small child.

Maria's piercing cry echoed as she fled the basement.

Speechless in turbulent waves of shock, disbelief, and bewilderment, the homeowners hurried to the Izhorsky-Fiat parked in the driveway.

Rigid in their seats, the traumatized couple never looked back at a home that was once everything to them as they drove away. Nikolai and Maria never set foot into the "bloody house of torture" again. Recurrent, frightful flashbacks kept them sleepless for a long time. After his cousin finally told him the truth, Nikola wrote in a journal:

In all the years of the existence of this house, no one had died in it. Eleven people lost their lives in my home. I cannot live with that!

If Nikolai Ipatiev had been a fly on the wall, he would have seen HELL firsthand— the evil that had befallen the eleven innocent souls.

Who were they? Why did it happen? Who was involved in this crime?

CHAPTER FOUR
"The House of Special Purpose"

*Those who show utter contempt for human life by committing
premeditated murder justly forfeit the right to their own life.*
—ALEX KOZINSKI, 1949

ON THE MORNING NIKOLAI AND MARIA VACATED their
home, a double-wooden fence exceeding the second-floor windows
was erected around the outer perimeter of Ipatiev House, closing
it off from curious neighbors. Two guard posts were placed inside
the enclosure, and eight posts to the outside secured the house.
Bolshevik sentries constantly stood on duty.

Mounted machine guns were installed in the attics of the neigh-
boring buildings. All the windows to this nineteenth-century abode
were blackened, shrouding the home in mystery. "The House of
Special Purpose" was ready for Bolshevik enemies of Russia. Why
did the Bolsheviks select *this* particular home?

The choice of location was selected by Commissioner Alexander
Dmitrievich Avdeev, who later wrote in his memoirs:

The House of Special Purpose is a place where its defense against an external attempt to free the family is less favorable.

Who was this family the Bolshevik government feared above all else?

CHAPTER FIVE
The Russian Imperial Royal Family

I am not prepared to be a Tsar. I never wanted to become one,
as I know nothing of the business of ruling!
—NIKOLAI ROMANOV, born 1894

THE ROMANOVS WERE NOT LIKE EVERYONE ELSE. Their quality of life with three square, hearty meals and *every* luxury at their fingertips was funded by the Russian population—many starving and homeless—during their long reign. These pretentiously superior rulers would pay dearly for these taken-for-granted advantages before the twentieth century ends!

On the introverted side, the acutely shy Grand Duke Nikolai Romanov, accustomed to this level of comfort, was uprooted when his father, Tsarevich Aleksandr Aleksandrovich–Emperor Alexander III, unexpectedly died on October 20, 1894, leaving the Russian throne to his only son.

Nikolai (Nicholas) was born in Pushkin, Russia, on May 6, 1868, the firstborn to Tsar Alexander III and Princess Maria Dagmar Feodorovna of Schleswig-Holstein-Sonderburg-Glücksburg, the second daughter of an insolvent Danish royal family. She was considered a great beauty, with shoulder-length curly, blond hair, flashing chestnut eyes, and a swan-like neck. Her marriage prospects improved significantly when her eldest sister, Alexandre, became betrothed to the future King of England, Edward VII, in 1861.

Maria, her preferred name after she converted to Orthodoxy, eclipsed her sister by marrying Tsar Alexander III in the Alexander Palace Chapel in St Petersburg in 1866.

The empress was warmly welcomed in the Anichkov Palace. She awed guests, having perfected the Russian language. In return, Maria expected utmost loyalty to the Imperial Crown and devoted much of her life to leading social functions and patronizing charities. Yet, she was extra careful to be excluded from politics, with one exception—She was vehemently anti-German.

Maria was angry when she heard of the annexation of Danish territories by Kaiser Wilhelm Friedrich Ludwig I, King of Prussia and the first head of state of a united Germany.

Maria's anti-German views weren't to be swept under a rug easily. German-born citizens residing in Russia wanted to kill her for openly airing anti-German sentiment, but their death threats didn't intimidate the strong-minded woman. Under the constant shadow of an assassin's bomb, knife, or bullet, Maria continued being favored at the Winter Palace, the Kremlin, and the Crimean summer palace of Livadia. A dark shadow struck the bullheaded Maria in another way.

Her beloved Alexander III passed away from nephritis, an incurable kidney disease, at forty-nine, leaving his son, Grand Duke Nicholas, to succeed the Russian throne. Inconsolable and poorly skilled in state affairs, the twenty-six-year-old Nicholas was prematurely thrust into ruling a country that, unaware to him, was in dreadful political turmoil. The country was a powder keg of mistrust for the Imperial monarchy.

Nicholas's autocratic father had ruled Russia with an iron fist, forbidding anyone within the Russian Empire to speak non-Russian languages, even in Poland.

Nicholas could not have known what he had become heir to—a giant melting pot of discontent that would bubble over and, in due course, bring about the Empire's fall.

Shortly after his father's death, Nicholas enlisted in the army. Passionate about his military duties and responsibilities, the nineteen-year-old eventually rose in rank to Colonel. He was not so passionate about government affairs and attended few political meetings. Nicholas aired his frustration to an army buddy, "I am not prepared to be a Tsar, and I do not wish to be one."

Nor was this ill-prepared new Tsar prepared for a *morganatic* royal marriage. (Morganatic means the marriage between a male from a royal or reigning house and a titled woman of lesser status.)

That would not work out too well either!

Of Maria's five children, Nicholas was the apple of her eye. She overindulged his every whim: "I want the finest tutor, Mother." "I want this." "I want that!"

The renowned University professor, Konstantin Pobedonostsev, was officially summoned to tutor "Mama's boy."

Young Nicholas shined in history, math, biology, chemistry, and languages but refused to learn the language his mother despised. He *inherited* his mother's extreme anti-German sentiment. The spoiled child struggled to grasp the subtleties of politics and economics, which were imperative in taking possession of the Crown.

Would it be a hindrance? No. Contrariwise, a "she devil" will step up.

Nicholas II married Princess Alix of Hesse-Darmstadt (who went by the English name of Alexandra) within a month of his father's passing. He had little choice but to marry to secure a future heir to the throne.

Alexandra was born as Alix Viktoria Helene Luise Beatrix, of Hesse by Rhine, part of the German Empire, on June 6, 1872, in Darmstadt, Germany. She had an imposing lineage. Her father was Louis IV, Grand Duke of Hesse, who died of a heart attack in March of 1892 when she was nineteen. Her mother was Lady Alice Christabel Douglas Scott, who became the Duchess of Gloucester, England, by marriage.

Tsar *Nicholas* II   Princess *Alix* of Hesse
(Tsarina Alexandra Feodorovna)

Grand Duchess *Olga* Nikolaevna   Grand Duchess *Tatiana* Nikolaevna   Grand Duchess *Maria* Nikolaevna   Grand Duchess *Anastasia* Nikolaevna   Tsarevich *Alexei* Nikolaevich

Alexandra's godparents were the Prince and Princess of Wales.

Alexandra was Queen Victoria's granddaughter, who didn't think highly of her. "Even though she was tall and slender, with an exquisite complexion and the graceful neck of a swan, she had a sad and pathetic expression. Even her grey-blue eyes under those long lashes do not mirror the emotions of a sensitive soul."

Family members noted that even from a young age, Alexandra was melancholic. Her first cousin and childhood friend, Princess Louise, stated, "She has a permanent mindset of fatality."

Louise confronted her cousin one day, "Alix, you regularly play at being sorrowful. You profess to be extremely religious, but the Almighty will send you some real crushing sorrows one day."

Alexandra laughed, shrugging off this prediction without a second thought. If this emotionally disturbed woman had taken heed of her small voice to *Grow up and change your ways*, Alexandra could have turned her life around there and then. As prophesized by a German soothsayer, nothing good was in the future for her.

Of course, the full-blown haughty Alexandra renounced Tsarevich Nicholas's marriage proposal. She refused to convert from Lutheranism and join the Russian Orthodox Church, as would be expected of all wives of Russian Emperors.

"It grieves me terribly and makes me very unhappy not to marry you," Alexandra said, "but leaving the Lutheran church would be wrong!"

With constant pressure from family members, Alexandra eventually surrendered. When Queen Victoria heard of her granddaughter's pending marriage to Tsar Nicholas II, she was not pleased and aired her worry to a confidant:

"Alexandra is not prepared to possess great wealth, vast lands, and umpteen palaces, but my blood runs cold when I think of her so young and placed on a very unsafe throne. I believe her life, and above all, her husband's life would be constantly threatened."

In the early part of her marriage, Alexandra was financially generous to close friends. Her lady-in-waiting, Anna Demidova, inscribed Alexandra's charitable words in her diary:

Anna, I want to help others in life. I want to help them fight their battles and bear their crosses.

It's a pity the Tsarina of Russia did not practice what she preached!

The tall, slender Tsarina Alexandra walked with the grace of a ballerina and loved music. At a very young age, she "tickled the ivories" and often sang duets with Queen Victoria's Lady in Waiting, Minnie Cochrane. Alexandra meticulously translated Russian text and studied Russian music to improve her command of the language. She read all Leo Tolstoy's novels as if they held the truth like a bible.

Life was good for the newlyweds until they tasted the wrath of their people. In 1894, at the Coronation of Nicholas II, a narrow backstreet only three meters wide became too overcrowded, and people fell to the ground like dominoes. Under the almost ten-foot pyramid mile, women and children were crushed to death. For those who were still conscious, life ebbed.

What sparked the deadly stampede? It happened due to Nicholas' lack of planning for crowd control.

Hundreds of subjects were tantalizingly lured there with offers of free coronation gifts of bread, bags of sugar, a sack of potatoes, chocolates, and a framed photo of their new Tsar. This drew a large crowd.

What could have prevented this disaster? Nicholas failed to prearrange a proper government policy to set up barriers.

It seems people were expendable to the Tsarina, who, when informed about the dead and wounded souls, heartlessly said, "They will get over it. Time will heal."

The now-disliked Alexandra habitually ignored sound advice and did so on this occasion. She went ahead with the masquerade

Coronation Ball, which only the rich in society would attend at the Winter Palace, the Tsar and Tsarina's primary home, with affluence beyond peasant imagination.

The home had an extensive assemblage of priceless art, facades engraved with gold leaves, gold-framed mirrors, sculptured stone female figure carvings, gold and bronze lion masks, and a vast array of gold Faberge eggs, amongst other riches.

The grand royal palace, sporting twenty-seven bedrooms, was externally coated with a red brick color, and surrounded by extensive walled, landscaped gardens. The opulent home was just one of several dwelling places the new Tsar had inherited:

Alexander Palace was also located in Pushkin.

Catherine Palace was also located in Pushkin.

Grand Kremlin Palace was located in Moscow.

Peterhof and Nikolaevsky Palaces were located in St. Petersburg.

Gatchina Palace was located in Gatchina.

Alexandra's hosting of the celebration triggered public outrage among those struggling to process sadness. Many searched for loved ones. Most of the unidentified dead were buried in unmarked mass graves the day following the stampede.

This ghastly tragedy became a foretelling that "utter darkness would befall the Romanov family."

Nevertheless, it wasn't just Alexandra who was blamed for being apathetic. Nicholas's lack of compassion in his response, assuring his people this would never happen again, earned him the nickname "Nicholas the Bloody."

Not one of the royal family members could have foreseen what lay ahead for them because of the ill-fated Tsarina, an undiagnosed sociopath with no empathy for other people.

Her first child, a daughter, Olishka (Olga), was born in 1895. Her second daughter, Tatiana, was born two years later, and another daughter, Maria, arrived in 1899. Anastasia, the last daughter, came into the world in 1901. Alexandra knew Nicholas's heirs would be his brothers and uncles if she did not bear a son. Finally, the longed-for son, Alexei Nikolaevich, was born on August 12, 1904. Alexandra had secured the dynasty, or so she smugly thought.

Joy soon turned to utter despair when the royal physician pronounced that Alexei had "incurable" hemophilia. This hereditary bleeding disorder had taken Alexandra's youngest brother who died before adulthood. Was the only male heir to the throne cursed? Or was his mother simply the carrier of the disease? (It seems so, because DNA science has proved that this rare disorder *has* passed throughout the history of European royalty in the nineteenth and twentieth centuries). In Alexei's case, his great-grandmother, Queen Victoria, was the likely culprit. She had already passed her blood disorder through two of her five daughters, who transmitted the mutant disease to other royal houses. It became known as "the royal disease!"

Much to Alexandra's dread, Alexei's condition worsened. The royal doctors didn't have much hope, telling her that it was unlikely he would live to adulthood.

In desperation, Alexandra summoned fortune-tellers to the palace. "Tell me what you see," she asked. "Will my son live?"

When the psychics didn't give her positive answers, Alexandra called them blood-sucking frauds and sunk into a deep depression until a letter arrived.

"God has seen your tears and heard your prayer. I have healing powers given to me by God. I will cure your sickly child."

Alexandra was overjoyed. She summoned the writer to the palace. Unknowingly, she'd invited the Devil-in-a-frock, whose lascivious conduct had earned him the title of Debauchee!

Rasputin would bring ruinous beginnings to the royal family. The self-proclaimed monk with a hypnotic character, an oval face, hooked nose, heavy black beard, and set grey eyes in deep sockets was hardly a man of God. He was nothing more than a con man. If Rasputin had told her the moon was made of green cheese, she would have replied without hesitation, *yes.*

Nicholas's shoulder wasn't there for her to cry on. He was constantly absent from the onset of their marriage. But who else could Alexandra have turned to in her hour of need? She had tried everything—fortune tellers, spiritualists, and alternative medicines.

The self-absorbed woman couldn't care less about Nicholas's military and state objectives which were to maintain the status quo across Europe. She didn't care that Russia was experiencing good economic growth, expanding industry into the Far East. Without her knowledge, commerce changed drastically.

The construction of the Trans-Siberian railroad had begun, connecting Russia with the Pacific Coast. As a result, Japan felt increasingly threatened. Japan attacked Russia, and Nicholas II's army surrendered Port Arthur.

By the spring of 1905, his fleet was decimated in the Battle of Tsushima. In the wake of Russia's defeat, Nicholas II entered peace negotiations with Japan that summer, but more significant concerns demanded his attention.

Father George Gapon led a sizable but peaceful demonstration of factory workers in St. Petersburg. The demonstrators demanded the Tsar boost the working conditions and establish a practical Assembly. That day, troops opened fire on the demonstrators, killing more than a thousand people in what would become the infamous "Bloody Sunday," earning the Imperial ruler another sobriquet nickname, "Bloodthirsty Tsar."

Following the protesters' bloodbath, workers downed tools, sympathizing with the cause. Nicholas's troops suppressed thousands of uprisings, further increasing tensions.

Although the Tsar deluded himself as being ordained by God to rule Russia, he had little choice but to concede in setting up an elected legislature, known as a *Duma*. He continued his fight against government reform, expressly with the newly elected Minister of the Interior, Peter Stolypin, Nicholas's nemesis, a man Nicholas would have been wise not to have crossed.

At the start of World War I, Russia's armies performed poorly. In response, Nicholas II appointed himself Commander-in-Chief to have direct control of the military against the advice of his ministers.

Nicholas spent much of 1915 to August 1917 away from St. Petersburg. As a result, Alexandra grew emotionally dependent on Rasputin.

Who is this man who controlled the Tsarina of Russia?

Grigori Yefimovich Novykh, "Rasputin," a self-proclaimed illiterate mystic, was born in Pokrovskoe, Siberia, on January 21, 1819. In his pubescent years, his reputation for immorality, exposing his genitals in public, is how he earned the title "Debauched One."

No one knows the reason Grigori acquiesced to religious conversion at age eighteen. He journeyed to Verhoture, a remote monastery in the Urals, and was introduced to the Khlysty sect. This underground spiritual Christian group had splintered away from the Russian Orthodox Church. Rasputin's perverted Khlysty beliefs were that one was nearest to God when feeling "holy passion," and the way to reach such a pious state was through sexual exhaustion.

After a few months, an intensely detested Rasputin left the monastery under the cloak of darkness. He returned to his birthplace Pokrovskoye, a village in Tyumen Oblast. Villagers steered clear of the returned wannabe monk.

Rasputin married Proskovya Feodorovna Dubrovina, an unattractive, chubby fifteen-year-old peasant girl who paid him attention. She bore him four children. But marriage and fatherhood failed to settle the habitually on-edge man.

The day after the birth of his last-born child, the insensitive man deserted his wife and children. Rasputin sailed on a clipper boat to Mount Athos in Greece. Then eventually, he voyaged to Yerushalayim (Jerusalem). Rasputin thrived by living off donations, pretending to be a *staret*, a religious teacher, and a spiritual mentor who could heal the sick and predict the future. The aspiring spiritual teacher's deceptions soon caught up with him when a mob of angry people threatened to lynch him.

"That man prophesized my son would not die of his illness, and he did!" screamed a woman.

"He told me my husband would be faithful to me, never cheat on me," shouted another. "Well, I found my *faithful* husband in bed with a whore!"

"He told me I'd become rich with my spice trade!"

Rasputin fled back to Russia but returned to a different Russia. After settling in St. Petersburg, by chance he met a man of his heart—Zatvoriniski, a reclusive warlock who informed him that using witchcraft powers and casting spells was no longer outlawed.

"Be not afraid to practice your beliefs," the warlock informed Rasputin. "Burning witches and warlocks is a thing of the past." With this get-out-of-jail-free card, Rasputin began to use his craft freely.

During one of Alexei's hemophiliac episodes, Rasputin was urgently ordered to the palace. The sickly boy smiled at his savior, who placed his hands on his head. "Do not be afraid. I'm here, dear boy, the blood flow will stop as God is by my side." And it did!

An elated Alexandra hugged Rasputin with little doubt that her son's savior had godly powers meant for her, too. Before leaving the boy's bedside, Rasputin proclaimed, "The destiny of your family is linked to me; don't forget that."

The charlatan had not only stolen Alexei's heart, but Alexandra's too. Not only did she give him all the court privileges, but the smitten Tsarina also bestowed him the royal title—Personal Advisor to the Empress of Russia.

From that day on, Rasputin basked in the royal appointment limelight. He had a "free pass" to all royal privileges. His handcrafted silk shirts sported embroidered initials, and he had access to luxury foods, the finest of wine and vodka, and whatever he desired at his fingertips. Despite that, Rasputin continued the pretense of simply being a humble and holy peasant sent by God to heal the royal family's sickly child.

Outside of the royal court was another matter. He returned to his depraved habits, telling women that physical contact with him would have a cathartic influence: pulling off this revulsive ruse, Rasputin seduced many gullible peasant women, cynical sex workers, and even high-society women.

When Rasputin's disgusting conduct reached the ears of Nicholas II, he did not confirm nor deny the charges, mostly coming from royal staff quarters, and turned a blind eye. He, too, had welcomed the "healer" after witnessing his ailing only son's happiness when Rasputin was present.

There was one man who wasn't going to tolerate Rasputin's degenerate behavior. Interior Minister Stolypin sent a warning letter to Nicholas, informing him about the perverted man's escalating obscene activities, notifying the Tsar that serious repercussions would follow if he didn't immediately stop Rasputin's visits to the palace.

To avoid friction, Nicholas banished Rasputin to Siberia. Nicholas presumed that would be the end of it, but he was mistaken!

While Nicholas was away with his troops in World War I, behind his back, Alexandra summoned Rasputin back to court.

When word of her actions reached Nicholas, he was enraged. "Don't insult me!" he yelled across the telephone line. "Stolypin will lobby against me. God knows what will happen!"

The self-important woman hung up, refusing to communicate with Nicholas in any form.

Her deliberate strategy to inflict emotional hurt and control paid off. After days of uncomfortable silence from her, the royal ruler admitted in a letter, "I understand, my beloved, I know you were only thinking of our son, and I'm fine with that." At that point, Alexandra and Rasputin became permanent fixtures in the palace.

Nicholas underestimated the conniving palace predator, who he allowed to remain as part of the family.

Rasputin stepped into Nicholas's shoes and took control of the Russian Empire's matters when the Tsar departed the palace on July 3rd, 1914, to mobilize his forces in military action against Austria-Hungary's (an ally at the time) declaration of war against Serbia. Prior, Tsar Nicholas dispatched an *ultimatum* to Vienna, warning Austria-Hungary *not* to attack Serbia.

Did the warmongers heed the warning? No.

Following Austria-Hungary's surprise attack on Serbia, Russia's pan-Slavic roles, in defense of Orthodox Serbia, mobilized their reserve army to their border with Austria-Hungary. Although they had no formal treaty obligation to Serbia, Russia's desire to control the Balkans had a long-term perspective toward gaining the advantage over Austria-Hungary, which led to the decision to protect Serbia by military force.

Along came a deadly black spider and sat down beside....

July 13th, 1914, the Deutsches Kaiserreich (German Empire) demanded Russia's immediate demonization, but Nicholas refused to comply.

The Ottoman Empire declared war on Russia and France, sending vast infantry battalions through Belgium to surround Paris. Belgium's endangerment became a major concern to the British Empire as the country was created by King George V to prevent France's access to the harbors in Northern France, especially Antwerp.

Unavoidably, Britain entered the war on August 4, 1914, joining their Allies: Russia, Belgium, and France. For unsuspecting Allies, World War I gave birth to horror like no other of war.

On the brutally frigid winter morning of January 31st, 1915, in the village of Bolimov on the eastern front, the German Ninth Army, one hundred thousand strong, mounted an attack on the Russian lines in an attempt to push forward to take Warsaw, the capital of Poland.

The Germans underestimated the frigid weather, compounded by numbing, icy winds leaving them frozen to the bone. The cold weather didn't bother Russian combatants at home in these winter temperatures.

Waist deep in snow, the German infantry began pounding their enemy with artillery fire. When that tactic failed, the five-star German general in command dispatched a coded radio message to the German headquarters, asking for help.

The encryption came back: *21-19-5-9-20* (Use it).

Would the cryptic edict punch through the Russian line and get into their rear where the German infantry could kill, wound, or capture large numbers of their enemies, as they assumed?

"For the Fatherland, kill them all," slid easily off German fighter tongues as they prepared to launch an unthinkable offensive on their unprotected adversaries.

Each dawn, the usual time for a German attack, Russian volunteer fighters woke to the *stand-to* order to guard frontline foxholes. Unaware that on this bitterly cold day, the Germans had heinously discharged metal canisters packed with xylyl bromide (mustard gas) into artillery shells.

Explosions ruptured, and a thick vapor mist of mustard gas swirled and encircled the Russian fighters. As their lungs inhaled the chemical warfare, it instantly inflicted life-threatening skin burns, severe irritations to the nose, and blindness.

"Will I make it home?" a dying soldier asked the field medic.

Even though most of the gas froze in the wintry cold, it killed ninety thousand fighters from both sides, but more than half of those killed were Russian.

While his soldiers were fighting for their lives, Nicholas was safely in Warsaw, enjoying an extravagant blend of Russo-Baltique vodka and savoring "Almas," expensive caviar that only millionaires could afford. He was accompanied by an old friend, Stephan Rebonowicz, a retired Warsaw general appointed by Nicholas's father, Alexander III.

At a disciplinary hearing, Nicholas was chastised for his selfish actions.

It wouldn't be Nicholas's only regretful humiliation. Leaving his incompetent wife and Rasputin in charge of Russia's internal affairs would haunt the Imperial rule for the rest of his life.

"I'm humbled," Alexandra had said. "I will fulfill your trust in me, dear husband. Return to me after your triumphant victory." It wasn't the first of the two-faced Alexandra's lies.

Word soon spread about Nicholas's bad judgments. Government officials and the public accused their Tsar of ineffectual, poor military decisions, blaming him for the thousands of deaths of their loved ones. Incensed finger pointing was venomously directed to Alexandra for her questionable association with Rasputin. An angry mob, many of whom had lost their loved ones in the earlier stampede, gathered outside the Winter Palace, clutching the rails of the eleven-foot-high wrought-iron fencing, shouting at her:

"Tsarina, you are a harlot!"

"You are nothing but a low-life drug addict. I know this because my brother supplies the opium Rasputin gives you."

"A mad monk has possessed you!"

"You should be strung up!"

"You are a German spy!"

"Tsar Nicholas must have been drunk when he agreed to marry you!"

"Come out and face us, bitch," a burly man spat.

Alexandra heard the crowd and demanded that her staff turn off all lights and ordered extra palace guards to the gates.

Nicholas was blindsided, unaware his wife had bestowed Rasputin with a royal title, giving the insane man enough power to appoint church officials and select cabinet ministers, most of whom were merely incompetent opportunists.

Rasputin also intervened in certain military matters, much to Russia's detriment, and was an aggressive opponent of anyone criticizing his egotistical self.

Hatred brewed like an evil potion in a witch's cauldron.

"He must be stopped," a church official said.

Several attempts to end the villainous Rasputin's life and save Russia from his evil clutches failed until Vladimir Purishkevich, a member of the "duma," and Prince Feliks Yusupov, the husband of Nicholas's II niece, Irina, met at a private club for aristocratic members only and agreed that enough was enough!

The patriots had something in common. They were steadfastly strong-minded to shield the monarchy from Rasputin's malicious influence over Tsarina Alexandra and to give Nicholas II one last chance to restore the reputation of the throne.

That evening, Rasputin's fate was sealed on December 16th, 1916. Yusupov lured him, a known womanizer, to his home to meet his wife, who was actually away visiting a cousin.

The bell rang at Morka Palace in St. Petersburg.

Without a flicker of emotion, butler Ivan Mikhail ushered the guest into the stately dining room.

"Prince Yusupov will be with you shortly," the servant announced, standing to attention, awaiting his master's entry.

The twenty-nine-year-old nobleman in a brown velvet, gold-embroidered jacket and pants faked a warm smile. "*Dobriy vecher* (Good evening) Grigori. Please take a seat," Yusupov said in a mellow voice, waving towards the dining table. "I invited you to my home to tell you it warms my heart for the great help you have given the Tsar and Tsarina in assisting their son to recover from his sickness. I am informed that Grand Duke Alexei is recovering well. Thank you."

"Thanks to God first," Rasputin replied in a voice like butter. "It has been an honor to be of comfort to the royal family in their distressing times. I'm honored to have received this invitation to dine with you, and I am yet to meet your wife."

"My apologies, but my wife will not be joining us. She was called away on an urgent matter."

"Maybe another time," Rasputin returned.

The mad monk, who had no table manners, sat at the baroque, hand-carved table and was served the finest of wine and Black Forest chocolate cake laced with lethal doses of ground cyanide powder sufficient to kill several men instantly.

Eating noisily, Rasputin devoured every cake morsel. Much to Yusupov's astonishment, he showed no ill effect to poison. The nobleman stared at Rasputin in utter disbelief.

Rasputin purred, "That was delicious. The best I've ever had."

Is he protecting himself with the supernatural powers he claimed to possess? Yusov wondered. *Or is it that the EVIL ONE really does take care of his buddies?*

Twitching nervously, the prince said, "Will you please excuse me for a moment?"

"No problem," responded Rasputin.

Waiting outside the room, Vladimir Purishkevich probed, "Is he dead?"

"Incredibly, no," Yusupov replied.

"Shit!" Purishkevich cussed. "Plan B goes into effect *now*! I'll see you in the wine cellar."

Yusupov returned to his guest. "May I offer you a glass of vintage Rémy Martin?"

Rasputin's eyes lit up like a Christmas tree. He wasn't going to refuse a tipple that he could not afford. "I would love a cognac."

"Then please follow me to my basement wine cellar and select a fine year."

Rasputin and Yusupov entered the wine cellar. Purishkevich sprung from the darkness, striking Rasputin several times with a heavy metal pipe. Blood gushed from his head and mouth, and his eyes bulged from their sockets as the injured man howled like a wounded animal. But he wasn't going to die quickly.

Rasputin, twitching in spasms, got up and walked out a side door into the courtyard, muttering, "Why, why, why?"

"This is a fucking disaster," Purishkevich spat.

He withdrew a Browning pistol and fired at close range into the most hated man's head. But even that didn't kill him. The human had been poisoned, beaten, and shot, and still he was alive. He must have had supernatural protection.

Rasputin lay in the courtyard like a broken doll, moaning, and then stillness prevailed. Purishkevich placed his middle finger on the side of Rasputin's Adam's apple.

There was no possibility of doubt. "The bastard is finally dead," he stated.

Yusupov heaved a sigh of relief. "Thank heavens for that!"

Upon instruction, his servant wrapped Rasputin's lifeless body in a carpet, tied chains around it, and then dragged the corpse to a horse-drawn carriage. Mikael steered the buggy to the Neva River, the main waterway in St. Petersburg, and tossed the rolled-up carpet off a bridge and waited until it sunk underneath glacial waters.

Now convinced that Rasputin had supernatural powers, Yusupov quoted his favorite novelist Feodor Dostoyevsky (author of *Crime and Punishment*) to Mikael upon his return from the river. "The holy man takes your soul and will and makes it his. When you choose your holy man, you surrender your will. You give it to him in utter submission, in full renunciation."

Seven days later, a river policeman, walking on the frozen river, noticed a large formation bobbing up and down under the ice. He sent for help.

The carpet, with its chains intact, was hauled to the riverbank.

Rasputin had been found! His autopsy did not disclose poison, but a fatal shot to the head.

Were his killers held accountable? No!

Major Popel, the head of the Water Police, carried out the murder investigation and, although he had an idea who had carried out the murder, no charges were ever laid.

The public, the elite, and outsiders celebrated the unknown killers. To all, Rasputin symbolized the corruption at the heart of their rulers, Tsar Nicholas and Tsarina Alexandra.

To Rasputin's executors' consternation, the murder did not lead to any radical changes in Nicholas's policies.

In the aftermath of the Russian revolution, Alexander Kerensky, the now leading political figure, stated, "Without Rasputin, there would have been no Lenin!" Was this self-proclaimed "holy man" missed? Not by his deserted wife but by his children, Maria, Varvara, and Dmitry.

But then, there was the crazed Alexandra, whose heart, mind, and soul had been stolen by the mad monk. When she heard the news of her lover's death, she ordered everyone at the palace to dress in black. Anyone who didn't obey was sent away to Siberian work camps. It was just the beginning of the bedrock of hatred!

After discovering Rasputin's body, allegations raged like an uncontrolled wildfire. People accused the mad monk and his lover Alexandra, a German spy, of deliberately harming Russia in its fight with the Ottoman Empire. Nicholas was utterly unaware of the escalating tensions back home caused by his wife.

Headquartered in eastern Belarus, Nicholas felt humiliated for his reckless participation in the home of the Warsaw aristocrat and was unaware that Rasputin had met his death. Millions of people struggled to survive. Workers who put in sixteen-hour days still struggled to support their families after the extortion taxation deductions for the Tsar's ill-planned Word War II.

Millions of people, poor as beggars, lived in awful conditions.

Many who could not pay the rent increases were homeless.

It was only a matter of time before all hell broke loose.

A month after Rasputin's burial, there was a rush to the door of lawlessness. Rioting and looting of bakeries and other food stores was rampantly out of control. The anarchy energized the well-prepared man waiting in the wings to bring about change to his beloved country.

As volatility intensified in the streets of St. Petersburg, a worried Tsarina sent a telegram to Nicholas on the front lines in Petrograd (St. Petersburg). Dated March 3, 1917, the message was loud and clear. *Return immediately. Our children and I are in danger, in fear for our lives.*

Upon receipt of the message, Nicholas immediately commanded the Imperial Pullman, his temporary quarters and military field office, to be ready for his return home. That wasn't going to happen.

Unbeknownst to the Imperial ruler, his duma government had turned against him while he was with his troops on the front.

The boycotted royal transport, decorated with dark blue and gold trim with coats of arms displayed between windows, was seized by duma-appointed agents.

Forcibly detained on the train, Tsar Nicholas II, under vexatious political pressure, signed the Decree of Abdication. Renunciation of the throne opened the "dark door" to the Russian Revolution just like a fortune-teller had forewarned: "You are being dominated, controlled by a stronger-willed person. If *she* is not put in her place, your power will end dreadfully!"

Suppose Nicholas, who did not wish to rule, had credited the mystic's forewarning to keep his wife in check. In that case, he could have prevented a tragic direction, gloomier than a Shakespearian tragedy.

Nicholas returned home to Russia, a country he no longer *knew*! Unintentionally, Nicolas fulfilled Lenin's leadership dream.

There were things Lenin would rather forget but couldn't because his heart burned with the longing for revenge. The Bolshevik leader had old scores to settle—to punish the wrong done to him, his family members, and the Russian people. Lenin's memory was still fresh from being crushed by exile and the murder of his brother. Revenge was foremost.

Will Lenin get that wish?

Yes, but in the most sinister way.

In early April 1917, the overthrown Tsar was finally allowed by Lenin to return home to his wife and children. Lenin then placed the Romanovs under house arrest at Alexander Palace. On Lenin's orders, the Romanovs were not allowed visitors except for Orthodox priest Father Afanasy Belyaev, who performed prayer services for Alexei's thirteenth birthday. It would be the last time the priest would conduct prayers for the royal family.

An excerpt from Belyaev's published book in 2018, *The Romanovs Under House Arrest*, begins by describing the faith of the Russian Imperial family:

In my presence, for the last time, the former rulers of their own home gathered fervently to pray, tearfully, and on bended knee, imploring the Lord's help to intercede for them in all of the sorrows and misfortune.

Five months under house arrest in the palace ended when the royal family, along with Dr. Botkin, three servants, a lady-in-waiting, a cook, and a footman, were escorted by armed military guards and transported by train to Tobolsk, Siberia.

The unwanted people were held in a former duma governor's mansion, retitled, "The House of Freedom," by the Bolsheviks. But the banishment of the Romanovs to Siberia was not enough punishment in the minds of their once loyal subjects, who wanted Nicholas's execution with no formal trial hearing.

Here and now was the outcry. Fearing murder by mob retaliation, the Romanovs and their servants were relocated to Yekaterinburg for a more sinister reason—to guarantee the Romanov dynasty would never again rule.

One of the Yekaterinburg detainees would be given a glimpse into the future.

The night afore, the man awoke drenched in perspiration and hyperventilating. He couldn't shake off the engulfing fear and heavy sadness that weighed heavily on his mind like a boulder. The man believed the nightmare was indeed a premonition of doom.

Who was this fifty-three-year-old?

Why was *he* under house arrest in Ipatiev House?

CHAPTER SIX
Dr. Eugene Botkin,
Russian Physician

From caring
comes courage.
—LAO TZU

AT MIDNIGHT ON WEDNESDAY, July 17th, 1918, Dr. Eugene Botkin was awakened from a deep sleep by a clenched hand tugging at his nightshirt sleeve. A voice as aggressive as the sleeve yank boomed, "Wake up!" Commissioner Yakov Yurovsky demanded, "You're to tell them to hurry and get dressed!"

Botkin's bushy, greying eyebrows furrowed. "Can you tell me the reason?" he sleepily asked. The soulless eyes of the Commissioner in charge of Ipatiev narrowed. "It's none of your damn business," he snapped. "Let's say—"

Yurovsky cut off his speech to shoot Botkin the evil eye. "It's for their fucking protection, okay?"

The heavy thud of military boots resonated on the wooden floor as Yurovsky marched out of the room. With a queasy feeling in his gut, the doctor ran his fingers through his unkempt salt-and-pepper beard and then rose from his cot bed. While dressing, the doctor reflected on his former life.

Born in St. Petersburg, Botkin was the oldest son of Anastasia Alexandrovna and Sergey Botkin. His father, Sergey, had been the appointed court physician since 1870 under the former Tsars Alexander II and Alexander III. Sergey Botkin was considered a Russian medical science founder who introduced pathological anatomy and autopsy diagnostics into modern Russian medical practice.

Eugene Botkin followed in his renowned father's footsteps, receiving his Ph.D. degree in the properties of blood hematology at Kirov Military Medical Academy. He was appointed Chief Physician at Saint George City Hospital in St. Petersburg.

While practicing at this hospital, Eugene received the chance of a lifetime. When Dr. Hirsch, Alexandra's physician, succumbed to pneumonia, Botkin was highly recommended to take the former doctor's place.

Over time, the profoundly religious Eugene developed lots of patience for Alexandra, whose deluded conviction was that she had a life-threatening disease. Botkin learned the Tsarina did not like to be contradicted:

"You don't know your backside from your elbow," she spat. "I *know* I have a heart condition."

The Tsarina had persuaded herself that she had a bad heart condition, but her doctor knew otherwise. Botkin diagnosed the mentally unstable Alexandra as a hypochondriac.

To ease her preoccupation from the self-induced, debilitating neurosis, Botkin curbed Alexandra's court duties, advising rest periods and the use of a wheelchair when accompanying her children for lengthy walks around the palace gardens.

Eugene devoted much of his time to Alexandra and Alexei, treating his hemophilia with the only medical option available—blood transfusions obtained from Siberian peasants, who were paid the equivalent of ten cents (by today's calculation) per blood donation.

But Eugene Botkin's devotion came at a price. His marriage to Berliner Olga ended. Olga accompanied him on an Imperial engagement to Crimea in the fall of 1909. She saw so little of him that she left Crimea and headed back home to be with their children, Dimitri, Yuri, Tatiana, and Gleb.

Eugene was not expecting the consequences of his spousal neglect. Olga was having an intimate affair with Friederich Lichinger, her children's German tutor. She wrote to Eugene: "I want a divorce to be with the man I love."

A stunned Eugene reluctantly agreed but stressed he wanted custody of the children. "Not happening," was her stance.

But a Russian court order decided in Eugene's favor. His custodial children then joined the Romanov children at Alexander Palace until they reached adulthood and then went separate ways.

Shortly after the kids were housed at the palace, Botkin learned that his ex-wife had been killed in an Allied bombing raid in Berlin. He blamed himself for not being an attentive husband to her.

Eugene Botkin's adult children had not forgotten or forgiven him for not putting their mother first before his royal duties:

"It was all about *them*, Father, and not our precious mother," Gleb admonished. "Shame on you; I hope your soul never finds peace!"

Dr. Eugene Botkin never remarried and never spoke to his children again. True to the accusations, he remained loyal to his employers for the remainder of his life.

Now, the devoted royal physician, of free will, joined the Romanovs into exile.

This correspondence was penned before he was rudely awakened on July 17th, 1918:

I am making a last attempt at writing a letter, at least from here, although that qualification, I believe, is utterly super-fluous. I do not think I was fated to report to anyone from anywhere. My voluntary confinement here is restricted less by time than by earthly existence. In essence, I am dead, dead for my children, dead for my work. I am dead but not yet buried in the ground or buried alive, whichever, the consequences are nearly identical. As I was calmly reading the day before yes-terday, I saw a vision of my second-born son's face, but dead, in a horizontal position, his eyes closed. Yesterday, at the same reading, I suddenly heard a word that sounded like Papa. *I burst into sobs. Again, this is not a hallucination because the word was pronounced, the voice was similar, and I did not doubt for an instant that my daughter, who was supposed to be in Tobolsk, was talking to me. I will probably not hear that voice so dear or feel that touch so dear with which my little children so spoiled me. If faith without words is dead, then deeds can live without faith if some of us have deeds and faith together, that is only by the special grace of God. I became one of these lucky ones through a heavy burden—the loss of my firstborn, six-month-old Serzhi. This vindicates my last decision when I unhesitatingly orphaned my own children to carry out my physician's duty to the end, as Abraham did not hesitate at God's demand to sacrifice his only son.*

I quote the philosopher Robert Burton: What cannot be cured must be endured.

CHAPTER SEVEN

The Final
Sunrise
- July 17, 1918 -

*Murdering the innocent to advance an
ideology is wrong, every time, everywhere.*
—GEORGE W. BUSH, 2002

A FEW MINUTES AFTER MIDNIGHt on July 17th, Nicholas II, dressed in his Russian Imperial uniform made of dark-green cashmere, entered the Ipatiev basement with Alexandra, wearing a full-length silk gown embroidered with gold and silver threads, and their children: Olga, Tatiana Maria, Anastasia, Alexie, with Dr. Botkin and servants in tow, believing they were there to have a family photograph taken before another relocation, as Dr. Botkin had relayed.

No one took any notice of the absence of camera equipment. In the chilly room, Commissioner Yurovsky ordered Nicholas to sit on one of the two chairs in the center. Then, Yurovsky instructed Alexandra to occupy the remaining chair.

Not waiting for his instruction, an ashen faced, slightly grey Alexei dashed to his father and climbed onto his lap. Yurovsky instructed Dr. Botkin, the Romanov girls, and the servants to stand behind the seating arrangement. Faces turned to each other without real concern. After all, it was only a photoshoot before being taken somewhere safer.

Yurovsky's right-hand man, Pavel Medvedev, and several uni-formed men entered the basement, lined up, and then aimed M1895 revolvers embossed with a Red Star at the wide-eyed captives with trembling insides and blood draining from their faces.

Nicholas II was shot at point-blank range first. Then a volley of bullets found their marks.

Alexandra died instantly, as did Dr. Botkin and the servants. Thirteen-year-old Alexei, his thin body spattered with his father's blood, moaned. Yurovsky silenced the boy with a bullet to the head.

The executioner's attention was drawn to the crumpled Ro-manov girls.

"It's not possible," Yurovsky growled in disbelief. "They are still fucking alive!" The flummoxed murderer could not have guessed the reason.

Underneath their dresses, the girls wore bulletproof corsets—girdles stiffened with copious amounts of jewelry sewn into the fabric the day before their supposed photo shoot.

Was it intuition when their mother's sixth sense kicked in, and she made them sew the gems into their underwear?

Stumbling over each other, the Grand Duchesses bolted for the door. An incensed Yurovsky bellowed, "Enough of this drama. Bayonet the bitches, *now!*"

Sharp steel finished off the living, or so the executioners believed. With blood running in streams, the slain humans were dragged out by the firing squad and flung onto the courtyard.

The murderers thought they had ultimately wiped out a dynasty, shrouded in mystery and religion, which had reigned in the Empire of Russia from 1613 to 1917.

They were wrong.

CHAPTER EIGHT
Betrayal
- Summer, 1918 -

It is in your moments of bad decisions
that your destiny is designed.
—LUCIA MANN

BEFORE HIS DEMISE, NICHOLAS REALIZED there would be no access to the outside world. Still, he kept hope alive that his cousin, King George V, whom he reached out to by mail before being relocated from Siberia to Yekaterinburg, would come to the rescue.

The two royal monarchs had a warm, close relationship and bore an uncanny, twin-like physical resemblance. Presumptively, Nicholas believed George would grant him and his family immunity in England without hesitation.

Alexandra didn't share her husband's optimism:

"Sometimes things don't work out as one wants them to."

"How dare you take hope away," Nicholas snapped. "George will not let us down."

That day, the optimist wrote in a diary: *I have sorted my belong-*

ings and books and the things I want to take with me when I go to England.

He told himself to be strong because things would get better. He didn't know that he had been forsaken in the darkest times.

In the spring of 1918, a mob of angry protestors rallied outside the gates to Buckingham Palace, with rally cries:

"Hats off to the Russian Workers' Revolution," one person praised.

"We want the same independent rights for the working class."

"Down with the Romanovs!"

"We don't want them here."

Sighing heavily, the British monarch watched as the riot police used water cannons to disperse the protesters. His private secretary, Lord Stamfordham, entered his office, placing several daily newspapers—The Daily Express; The News of the World; Sunday Express, on the king's writing bureau.

Splashed on all front pages:

KING GEORGE GIVES REFUGE TO THE BLOODTHIRSTY TSAR, IMPRISONED BY THE SOVIET UNION LEADER VLADAMIR LENIN

George turned to Lord Stamfordham. "This is ghastly. I don't know what to do."

"In my respectful advice, Your Majesty, bringing the Romanovs here to England will probably bring civil unrest."

George sighed. "I agree. We *must* handle this dreadful circumstance tactfully."

That same day, George wrote to Nicholas:

Alicky (his nickname for Alexandra) is the cause of everything, and you have been too weak-willed, dear cousin. I regret that I cannot help you. But I want you to know I am in despair over this decision.

Please keep in touch.

I am your faithful and devoted cousin, George.

The correspondence was intercepted by the Bolsheviks and destroyed. Nicholas would never learn his cousin had betrayed him because he believed blood makes you relatives; loyalty makes you family.

When George was informed of his cousin's execution, he was bereft. The British monarch unburdened his heaviness to Sultan Aga Khan, a close friend, "More than once in our private talks, Nicky had no hesitation in opening his heart to me and telling me of his sorrow. I feel wretched. They are all dead because of me. I will take to my grave this cowardly change of heart when my cousin needed me the most. May God forgive me for being a vacillating fool!"

"Do not place the blame solely on your shoulders," the Sultan consoled. "There were other prominent figures that didn't lift a finger to help them, including myself. How could any of us have known they were to be murdered? But we must do something to help the Dowager and other royal members who are in hiding."

George nodded in agreement. "You are right! I will get on it straightaway."

He placed a call on a secure phone line, "Good afternoon, Vice-Admiral Pridam. I would like you to ready the HMS Marlborough for its voyage to the Black Sea."

The vice-admiral was alarmed about a British battleship traveling through Russian waters. "May I ask what this is all about?"

"No, not over the phone," George returned. "An MI-5 agent will contact you shortly. He will fill you in."

George sent an encrypted message to the British Embassy in Russia regarding the plans to rescue his aunt, Dowager Maria, his cousin, Grand Duchess Xenia, and other Romanov relatives in fear for their lives. His message also stated that an undercover agent had their safe houses' addresses and would inform them of the pending rescue.

The secret operative was told to inform them help was on its way.

On a misty September morning, the unescorted Marlborough moved silently from the anchorage off Yalta on the southern coast of Ukraine, heading into the mist of the Black Sea. Onboard was Empress Dowager Maria, who did not believe her son was dead. Her daughter Xenia, her six sons, the oldest twenty and the youngest, Vassili, twelve, and thirty-five other unexpected passengers stood on the deck.

The asylum seekers arrived unheralded in the United Kingdom six weeks later.

In 1924, six years after the Romanovs' executions, the Labor government under James Ramsay McDonald, the First Labor Prime Minster who had vehemently opposed Britain's entry into World War I, established relations with the Soviet Union. King George adamantly rejected James's plea to leave the past behind and receive Soviet representatives at his residence. His face reddened with rage, *"I will not shake hands with the murderers of my relatives, and that is that!"*

The British government hushed up their sovereign's rejection of Romanov asylum, and Lloyd George became the perfect scapegoat with the dictated statement:

I understand that Lloyd George was not responsible for denying exile to the Romanovs, but it is not expedient to say who was.

Ultimately, King George V failed his cousins when they needed him most. That fateful decision troubled him till the end of his days.

Two days after the execution, Ekaterinburg was occupied by the Czechoslovak Corps, an anti-Bolshevik military Cadre of Czechs, Slovaks, Russian exiles, and former prisoners of war.

General Nikolai Nikolayevich Yudenich, a Russian citizen born in Moscow, led the Civil War invasion. A staunch monarchist, Nikolai's strategy was to overthrow the communists and bring law, order, and salvation to Russia.

Alas, Yudenich arrived too late to save the royal family.

Bolshevik Commissioner Yakow Yurovsky had made sure of that. He had been pre-warned by Russian intelligence that the White Army was nearing Yekaterinburg. The White Army was greatly feared by the Bolsheviks.

"Kill them all and make damn sure they are never found!" was the higher Bolshevik directive.

On September 22nd, 1977, Boris Yeltsin, First Secretary of the Sverdlovsk Regional Committee of the Communist Party, ordered Ipatiev House to be demolished.

"Sooner or later, Russia will be ashamed of this piece of barbarism," Yeltsin later stated.

The *true* motive behind the bulldozing of the infamous abode was because the Russian government had learned from a credible source that the Russian Orthodox Church would turn it into a holy shrine for the Romanov martyrs! Yeltsin couldn't let that happen.

A few pages from Nicholas II's diaries that he had penned before his death were discovered among the rubble by a construction worker during the 1977 demolition:

All around me is treason, cowardice, and deceit. The guards surrounding my family are rude, cocky, and constantly drinking vodka and smoking. What is to become of us?

A lingering matter remains unanswered: Why wasn't the "death" room washed clean as other Ipatiev rooms after all those years? Was it an oversight, or did the hired local cleaners purposely leave the Ipatiev basement untouched?

During the seventy-six days they were locked up, the Romanovs were blamed not only in Russia, but around the world.

The collapse of Imperial rule and their demise was brought about by Alexandra, whose mind didn't speak of royal loyalty, but of desire for another man.

A Winter Palace Court consultant had this say after her imprisonment:

"That crazy woman let our country fall to its knees because of her wild infatuation for the mad monk. His somnolent hypnotic powers controlled her. I'm convinced the true *fall* of Imperial dominance, which thrived for over three hundred years, is all *her* fault!"

The Russian public generally believed Alexandra *was* a German spy. They also believed (incorrectly) that the perverted Rasputin *was* ruling the country.

It *was* the deranged Alexandra who wore the palace pants! Her rallying cry to royal followers was "Trust me!" But her message fell short among all the tight-knit, all-seeing palace servants. Several of them had witnessed Alexandra's lack of physical restraint while in the presence of Rasputin. Flirtatious flashing of eyes, hugging, and often giggling like a schoolgirl with a crush on an older man left little doubt of their intimacy.

"I'll *not ever* trust her," a maid exclaimed. "I've seen things that could send her and that mad monk into the fires of Hell!"

"Oh, please, *tell*," urged another servant.

"I can't," the girl replied softly. "If she learns of my telling, I will disappear for good."

There were many reasons why the royal staff feared retribution from the cruel woman. The abuse came easy for her.

A fifteen-year-old chambermaid was viciously beaten with a walking cane when she knocked over the Tsarina's nighttime porcelain chamber pot, spilling urine onto a wedding gift, a Russian handmade floral rug. Another servant received a smack across the face when she gawked at Rasputin. A cook was scalded with hot broth after the Tsarina complained it was tasteless.

An incensed Alexandra attacked her cook, whose regulatory white cotton pinafore was slightly soiled and headband ties hanging loosely instead of tied back. "How dare you serve food with that dirty clothing!" she snarled. "Remove yourself. Your service is terminated!"

Evil has never-ending depths for a person who cares little about others! The woman born with a silver spoon was unaware that she had become the most hated woman in the palace world.

Alexandra's unpopularity reached the ears of her grandmother, Queen Victoria. "She depends on her superb intellect rather than on emotions or feelings for others," stated Victoria. "She is indeed troubled and needs help. Her behavior is not normal!"

Was this the pot calling the kettle black? Nonetheless, the United Kingdom had never been mightier under her rule.

Her Majesty, Queen Victoria, the longest reigning British monarch at the time, died from a cerebral hemorrhage on the Isle of Wight in 1901, at eighty-one. She became Queen of England after her father, Prince Edward, Duke of Kent, and son of King George III, died of pneumonia in January 1820, shortly after her birth. Princess Victoria's three uncles, who were ahead of her in succession—George IV, Frederick Duke of York, and William IV—had no legitimate children who survived.

The rightful heir to the British throne had been raised in seclusion in Kensington Palace by a detached mother, German Empress Victoria of Coburg-Saalfeld. The young princess was tutored by a governess, Baroness Lehzen, with whom Victoria developed an emotionally dependent bond. Her cold mother never had the time of day for her.

Victoria was crowned Queen of England in 1837, at the age of nineteen. Two years later, following traditional royal protocol, she married Prince Albert of Saxe-Coburg and Gotha, her first cousin, in the Chapel Royal at St. James Palace.

Albert was handsome—tall, slim, with a creamy complexion, high cheekbones, perfect unstained teeth, fine flaxen hair, trimmed mustache, sideburns, and sparkling lake-blue eyes.

Was the bride as appealing as her groom?

Alas, no.

Victoria could never be described as beautiful because she came from a "diluted" stock—epochs of interbreeding by her German ancestors. Her slightly hooked nose, protuberant Habsburg bottom jaw (congenital deformity), tiny child-like feet, and diminutive stature of less than five feet were not flattering. Victoria griped to her mother, "Everyone in my family grows tall but me!"

The new queen did have some favorable attributes, however: a flawless face like a porcelain doll with dimples that drew attention to her soft smile; fair long, straight hair; and the intonation of a singing voice like that of a Nightingale bird. She loved music— trendy popular gospel songs such as *My Mother's Bible* and classical music by the Hungarian composer Franz Liszt were her favorites. She also loved dancing and staying up late.

Why did a handsome prince marry an ugly duckling? The German Prince was given little choice! Royal intermarriage, a centuries-old tradition, is a calculated, shrewd political strategy by heads of state to secure alliances between royal dynasties. Of course, the dreadful consequences of blood-related unions were medically undiscovered. Now, recessive defects are evident:

- Reduced fertility
- Reduced birth rate
- Higher infant and child mortality
- Smaller adult size
- Reduced immune function
- Increased risk of cardiovascular disease
- Increased facial asymmetry
- Increased risk of mental disorders

Born just three months apart, with Victoria being the older, her marriage to Albert was considered a love match by her subjects. Albert wasn't so thrilled with his new label of prince consort (an old imperial rule stated that if a man married a reigning Queen, he would be known as prince consort). He wasn't the first to be locked in an arranged marriage by zealous monarch rulers.

The Queen of England, who spoke English with a strong, distinctive German accent, bore Albert four boys and five girls with her blond hair and Albert's lake-blue eye color. The children were named: Victoria, Albert "Bertie," Alice, Alfred, Helena, Louise, Arthur, Leopold, and Beatrice.

At the start of her first pregnancy, Victoria's true colors came out in a callous comment to the royal midwife, Dorothy Thornley, "If it's a girl, you will drown her!"

The fifty-eight-year-old nurse who delivered baby Victoria into the world was so shocked, she never set foot in Windsor Castle again.

Throughout her pregnancies, Victoria suffered from mid-backaches, severe headaches, abdominal cramping, and severe post-natal depression, hindering her royal duties.

She became dependent on Albert to run the country. This transitive dependency sent Victoria into clinical depression. Her doctor reasoned (speaking in German) that she resented being robbed of her air of command when Albert became more admired than her. But mostly, Victoria resented what pregnancy had done to her.

Following the birth of her last child, she became a human wreck, losing all sense of reality. Her volatile mood swings of cussing and hurling stuff in an uncontrolled rage finally sent Albert to seek solace away from her. Her children were not far behind him. They avoided their mother, whose weight gain, bordering on morbid obesity, made her short stature look even more diminutive. After a lifetime of overeating, the stony-faced, humorless monarch with bulgy eyes and a protruding chin under flabby flesh tried everything to get back in favor with her husband, but time ran out. She was unprepared for the worst day of her life.

At 10:50 p.m. on December 15, 1862, the forty-two-year-old prince consort was pronounced dead by his physician Dr. Jenner: "Prince Consort Albert has died from typhoid fever."

Contradicting Dr. Jenner, royal physician Dr. Watkins diagnosed Albert's cause of death as the Russian flu, the virus responsible for the respiratory pandemic that took the lives of over one million people from 1891 to 1894.

Another medical specialist queried Albert's diagnosis: "I have deep suspicion that the prince consort's death was *not* due to contagious viruses, but instead due to the stresses of taking on the burdens of the queen's duties. It was well known that she had depended upon her husband in every way, from writing official letters and sending dispatches to his approval of clothes and even bonnets."

"I cannot disagree or agree to your hypothesis," Dr. Watkins responded to the specialist. "In my opinion, the prince's depression, insomnia, loss of appetite, bloody diarrhea, and generally not feeling well in the days before his death was probably the cause."

Albert's death brought various medical debates about whether the prince consort succumbed to typhoid fever or flu. Pathologists argued that a virus had not been the result of Albert's demise. They were correct in presumptuous arguments because Albert was suicidal, articulating his wish to leave the world. "I do not cling to life," he snippily remarked to Victoria. "You do! But I set no store by it. If I knew those I love were well cared for, I would be quite ready to die tomorrow. I am sure my days are numbered. I should give up at once. I should not struggle for life. I have no tenacity for it anymore."

Victoria cried, "My beloved husband. Let's love, forgive, and grow old together. Please fight for your life; don't leave me. I will be *nothing* without you."

Albert's passing crushed a heartbroken Victoria. She composed those last moments with Albert:

He drew three long but perfectly gentle breaths with his hand clasping mine, and then all was over. I kissed his cheek and called out in an agonizing cry, "My sweet darling." I fell to my knees in mute, distracted despair, unable to utter a word or shed a teardrop. Ernst (Prince Leiningen, captain of the royal yacht HMY VICTORIA AND ALBERT) lifted me and led me out of the room.

The inconsolable widow ordered Albert's private rooms at Windsor, Balmoral Castle, and Osborne House to be kept as her husband had left them. Victoria also instructed her maidservant, Molly Baker, to place a large jug of hot water, clean towels, and Albert's night attire in his dressing room.

With compassion for their hurting queen, her royal staff supported her bereft bidding, although whispering behind her back was rampant: "She's off her rocker!"

"Yes, she has lost her mind!

"She's crazy."

The widow spared no expense for Albert's funeral.

His coffin was carried in a six-horse drawn carriage with heavy velvet curtains and outsized black plumes. Carved images of angels and doves, custom-made with his initials, adorned the Royal hearse. It was escorted by the Regiment of Life Guard to the Royal Vault in St. George's Chapel at Windsor before being taken a half mile south of Windsor Castle to a mausoleum at Frogmore set in thirty acres of private gardens.

Laid to rest in a tomb, Albert would have to wait thirty-nine years for his wife to join him.

The day after Albert's internment, the devastated widow, numbed with depression, went into seclusion at her oceanfront summer home, Osborn House, perched on the north coast on the Isle of Wight. Prince Albert's love of the beach motivated Victoria to pay £28,000 to buy this mid-19th century seaside mansion from Lady Isabella Blatchford in 1845. Isabella was the daughter of the Duke of Graftin, the eleventh Prime Minster of England. The love-struck Victoria would have gone to any length to please the man she adored.

The mansion that had impressed visiting dignitaries such as Emperor Napoleon III and Tsar Nicholas II now accommodated an unhappy queen who was withdrawn from her official duties.

In her now self-imposed reclusiveness, Victoria commissioned full-size statues, figurines of Albert, and umpteen gold-framed photographs of him to be displayed in all her abodes.

Plaster casts of his hands and locks of his hair were ordered to be treated as sacred relics, as she expressed to all who entered her homes.

Queen Victoria mourned Albert in the widow's weeds for the rest of her life, which ended on a dreary winter's evening in January 1901. That day, she summoned physician Sir James Reid, reporting that she was feeling unwell. The doctor examined her, but he was not overly concerned, and he administered electrolytes for suspected dehydration. But as daylight began petering out, her symptoms worsened.

At half past six that evening, with her son and successor, Edward VII, and her grandson, Wilhelm II, at her bedside, she asked that Turi, her Pomeranian dog, be brought to her. It was the eighty-one-year-old's last request.

A British monarch who had reigned for almost sixty-four years and had survived eight assassination attempts took control of her own funeral arrangements with explicit instructions: No embalming, no lying-in-state, no mourning in black. She did not want a royal hearse, but instead she requested a gun carriage to rest her coffin, with six white ponies to pull the carriage and a naval guard escort.

Victoria's precise funeral arrangements were not the only bone of contention for the royal funeral director, William Banter. She expressed her last wish on an official letterhead displaying her royal monogram:

VRI, VICTORIA REGINA, IMPERATRIX

(Latin for Empress)

I will not be buried within the confines of Westminster Abbey. My last and only wish is to be buried at Frogmore with my beloved Albert.

She was the first monarch to break royal protocol since King George I, who reigned from 1714 to 1727. At age fifty-four, George Ludwig was the first monarch of the Hanoverian dynasty. He was King of Britain and Ireland for thirteen years before dying of a stroke on a visit to Hanover.

Queen Victoria carted the jewelry obsession she'd had since she was a little girl to her grave. On her deathbed, she requested her substantial jewels be buried with her.

From her gem-encrusted brooches, bracelets, necklaces, tiaras, and rings, she picked out two brooches and pearl and diamond necklaces to decorate her burial wedding dress. She also selected rings, gifts from Albert, to be placed on every finger.

After lying in state at St. George's Chapel for three days, the soulmates in life were now souls in Heaven, entombed together for all eternity at Frogmore. As requested, full-size white and blue-grey Carrara marble effigies of her and Albert later adorned their resting place.

Victoria's death marked the end of the Victorian era, a period of Queen Victoria's reign from 1837 to 1901. It was a period of political reform and social change—the Industrial Revolution, marvelous writers such as Charles Dickens and Charles Darwin, a railway and shipping boom, and the first telephone and telegraph.

There was one fragile, very close relative who fell apart at Victoria's funeral service. Funerals are a chance to lean on each other and come closer together, but not in this case!

CHAPTER NINE
Forever Gone But
Not Forgotten
- Saturday, February 4, 1901 -

Grandmothers hold our tiny hands for a while,
but our hearts forever.
—LUCIA MANN

SITTING BESIDE HER HUSBAND and her three very young children in St. George's Chapel was a twenty-nine-year-old, heavily pregnant Alexandra, who was dressed as "Empress of Russia" in a head-to-toe white lace maternity dress with an impressive diamond brooch pinned to an embroidered bodice. She wore an exquisite heirloom, a four-stranded Akoya pearl necklace looped around her swan-like neck, and her auburn, long enough to sit on tresses which had never been seen unbraided publicly hung like a weighty tiara under her full-length tulle veil.

Alexandra wailed, drowning out the choir singing Tchaikovsky's hymn, *How Blest Are They?*

Victoria's nine children, monarchs from fourteen countries (including Kaiser Willem II of Germany), and other mourners turned their heads to the back pew. The Archbishop of Canterbury conducted the faithful to pray for the departed Queen and raised his tone a notch.

Also attending the service were several Russian aristocrats, including Prince Yusupov (Rasputin's archenemy). They all bore "What in the world!" wide-eyed expressions. Yusupov, who always considered Alexandra as a cold-hearted woman, glared at the Tsarina making a spectacle of herself, then averted his scowl at her companion: *Are you going to do something about her behavior or not?*

The Tsar of Russia, in a white military uniform encrusted with gold loops, took gentle hold of his wife's shaking hand. "I, too, greatly mourn her," Nicholas whispered. "Time will heal the loss, my precious wife."

Alexandra recalled her beloved grandmother's words and spat them out, "My wish for you is not to be morally or bodily a husband's slave. My grandmother was right. I have been a slave to your Crown!"

The Tsar's expression was blank with no articulation to counteract her insult. Neither was he expecting her next move, as Alexandra dug her fingers into his gloved hand to release his clasp. She seethed with a contemptuous grimace underneath her heavy veil, "Leave me alone!" She never had any real feelings for the man she married.

At this moment, another memory remained unopened:

"You think the world is just about you, Alix," Victoria scolded, "Mark my words, one day, you will pay an awful price for not trying to change your arrogant mindset!"

Queen Victoria did not trust the Romanovs, referring to them as "Horrid Russia." During her lengthy reign, Victoria met all the Tsars, Nicholas I, Alexander II, Alexander III, and Nicholas II, whose sovereignty coincided with hers. Victoria was deeply disturbed when her favorite granddaughter, Alexandra, occupied "the thorny unsafe throne," as Victoria put it.

With her differences thrust aside, Victoria warmly welcomed Nicholas, Alexandra, and great-granddaughter Olga to Balmoral in September 1896. But a smooth reunion, it wasn't!

News of Nicholas's contentious political arguments conducted behind her back soon came to her royal ears. Her Prime Minister, Wilfred Laurier, aired his upset feelings to his queen. "Your Royal Majesty, if you don't mind me saying, the Russian Tsar is a pain in the buttocks!"

"I agree," she chuckled. "This family has been a pain in *my* backside for years!"

The feuding politicians and their Queen had this in common: *mistrust of Wilhelm II.* Barely two years later, in 1898, their mistrust was proven warranted.

Following a long battle with cancer, Wilhelm's father, Emperor Frederick III, died. His successor Wilhelm II became King of Germany and Prussia. Kaiser Wilhelm II began building Germany into a naval, colonial, and economic power second to none. The twenty-nine-year-old new German ruler pressured Chancellor Otto von

Bismarck to resign in 1980. Domestic and foreign policies rested in the hands of a power-crazed inept ruler.

The Kaiser's pigheadedness would strain Germany's relations with Britain, France, and Russia, which led to World War I. What enraged the British Queen was that Wilhelm had sent his congratulations to Dutch South African Boer War leader Paul Kruger following the defeat of the British raid into Boer territory. (South Africa was a British colony at this time).

Not long after this unthinking blunder, Wilhelm rallied the German infantry to fight in the Chinese Boxer Rebellion (1899-1901), nicknaming his soldiers "Huns," pushing them to fight like Attila's troops. Attila was a fearsome warrior of a tribal empire (present-day Hungary) of Huns, Ostrogoths, Alans, and Bulgars, who dominated from 434 A.D. until his death by natural causes in 453 A.D. Attila, a non-Christian, of Mongolian descent, was nicknamed "The Scourge of God" for sacking and pillaging Roman cities to feed his starving people.

Nicholas, Alexandra, and baby Olga left England to return to Russia. Victoria feared never seeing them again. She would never learn that this would be a fact or learn the *truth*. Alexandra's selfish needs and wants didn't resonate with sound advice, as if rules didn't apply to *her*. To the Tsarina of Russia, advice of any kind was seldom welcome because it did not suit her own agenda.

"I rule, you don't. Don't tell me what I can or can't do."

Without doubt, Alexandra's theatrical refusal to heed counsel contributed to the royal family's horrendous fate in the summer of 1918.

CHAPTER TEN
The Death of the Last Russian Tsar
- 1918 -

Three things cannot be hidden, the Sun,
the Moon, and the Truth.
—ELVIS PRESLEY, 1977

THE UTTERLY EVIL-MOTIVATED 1918 Romanov execution had been a *taboo*, governmentally censored subject matter at the hand of the USSR. That was about to be changed in the fall of 1977, fifty-nine years after the royal family's deaths.

Muscovite filmmaker Gueli Riabov had planned to make a documentary about the infamous Ipatiev home, but other pressing engagements had distracted him until he heard of plans to demolish the site. He drove in haste from Moscow to Yekaterinburg, the city named after Peter the Great's wife, Catherine I, to create this documentary.

Riabov was unaware that the secret agenda to demolish the Ipatiev House by Russia's Communist Party leaders had failed.

Yekaterinburg locals saw heavy equipment turning up at the site and protested outside.

Handing over his business card, Riabov addressed a security guard, "I need to go in."

"I can't let you in. I will lose my job, or worse," the man nervously announced.

Riabov reached into his trouser pocket and pulled out a magnetic money clip. "Will this change your mind?" he held up a thick wad of American dollars, offering it to the guard.

Ivan tucked the money, equivalent to six months' pay, into his service uniform pocket. "Follow me—"

Ivan spotted the Zorki 35mm camera strung around Riabov's neck.

"No. No," Ivan stressed. "It's absolutely forbidden. You *cannot* take pictures!"

Riabov nodded.

"Follow me, but do not touch anything!"

With Riabov's escort leading the way, Riabov and Ivan entered the undisturbed crime scene. The hairs on the filmmaker's neck stood erect and cold shivers ran the length of his spine.

The brown-stained wallpaper, bullet holes, and stained chairs left little doubt about what had occurred here. The rationalizing of this evil sent Riabov's stunned brain into two thoughts: *Someone knows, and that someone isn't telling! and damn it! I must photograph this. Think, man, think!*

"Do you like American cigarettes?" Riabov asked his escort, having observed the smoke-laden smell on his clothing. (Russians loved American cigarettes, which they prohibited at that time.)

With his happy guard taking a smoke break outside the cellar, Riabov clicked away. After the Ipatiev tour left him numbed, Riabov decided to remain in Yekaterinburg until he got answers. The filmmaker checked into the quaint Podvorye Inn.

As luck would have it, he was introduced to Alexander Avdonin, an ethnographer (a branch of anthropology), at the bar that night. Riabov was happy to learn that Alexander Avdonin was an expert in earth science. The sixty-five-year-old ethnographer had shoulder-length, blond hair, dove-gray eyes, and the dark-skin of Jewish descent. They became of one mind—to find the Imperial family's remains.

Born in Yekaterinburg, Avdonin informed his new friend that he met up with one of the Romanov executioners. "I also have information about the possible whereabouts of the Romanovs from other sources," Avdonin informed. The two men discussed how they, as a team, could go about finding the missing bodies.

"I will try to set up another meeting with Alexander Yurovsky, the son of Commissioner Yakov Yurovsky, who I'm led to believe headed their execution."

Avdonin handed Riabov a four-page confession, which his father Yakov had penned after the execution:

We dumped the eleven bodies in a mineshaft. We were then ordered to remove them and take them to the forest, where we buried them in a mass grave. I've forgotten the whereabouts, the forest location, and I believe the gravediggers don't know either. I'm told that the lazy bastards did not fill in the grave after we left, either.

The last note on the back page of the confession read:

Ekaterinburg has fallen to the White Army Infantry, and my Commander has left little doubt in my mind that they would have freed the Tsar and restored him to the throne. Just as well, we are rid of them!

Why Yakov's son turned the confession over to Avdonin wasn't discussed.

Exactly eight months after the executions, "the White Army (anti-communist forces) did seize Ekaterinburg. If it wasn't for one of their foot soldiers, Nikolai Alexeievitch Sokolov, the details of the Romanovs' demise might have remained in the dark forever.

The monarchy sympathizer with a degree in criminal law was summoned by White Army commander Alexander Kolchak, "I'm assigning you to a highly confidential investigation, a very sensitive case investigation of vital significance not only to Russia, but the whole world in general." Commander Kolchak handed Sokolov a manila file stamped: CLASSIFIED.

"Get back to me as soon as possible. I'm informed the Red Army plans to take back Ekaterinburg from us."

Sokolov perused the contents in the privacy of his barracks room. It was an investigation dear to his heart.

In the dead of night, following the information given by the monarchy sympathizer informer, Nikolai Sokolov snuck into the basement. With the aid of a powerful flashlight, he stood still, eyes glued on the wallpapered wall.

Sokolov dug out the bullets with a penknife, picked up a couple of shell casings, and rushed past the chain-smoking Ivan back to the army vehicle.

The following day, Sokolov headed to the Four Brothers Mine. A Bolshevik informer disclosed where the bodies were dumped. To Sokolov's disappointment, the mineshaft held no human remains. However, above ground were the telltale signs—a small piece of delicate lace belonging to a female and a lower denture made of animal bone were verification that, at some time or other, the dead had been there.

On a whim, Sokolov drove to the nearby old mining village.

As expected, terrified of unknown Bolshevik repercussions, the villagers knew and heard nothing. Sokolov was driving away when he spotted a boy sprinting behind his Lada truck. He quickly applied the brakes and rolled down the driver's window. The out-of-breath lad made eye contact. "Mister, I heard you are looking for the dead people, right?" He cheekily countered, "For a price, I will tell you."

Sokolov removed fifty-ruble banknotes (about one American dollar) from his wallet. "You're not getting any money until I hear what you say."

The boy pulled a face. "I helped my father make the rope ladders. I was there with my father when he handed them to the Bolshevik soldiers waiting by the mine hole. A soldier paid my father and told us to leave, but we didn't do as he said. We hid behind a tree and watched them throw lots of dead people into the pit. My father told me never to say a word, but I need the money to buy food." Sokolov sighed heavily.

Throngs of wretched people, mostly women with young children, had run alongside army vehicles begging for food when the army arrived. "Help us. We are hungry," they cried.

Sokolov returned to his barracks. He noticed an envelope lying on his bunk bed.

Get the hell out now! the unidentified writer urged. *Ekaterinburg is going to be recaptured at two o'clock tomorrow afternoon.*

The White Army was forced to retreat after a series of defeats. Sokolov sent the evidence in diplomatic seals on a warship headed for Paris, where he settled in March 1920.

Sokolov recorded his Ipatiev findings, the unsuccessful visit to the mineshaft, the silent villagers, and the boy's revelation. He told friends that it was an unholy execution, punishable by God. Of course, the Romanov refugees disputed Sokolov's story, referring to his writings as *a figment of imagination.* They believed that the Tsar and his family were still alive! Sokolov died of heart failure in 1925. *The Murder of the Royal Family* was published posthumously.

Fifty-four years after Sokolov's death, armed with his book and Yurovsky's written accounts, Avdonin went to the abandoned mine and descended into the mineshaft. Pieces of rotted wood remnants lay under heaped coal dust, but no human or animal remains.

Avdonin drove into the Koptyaki forest and set up camp. At the crack of dawn, Avdonin began a detailed search using ground-penetrating radar equipment to locate the burial site.

After months of scanning, Koptyaki finally revealed its secret to

Avdonin, ending the mystery surrounding the whereabouts of the remains of the Imperial royal family, Dr. Botkin, and the servants.

Avdonin took his hat off, bowed his head, and cried.

Recomposed, he spoke to Riabov by radio phone. "I have found their skeletal remains. It's a joyous day, my friend. God rest their souls."

"Congratulations, my friend. I'll be there as soon as I can. Barricade the site, and don't let anyone near."

The unearthing the remains did not sit well within the changing political climate in Russia. Brezhnev immediately prevented this news from getting out to the Russian public by blocking radio transmissions and banning any airing on their government-controlled television network. Brezhnev's blocking measures failed.

No sooner off the telephone, the Moscovite filmmaker began imparting this shocking report to all media outlets across Europe. A French newspaper's headline announced:

THE REMAINS OF THE ROMANOV FAMILY ARE FOUND IN A REMOTE RUSSIAN FOREST. THE REMAINS OF ONE OF THE ROYAL CHILDREN HAS YET TO BE FOUND.

An American scientist, Dr. Meyer, with the up-to-date photographic superimposition technique, positively identified all the exhumed skulls of the murdered family, except for one. Another forensic scientist, Dr. William Fitzgerald, from the University of Florida, arrived at Ekaterinburg on July 25, 1991, and concluded that superposition was undeniable. After further studies of dental and bone fragments, Fitzgerald announced that *one* family member's skull was not among others.

In 1992, Peter Gill of the British Forensic Science Service suggested that mitochondrial analysis would ultimately be conclusive. Queen Elizabeth's husband, Prince Philip, Duke of Edinburgh, provided a DNA sample. When the investigators compared his DNA with those of the bone fragments, they got a 98.5% match to Nicholas II, Alexandra, Olga, Tatiana, and Alexei.

The DNA sample supplied by Dr. Botkin's granddaughter, Marina Borkina Schweitzer, was instrumental in positively identifying her grandfather through partial dentures and his skull. Also recognized were the servants—Anna Demidova, Aloysius Trupp, and Ivan Kharitonov, whose families had also supplied samples of their DNA.

In 1978, the remains of the last Tsar, Nicholas II, Alexandra, Olga, Maria, Tatiana, and Tsarevich Alexei, were transported to St. Petersburg and laid to rest in the stone chamber of a side chapel in Peter and Paul's Cathedral, their final resting place. Dr. Botkin's remains, along with those of the servants, were interred in the Catherine Chapel, also in St Petersburg.

In August of 2000, the Romanovs were canonized by the Russian Orthodox Church. Why the Russian Orthodox Church chose to make them into Saints is problematic when the Tsar and Tsarina were like a bleak winter, forever cold to what was happening around them. With bottomless superpower rule, these monarchs had transparently irked their subjects with lavish lifestyles while thousands died during this lavish coronation celebration. Hundreds of poor souls were homeless and begging for food on the streets.

Where were the priceless gemstones sewn into undergarments before the execution? What happened to the Romanovs' priceless Fabergé eggs, artwork, crowns, tiaras, gold dinnerware sets, silverware, furniture, clothing, and other effects plundered by the Bolsheviks from the six royal palaces?

After the fall of the Imperial reign and the ensuing civil war, the Bolsheviks sold royal belongings to raise funds for their new state. The possessions were auctioned off or sold directly to billionaires from the U.S. and Europe. Alexandra's sizable trinkets of emerald and diamond-studded tiaras were discreetly sold to other royal families. The Imperial crown was returned to Russia anonymously in 2001.

Russian monarchs had worn it since Catherine II, known as Catherine the Great for her long-standing reign and numerous successes as ruler after the death of her husband, Tsar Peter III. The Russian public didn't know that her given name wasn't Catherine, and she *wasn't* Russian!

Born Sophie von Anhalt-Zerbt, in 1929, she was the eldest daughter of an impoverished Prussian prince. (Prussia does not exist on a map today, not even as a province of Germany. It was banished, first by Hitler, who abolished all German states, and then by the allies, who singled out Prussia for alienation as Germany was being reconstituted under their occupation.)

The remains of Catherine II, the longest-ruling Russian Queen, are held in the Kremlin, meaning "fortress inside a city," the former home of the governor of Russia and the Soviet Union citadel in the center of Moscow. Catherine's skillfully-crafted headpiece had been created by then Court jeweler George Friedrich Eckart and his associate, a diamond craftsman, Jeremiah Posier. The crown was decorated with 4,936 diamonds (2,858 carats), 75 large pearls, and a 398.72-carat spinel.

A piece of royal jewelry that survived the Bolsheviks' sell off is the Kokoshnik Diadem (a traditional headdress decorated with priceless diamonds of various cuts and sizes, with a rare pale pink diamond as the center stone, surrounded by pearls embedded in rich gold-spun cloth). Passed down from Queen to Queen, Queen Elizabeth II owned the diamond. Who owns it now after her death is unknown.

Alexandra's diamond, sapphire, and pearl-encrusted necklace and other pieces of jewelry were snapped up by Marguerite Bowes-Lyon, wife of King George VI (Queen Mother) for an undisclosed amount. After she died in 1953, the priceless pieces were left to her daughter, Queen Elizabeth II.

Alexandra Romanov's exquisite necklace was seen around the neck of Princess Anne, Elizabeth's daughter, at the wedding of William, Prince of Wales to Catherine Middleton on April 29, 2011.

To this day, priceless objects such as Fabergé eggs will probably never come to light. But *someone* knows who has them!

Even so, Romanov jewelry and uncut diamonds *did* escape the sticky fingers of thieves.

Surprised? So was I!

CHAPTER ELEVEN
Ghosts Within the Russian Mountain Wilderness
- July 1918 -

A cat has nine lives. For three, she plays. For three,
she strays. For the last three, she stays.
—ANCIENT PROVERB

MILES AWAY FROM ANY SETTLEMENTS, a low door to a crude timber home with hand-hewn hinges creaked open, and the figure of a tall yet stooped-over male with a pronounced hump on his shoulders stepped onto a pallet deck and into a beautiful summer morning in 1918. Though his aged physical appearance resembled someone with a foot in the grave, he was still spritely, strong as a tree.

The seventy-two-year-old stood in front of a six-hundred square foot single-room cabin constructed of rough timber and heated by a simple barrel woodstove made from scraps of salvaged steel gathered by his deceased parent, Constantin Boris Vladislav, seventy-three years prior. Boris's parents had never spoken openly about their reasons for setting up a home in the unforgiving Koptyaki (Eternal) Forest. Boris knew nothing about their lives before settling in the mountains or of the traumatic reflections they suffered. It was one of their best-kept secrets.

In 1845, fearing merciless persecution from Imperial rule for allegiance to the Christian Ritualists, a sect that refused to obey the Yarovaya laws, the illegal preaching of any religion other than that of the Russian Orthodox Church, Reverend Sergei Polykov urged followers to find peace and safety and leave Poland until this persecution of their beliefs came to an end. Little did the ritualists know that it would be decades before this would come to pass!

Amid the backdrop of the terror of tongues being cut out, or worse, being burned alive, Constantin's father beseeched his son, "Hurry, pack warm clothes. We are going home to Russia."

The destination for the dissenters was Aidara, a remote village on the plains in Western Siberia, the family's birthplace.

Although Constantin feared for his life, the nineteen-year-old was harboring a secret he couldn't divulge to his father. "Go ahead," he glibly said. "I will follow you soon. I must finish stacking hay for farmer Bielec, or I won't get paid. May God keep you safe until I join you."

After tearful goodbyes, Constantin made his way to his lodgings on the 345-acre property where he had worked for over ten years cutting grass and piling up haystacks for cattle feed. His father had overseen a large herd of bulls and cows and his mother cooked three meals a day for the wealthy widower, Mr. Bielec. The family were given free lodging and food and paid approximately forty dollars per month in zloty currency.

Constantin entered the dingy room where a young girl was resting on a sacking sheet stretched between two beams to create a hammock bed. Constantin approached. "I promised to take care of you," he tenderly said. "But you are no longer safe here. We must leave Poland."

Without question, twelve-year-old Bronya helped Constantin pack his few possessions and the hundreds of tiny potato seeds stolen from his employer's store.

As night set in, Constantin strapped their survival items onto the back of a 145 cm tall brown and grey in-foal Yakut filly with a short neck, broad body, and low withers that were bred for milk and meat. (Mongolian Yakutian breed, considered sacred by Russian Cossacks, are frost-resilient horses that can tolerate frigid weather below zero temperatures and are known to dig through as much as five feet of snow to find food during winter).

On this moonless night, the runaways crept out of Bielec's property on the stolen horse used during haying. With little money, only the clothes on their backs, meager food supplies, and a full-sized prayer book, Constantin and Bronya walked an average of twenty kilometers a day through icy Poland, only breaking their journey when tired leg muscles cramped and breathing became too difficult.

Two weeks later, nearing starvation, they arrived in Wisztyniec, a small village bordering Russia. Mistrustful of outsiders, many devout Catholics initially did not welcome the couple but were stunned when they learned the couple had traveled on foot to reach Russia. "Why?" a village elder asked. Constantin's evasive answer was that of being unable to practice their faith as Jews!

If their new hosts had learned the truth, Bronya, surely, would have been handed over to Russian security.

The Wisztyniec community gave them shelter and food in exchange for menial work, but they had not succeeded in leaving their past life behind in Poland as they had hoped!

A visiting family member from Warsaw accosted Bronya. "You look very familiar..."

The former royal servant looked her up and down. "You remind me of Princess Anna."

That did it!

Bronya rushed to find Constantin at the blacksmith's, sharpening an axe. "We can't stay here," he said in a fixed tone. "We must leave *now*!"

With no thought-out escape route, Constantin and Bronya fled Wisztyniec into the eighty-four-million acres of Urals, a mountain range of eternal winter.

After a grueling trek across mountainous crusty spring snows, lingering on animal tracks through dense growth with the probability of awakening ravenous brown bears, Bronya felt the mountains would swallow her up.

"We are going to die out here!" she cried.

"No, we will not," Constantin assured her. "We are tough and will *survive* out here."

Constantin spotted an elevated clearing between the scant pine and larch groves. The weary travelers were overjoyed, agreeing it was the perfect spot for a rest, especially with a fast-flowing creek running alongside one edge of the woods. *This is a practical site to build a forever home*, he thought.

Although summer weather would soon be upon them, Constantin and Bronya knew they didn't have much time to spare. They had to overcome fear and anxiousness and hurriedly made a temporary shelter under a large fallen tree with ample space for two. Constantin began weatherproofing the temporary survival dwelling with thick branches to prevent windstorms and pesky flying insects, such as mosquitoes, from getting in.

Bronya filled the tree cavity with leaves and twigs. While she rested in the hollow, her companion led the tired and sweaty Yakut filly, laden with the liberated tools from Wisztyniec, to a nearby pine spruce, tethered him to the tree, and returned to the clearing. It was at this spot that he would achieve the seemingly impossible.

At the crack of dawn the following day, Constantin marked the borders for the foundation with stakes. He dug six holes on each side in preparation for the framing. The young man toiled unfalteringly, felling trees, stripping bark, and carving semi-circle notches into the twelve-inch logs.

Eight months later, although not so weather-tight with breezes whistling through cracks, the structure was ready to call home! It was a moving moment.

Their new house had extra-wide eaves to propel rain and snow and a low entrance door to help reduce heat loss. It also had out-buildings, including a toilet with a wooden seat over an earth pit, a firewood shed, and a small storage shed attached to an outer cabin wall for dried, cut-up potatoes after the harvest.

The untrained builder constructed a ventilated winter horse stable, divided into two box stalls with a hay loft above to make the pregnant Yakut and her newborn foal snug. Next to the stable was a two-wheel horse cart to haul firewood.

With no interaction with other human or creature comforts, the new homeowners lived like 17th-century peasants, sleeping in their clothing on mattresses stuffed with straw placed atop rough timber planks. Existence for the runaways was a heartless struggle with a minimal diet and little comfort from unpredictable weather, including heavy blasts of snowstorms and temperatures plummeting below minus sixty. Nevertheless, the happy couple worked tirelessly, awakening at 3:00 a.m. each day between the last frost of winter and the first frost of fall, collecting firewood and tilling soil hardened by wind, water, and ice deposits to plant potatoes in the short growing season. Animal snares were checked daily while avoiding dangerous animals such as grizzly bears, wolves, and even Siberian tigers.

Constantin and Bronya fell in love and exchanged wedding vows two years later. They were as happy as pigs in mud, even more so, when their twins were born two years later. Baby Boris and Sophie made the proud couple's lives complete.

The former Princess and, for a brief time, countess had exchanged a life of luxury for being happily poor, as she and Constantin set about teaching her children to read using the only reading material available—her prayer book—and taught them to write utilizing birch bark for paper, birch sticks made into fine charcoal pencils, and berry dye for ink.

At bedtime, Bronya would recite Polish fairy stories from memory. Life was blissful until ten years later when Constantin made his way to one of the animal snares on a nearby slope. His sudden presence startled a black bear weighing about four hundred pounds that was accompanied by two scrawny cubs, tearing at the flesh of a wolverine. The sow clapped her jaws and huffed, letting him know she wasn't happy with the interruption. Although this was not Constantin's first encounter with a bear, he lost his nerve, making the fatal mistake of turning his back on a wild creature. The trapper ran like a mad man as fast as his legs would allow before stumbling over a decaying tree limb. With his wits about him, he huddled in a fetal position and held his breath. Pretending to be dead didn't work. With a death grip, the sow attacked, sinking her razor-sharp incisors into Constantin's face and skull.

As the injured man stared death in the face, he cried in agony. The trapper knew the odds of surviving this mauling were firmly against him. He closed his bloodied eyes as his brain lapsed into unconsciousness, freeing him from agonizing pain. Satisfied that an additional food source was immobilized, the mama bear returned to her wolverine feast.

After what seemed an eternity, the severely injured trapper regained consciousness. Vivid images of his loved ones flashed before his mind's eye. He raised his hands to Heaven and muttered in slurred speech, "My beloved Polish countess and beloved children, remember I will never leave you. I will protect you all from Heaven—" With a final labored breath, Constantin succumbed to death's embrace.

As daylight turned to twilight, with no sign of their father bringing home the evening meal, twelve-year-old Boris turned to his mother, "We must go and search for father," he pressed. "Maybe he is hurt."

No one in the room could have imagined the ending fate of the fellow who had been their loving father and provider. Bronya's heart skipped a beat as intuition instantly kicked in silently: *Something had gone terribly wrong!*

In a soft, composed voice, she hid her unnerved demeanor, "Yes, Boris, *I* will go and look for him."

"We will come with you, mother," the twins said in unison.

Shaking her head in disagreement, Bronya ordered, "No, you must wait here. I will find your father, and *we* shall return together."

Two disagreeing faces were as sullen as three-year-olds could be.

Bronya lit a copper lantern filled with hemp seed oil, then set the braided sack-cloth wick alight. Clutching the brightly lit lamp, Bronya lifted Constantin's axe that was propped against a stack of firewood. Her fine-boned features creased with apprehension.

In the unsafe darkness, a fretful Bronya walked briskly along the familiar trail Constantin had trod hundreds of times to check his traps for forest-dwelling animals such as squirrels, sable, and other small omnivores.

On a moonless night, Bronya's happy life changed for the worse. Her lantern fell to the ground. Bronya sunk to her knees as she saw the outline of her half-eaten partner, dragged over one hundred feet from the trap. Piercing cries cut through the night sky as she rushed back home.

There, with the corners of her mouth drooping in sorrow, a heartbroken Bronya broke the news to her children, who had remained awake awaiting her return. All were in tears, their mournful wailing echoing eerily throughout the cabin.

The wide-eyed children had known animal death, such as the Yakut mare found dead one morning not long after giving birth and whose flesh and afterbirth had sustained their lives throughout a brutal winter.

The children had not experienced the loss of human life or the nature of such death until now.

But the death's shadow would soon again revisit.

Bronya gently stroked the children's traumatized faces. "Father isn't here anymore. He has gone up into the sky to be with God," she consoled.

Boris, his eyes puffy, asked, "What is to become of us now that father is—"

Sophie interrupted, "I can set the traps. I watched father many times."

Boris condescendingly countered his sister, "I went with him more times than *you!*"

Bronya smiled. "We are a strong family, and we will get through this together."

The wannabe adults nodded in agreement.

"As soon as the sun rises," Bronya said, "we will go and get your father and bring him home for burial. But now we must remember him in prayer." All on knees and heads upwards, Bronya recited in Polish, "*Wimię ojca i syna i Ducha Świetego*"—In the name of the Father, the Son, and the Holy Spirit.

At daybreak, the twins, with sad eyes and running noses, walked alongside their forlorn mother, leading a wild horse that Constantin had previously roped and broken, pulling their only cart.

At the site, Constantin's bloodied, mangled body was lifted into the two-wheel wooden carrier he had built to collect firewood and now carried the dead. The grief-stricken family headed home with their departed loved one.

Back at the cabin, Bronya imperceptibly now had concerns that having a grave so close to their home could attract predators. What if *living* flesh was more enticing than any *decomposing* flesh? That thought made her quiver. Bronya instructed, "Gather branches, twigs, and driftwood from a nearby stream."

Within an hour, the pyre, banked up with dried moss and leaves and soaked in hemp seed oil, was ready to receive Constantin Vladislav, the brave teenager who had, without a second thought, saved a damsel in distress.

Bronya ignited the pyre.

Forlorn faces watched the bellowing flames lick the still air, carrying the pungently sweet odor of burning flesh. Bronya sighed heavily. Cutting firewood and other daily chores was now her sole responsibility. That night, tears cascaded and her heart burst with heaviness:

Why did you have to die? Her inner voice cried. *I don't know what I'm going do without you, you are the only man I've ever loved!*

The following morning two young pairs of eyebrows knotted. The stove was unlit, and their mother was not in the cabin. Like clockwork, she got up well before dawn to prepare *bryjka* (porridge) made with crushed seeds harvested from a flowering plant, similar to rhubarb.

The twins rushed outdoors, calling, "Matka. Where are you?"

Baffled, the children began checking everywhere for her. Their world came crashing downhill once more.

They froze on the spot with wide eyes, looking at her spread-eagled body lying in the woodshed. She had blue-and-reddish-mottled blemishes on her face and hands. "Matka, *wake up!*" Sophie cried, tugging at the stiff shoulder of her mother, frozen in a snowdrift outside the woodshed. Sophie's wails pierced the frigid morning air.

Boris had an overwhelming desire to hug and comfort his mother but didn't. The more mature child gently took his sister's quivering, cold hand and led her indoors. Covering herself in blankets, a source of emotional comfort, little Sophie asked her twin, "Is mother with God in Heaven like father?"

"Yes, sister, they are together in Heaven."

Although traumatized by his dad's sudden death, the young boy with an old soul realized survival depended upon him as the de facto man of the house, even though he was still considered a child.

While his sister remained buried under covers, Boris carried handfuls of wood into the cabin and lit the barrel stove. Outside, he collected snow in the metal pot that Constantin had made at the blacksmith's forge in Wisztyniec, placed the pan atop the hot stove, added a handful of dried potato peelings, and called out to his twin, "Food is ready."

A teary-eyed child rose from her bed. The here-and-now head of the household hugged his sister. "Everything is going to be alright," comforted Boris. "We have each other. I'm going to take good care of you. It will be tough, but we must make our parents proud in Heaven."

They weren't children that cowered in fear of the unknown, for they had inherited their father's remarkable strength of character and their mother's steadfast tenaciousness.

Though the parentless children bore survival on their shoulders, they foraged in the sparse landscape for any edible nourishment and water. Boris chopped firewood to crank up the stove in bone-freezing winter months. The children planted potato seeds in the seasonal months. The most dangerous task was removing heavy snow from the sloped cabin roof to prevent a cave-in. The courageous boy fulfilled this winter chore without breaking his neck.

At bedtime, the inseparable twins cuddled on one straw-filled mattress, having vivid dreams that seemed to worsen as time passed. They no longer wanted to read from their mother's prayer book or compose sentences on birch bark as she had taught them. Instead, they invented imaginary stories. In a fanciful fantasy, Boris made up stories of mystical forest creatures dwelling in the Koptyaki Forest, who protected them from harm and would continue to do so even after they had passed from life.

Alas, the resilient twins, who endured hardships beyond imagination without other lifestyles to compare to, would not enjoy the protection of the forest spirits, as had been dreamed.

CHAPTER TWELVE
The Past Is
Never Dead
- Friday, July 19, 1918 -

Life is filled with twists and turns, but an unexpected
visitor can change a life forever.
—LUCIA MANN

WITH A FULL-LENGTH, DISHEVELED BEARD resting on his chest, Boris slipped on his shoes made only from birch bark and sauntered to an enclosure made of wood slats, with grass branches securing the panels together. Behind the slats, a horse was stomping the ground excitedly, braying loudly.

Boris's arthritic fingers gently stroked her mane, tangled with grass, twigs, and burrs. "We have much work to do before the day ends, *pozhilaya dama* (old one)."

Almost thirty years prior, Boris had encountered the foal, snorting in distress, with one front hoof held fast in a snare. "Be still!" he soothed. "You're not one I wish to harm."

Boris secured a rope around her neck before springing open the trap. The young filly fought hard to escape from this two-legged creature, but she was no match for the muscular cowboy, who was taught horse husbandry and how to rope an animal at age five by his father.

Boris harnessed the mare to the cart. With the horse reign held tight, Boris led the "Old One," as all the horses had been named from the pen, passing three rock-built mounds scattered with wild sage leaves.

Boris respectfully bowed his head to the dead as he passed the graves. Wood crosses on the graves were marked with blackberry dye: *Matka*, *Sophie*, and *Malyshka* "Baby girl." The aged man could scarcely have imagined that the cross bearing the name *Bronya* was not reflective of his mother's full name.

Princess Anna Sophie Bronya was, in the summer of 1833, the only child of Prince Sobieski of Warsaw, and Princess Sophie of the Austrian Habsburg dynasty.

Anna had inherited her mother's allure, visibly pleasing to the eye. Words could not do her beauty justice. Anna was her mother's "ray of sunshine," with golden hair, rosy cheeks, glacial-blue eyes, and a smile that could light up Poland.

Anna was educated by a Russian tutor, who taught her Latin, mathematics, ancient history, philosophy, and social science. She was unaware of her parents' diabolical scheme—hatched from the day she was born—to promise her to Count Alfred Wojciech Poniatowski, a descendant of William the Conqueror, King of Great Britain from 1066 to 1087.

Reputedly, Poniatowski was the wealthiest man in Poland after he inherited a medieval English castle from the mid-10th century in five thousand acres, surrounding farms, pastures, vast forests, and village properties, ills, mines, and a brick factory from his father Count Graf Alfred Poniatowski. Anna's marriage was a union of necessity, as her father was a heavy drinker and gambler verging on bankruptcy.

The prince habitually scrounged money (up to half a million dollars in today's currency) to pay off his gambling debts from Count Alfred. When the nobleman couldn't repay this debt in full, he offered his daughter's hand to the avaricious count.

In an intricate web of lies, the prince cunningly misled the naïve Anna, saying, "Your husband-to-be is a handsome fellow, and one day you will be the Queen of Poland."

Blinded by a daughter's love for her father, the twelve-year-old Princess Bronya (which became a permanent alias) imagined being swept off her feet by a good-looking spouse.

Still, her father's immoral plot to rid himself of debt became apparent when Bronya met her bridegroom on their wedding day. Count Alfred was not only short in stature, but he was also ruddy-faced, obese, and had only four of his teeth left. He was old enough to be her grandfather. In utter disbelief, young Bronya's bright brain couldn't grasp reality. She wanted to bolt but couldn't unclasp the firm grip on her arm as he treads her up the chapel aisle. Hatred surged through the daughter's heart for the father, whom she had adored. Not only had the man holding all the power betrayed her, but so had her mother, who she believed to be kind and loving. Why she had gone along with the prince's wicked dishonesty was mind-bobbling to the distressed bride.

This hypothetically joyous joining of two people in holy matrimony certainly would be nothing like the fairy-tale romance Bronya had expected, because her wedding night would reveal her groom to be a terrifying incubus!

The child-bride's body was forcefully pinned down onto a four-poster bed by an overweight drunk with unbridled flatulence. With one testicle missing he could not perform, which gave rise to explosive sexual frustration.

In drunken-fueled madness, Alfred beat Bronya within an inch of her life. She was unaware of Alfred's reputation of sexual abuse that included his two previous wives, who died under questionable circumstances. The traumatized bride, with her left eye swollen shut and numerous welts on her body, remained deathly still until she heard his loud snoring.

Bronya's legs sprang into action. The trembling child-bride hurriedly donned her white high-waisted, calf-length chemise wedding dress, then slipped out of the bedchamber.

Bronya tore like the wind from the count's stone fortress, nestled between Prussia and Habsburg in Austria and bordering Russia, into a dank, drizzly, starless night. The patter of bare little feet, making squishy sounds, trod through the sodden grass. Bronya ran and kept running until exhaustion overcame her rain-drenched body. In unfamiliar territory, Bronya slept soundly under an oak tree until she awakened from a slow-wave slumber.

"*Vy v pory adke?*" a concerned warm voice queried. Bronya stared up at the handsome teenager. Fluent in his Slavic tongue, she replied in a haughty intellectual tone, "Do, I *look* okay?"

The nineteen-year-old, who seemingly read her royal heart, pompously responded, "How may I be of service, *My Lady*?"

"*Mudak* (moron), don't speak to me in that tone of voice!"

Constantin Vladislav shut her up by placing a finger to his lips. "You don't have to insult me like that," he pouted. "You can stay under the tree for all I care, but something tells me you are far from home and very scared."

Bronya clasped hands over her face. With an emotional breakdown threatening her sanity, Bronya emptied her inner pain onto a stranger whose eyelids stretched high in disbelief. When she ended her sad story, Constantin wiped the tears off her cheeks with his fingers. "I was out of place to mock you. Not very kind, and I'm so sorry this has happened to you," he said, "I can assure you. I'll never let the *svoloch* (bastard) hurt you again," he vowed. "You will be safe with me. I have lodgings where I work. You can hide there until we can make other arrangements."

From that moment forward, they became inseparable. But alas, far from safe!

At his castle, an angry Alfred deployed his spies, instructing them to bring back his bride. When his scouts returned days later and informed him that his bride was nowhere to be found, he wasn't crying in his beer!

Often attired in effeminate garments, Alfred ordered his manservant to go and fetch local prostitutes, male and female, to the castle to satisfy his depraved needs.

There were no shortages of impoverished women, some were mothers who needed money to feed their children.

While Bronya's husband's public image akin to the mad monk

Rasputin was in full swing, Bronya, who had a world of reasons to harbor loathing, prayed for revenge against the count and her parents. The count's payback karma eventually came in the form of syphilis, commonly known as the "French Disease" amongst French troops during the war between their country and Naples in 1494.

His physician, Dr. Volanski, administered mercury-based pills, declaring the tablets would wipe out the infective agent.

Nonsensical unethical blather!

The side effects of mercury-based medication aggravated the open, pus-filled sores on his mouth, genitals, and anus, causing chronic constipation.

Bathed in sweat and with severe shortness of breath, the sixty-eight-year-old brute, whose naked dancing earned the name "Satan's Dancing Puppet," died alone (many of his repulsed servants had abandoned him) in his bed two months after Bronya had fled the castle.

Count Poniatowski was hated in life as he was in death. He did not receive a state funeral since the religious fractions deemed him to be an ungodly person condemned to the fires of Hell. For three days, his sealed burial casket rested in the castle.

His mourners, a handful of castle servants, and an emaciated young woman in her twenties holding a newborn baby in her arms placed offerings of food and wine for a man who had destroyed his respectable nobility. But according to Count Alfred's Will, the baby in the woman's arms was to become his legal heir to the Poniatowski estate holdings.

This deceased pervert could not have imagined that his bastard son would change the course of future history.

Bronya never revealed her royal blood or her dreadful forced marriage to her children. Only Constantin had knowledge. However, Bronya did conceal her darkest secrets to paper in a hollowed-out prayer book, which surfaced many years later, and found by a person with Count Alfred's DNA.

Bronya outlived her parents, whom she never wished to see again. Shortly after escaping to the wilderness, her father was stabbed to death, allegedly carried out on the orders of Count Poniatowski before his demise. Bronya's mother died a month later from smallpox. On her deathbed, Bronya's mother begged for her daughter's forgiveness. The princess never found forgiveness for either of her parents.

Constantin Vladislav never saw his parents again, either. He wouldn't learn of their debilitating hunger. Starvation had taken them while the Crimean war was in full swing. He also would never learn that the "Old Believers" had vanished without a trace from the village of his birth. Or the many executions carried out on the orders of Tsar Nicholas II.

Bronya had penned a letter yet to be found in her bible:

My darling children, time for me to go. I won't say goodbye, so look for me in rainbows in the sky. Ask the angels to go where you cannot. Just wish me to be near you, and I'll be there for you until we are never parted again. I love you.

CHAPTER THIRTEEN
A Forest Harboring Grisly Surprises
- Friday, July 19, 1918 -

*Koptyaki Forest spews its darkest secrets
like a vile witch's brew.*
—LUCIA MANN

SHORTLY BEFORE NOON, Boris and his horse, "Old One," plodded along a familiar path Boris knew by heart. He stopped to catch his breath and recalled a memory as if it were yesterday.

He had accompanied his father every summer to collect edible fungi, flourishing on dead or dying trees, fallen branches, and decaying stumps, a staple food during the winter. The father and son didn't go into the forest just to pick fungi. Arrows from bows made of hardwood often found their way into any forest creature that had the misfortune to cross the hunters' paths and become dinner.

Boris's fond musings abruptly ended when his horse sharply jerked her head. Stomping wildly and jumping sideways to flee, she bucked off her rider. Caught off guard, Boris landed on his backside. He caught his breath after a few minutes and checked himself for injuries. His ankle seemed to be sprained, but he was otherwise okay. Boris wondered why the quietest of all the previous horses had never displayed such behavior before. He petted her mane and neck to calm her. "What spooked you, Old One?"

Boris hurriedly notched an arrow in readiness. Cautiously, he approached the rustling sounds in the dense bush. He came across a girl lying on the ground. Mouth agape, Boris fell to his knees and dropped his bow. He'd never come across any other person since his father, mother, and sister passed away. His mind was going a mile a minute, wondering who she was and what caused her injuries, the shocked man internally asked:

Who is she? Who, or what, caused her injuries that looked like father's bear mauling?

Warily, Boris tapped the shoulder of her curled-up, thin body, and when the sound of moaning answered, he bolted upright.

"I need help," a faint voice pleaded.

"Who are you, girl?" he asked, towering over her.

No response.

"What are you doing here?"

No response.

Boris shrugged, gently lifted the teenager, and carried her like a baby in his arms back to Old One, placing his "find" in the back of the cart and setting the horse off at a gallop. Mushroom-picking or darting a creature for supper was furthest from his mind.

With starlight dancing above the cabin roof, Boris laid the teenager in a vegetative state on his bed. He covered her with a burlap over-blanket to keep her warm while he fired up the wood stove. Boris turned his head towards the bed where the shallow-breathing girl lay. "I will take care of you."

Without warning, a dichotomy of reminiscences resurfaced in Boris's mind. Flashbacks flooded through him. He tried pushing the memories to the corner of his mind, but his defiant remembrance wasn't to be denied. Tragedy replayed in his mind as if it were only yesterday.

"God is punishing us for our sins!" Sophie wailed, clutching a full-term, stillborn baby weighing less than three pounds with a misshapen skull, fused limbs, and cleft palate. (The effects of inbreeding with anyone closer than a second cousin are genetically endorsed! According to genealogical research studies, one in ten people is inbred. *Holy cow!* Interbreeding was a fundamental strategy amongst royal families to retain their power!)

Boris lowered his head as shame and guilt overflowed through him:

What if I hadn't—?

His past child-on-child intimacy hadn't been intentional; it had just occurred.

Shortly after their mother had died, puberty began, signaling sexual attraction, holding gazes much longer than usual, lingering touches, and kissing. The siblings were intimate, just like their parents had been under the same roof. Madly in love, the twins chose to disregard one of the bible lessons Bronya had read: *Cursed be he that lieth with his sister.* [Deuteronomy 27-22]

That day, with the rain turning into heavy snowfall, Boris pleaded, "I must bury our baby before the ground becomes too hard, Sophie." He held out his hands." Give her to me." In an abyss of grief, Sophie tightly clasped the dead baby girl to her breast. His eyes wet and swollen with tears, Boris removed the infant by force. She screamed at him, repeating her earlier words, "God is punishing us!"

Sophie went into an unreachable world.

With the dead newborn wrapped in hessian sacking, Boris headed outdoors, leaving his tormented sister staring at the wall. He couldn't think or process the moment and did not suspect further sorrow to come before the day was out.

Boris dug a small, shallow grave between two immature pine trees. He kissed the baby's head before laying her on the damp earth and backfilling the tiny grave. The grieving man scoured the forest for small stones to place on the grave. Afterward, he reached into his pants pocket and threw a handful of wild sage, Sophie's favorite herb, among the rocks.

"Rest in peace, innocent child," Boris intoned sadly. "Please forgive us."

Boris didn't ask God for this same forgiveness. He was done with religion.

A forlorn father returned to the cabin. Sophie was absent. Frowning, Boris went in search of her.

"Oh, no, no," he cried, his numbed mind unable to process what he saw.

Rope-tied to a rafter in the horse shelter, Sophie had hung herself. Boris fell to the ground, pulling his knees up to his chest. "She's gone! Both are gone!" he wailed. "I was here for you, and you never even said goodbye!"

That night, unbearable sorrow overcame him, blaming himself for his sister's suicide.

Death for her seemed the only answer for their shared disgrace. But it was the baby's death that got to the brokenhearted man. He started to cry, not sure if it would ever stop.

An unforgiving wilderness knows all about death and has snatched many an unfortunate soul who entered her domain, and now two more souls would join them.

Tragedy has consistently followed this family.

With lamplight guiding his way, Boris headed to the stream to get water. He returned to the cabin and pushed guilt and blame aside as he focused his full attention on the teenager. "Open your eyes," he charged.

With irregular breathing and no reflex movements, his visitor remained silent.

Unsure of how to treat her many wounds, Boris removed her bloodied dress that clung to raw, inflamed flesh. His loud gasp echoed when the shiny brooch encrusted with gemstones and a handful of uncut diamonds spilled out from her corset lining. He'd never seen such finery before. His mother only possessed a silver necklace suspending a crucifix.

Boris placed the girl's jewelry in a wooden box above the bed, then attentively removed several shrapnel fragments lodged in her arms and legs with the tip of a handmade hunting knife sterilized by fire. Satisfied he had gotten them all out, Boris reached for another wooden container housing wild marsh marigold seeds and balm made from wild sage mixed with fireweed. Boris sighed as he recalled returning home with bunches of red blooms picked from the creek banks. Fascinated, he had watched his mother wrap the stems of the flowers together with vine tendrils before hanging the upturned flowers to dry.

Boris soaked a handful of the seeds in the warm water, reflecting once more on how this herbal remedy soothed raw blisters when he burned his hand on the wood stove as a small child.

Would it help the girl's horrific burns, gunshot wounds, and knife slashes?

The spurred-on man tended to his patient's injuries, dabbing the marigold-infused water on wounds. After washing away clumps of dried blood that had been nestled in her strawberry blond hair, Boris applied horsetail weed salve to the single gunshot wound in her abdomen and the two stab wounds in her chest.

"You have to wake up," Boris implored. "You will waste away. I need to feed you to make you strong again."

The teenager remained in her silent world.

Boris slept on the floor beside her with little concern for his throbbing ankle. He had been so lonely for many long years. Just the thought of having the company of another human in his life brought a flood of tears.

She emerged from her coma two days later. Her eyes slowly opened as she blinked awake. A delighted Boris hugged her. "Devochka (Girl). I've made potato soup. It will do you good and make you well again."

The teenager in Sophie's oversized hemp dress had no conscious awareness. Her name and past a blur, the seventeen-year-old made eye contact. "Who are you?" she asked in an agitated tone. "Where am I?"

An exhilarated caregiver bombarded her with questions: "Who are you?" he countered. "How did you end up in the forest?" "Who hurt you?" "My name is Boris Vladislav. What is your name?"

The teenager stared at the old man who had saved her life. A faint voice revealed, "My whole family has been murdered." a fractured hand reached out to grab his. "Please," she pleaded, "you *must* help me get to St. Petersburg."

His injured brain had muted and slipped into the dark void of memory loss. Boris rubbed the back of his head in confusion. His hermit mind couldn't make sense of what she'd said. One thing, however, did make sense: His patient wouldn't live much longer. Her torn skin had the rank odor of a flesh-eating infection.

Unable to control his overly attached emotions, he broke down, sobbing his heart out. Boris cradled the unconscious teenager. "I can't lose you like my father, mother, sister, and baby daughter," he cried. "Please fight, girl. I love you."

Some things are never meant to be, no matter how much we wish they were.

Over time, with Boris's tender care, the mysterious teenager recovered from her horrific injuries but not from memory loss. She followed Boris around like a lost puppy. The old man was more than happy to be a surrogate parent, but darkness lurked within his being that would eventually lead to his undoing.

Four months later, their happy togetherness ended when Boris attempted to be intimate with her.

"Get away from me!" she shrilled, trying to fight off his groping hands from going any further. "Don't touch me!"

Her brain halted her speech, purging a raw remembrance of what happened at "The House of Special Purpose."

The teenager reached for the stone used to wedge the fire door open. The blow to his head was swift. Boris groaned in agony. The violent impact had caused a copious amount of blood that flowed from ruptured blood vessels. Boris gasped and then stopped breathing.

His assailant dropped the bloodied weapon and fled outside into the cold November night air. Quivering from head to toe, she thought that her attacker might come after her. The shaking girl had no clue Boris was dead.

CHAPTER FOURTEEN
Grand Duchess,
Anastasia Nikolaevna Romanov
- Born June 18, 1901 -

The past beat inside her like a second heart
that did not wish to resurrect.
—LUCIA MANN

TUCKED AWAY IN THE OLD ONE'S SHELTER, Anastasia lay in darkness under bundled hay as she suffered from auditory hallucinations:

Survive, precious child, a voice in her brain urged. *We will not give up on you; don't give up on yourself.*

Was it a deceased family member whispering to her broken heart?

As daylight broke, she waded in waist-deep snow to the cabin. She didn't hear the high-pitched noise from a light aircraft circling above.

"Is that what I think it is?" the pilot commented to his passenger, pointing his finger at the pillars of smoke funneling upward into the dark-blue skies.

Vadim Vavilov, a Russian geologist who commissioned Andrzej

Poniatowski to fly him from Moscow to Yekaterinburg to attend a meeting, followed the gesture, looking out the cockpit window. "Yes, I see it. That's odd. I've never witnessed a wildfire at this time of the year. Let's check it out."

Poniatowski, who had bought the THULIN two-seater plane of a retired Finnish Air Force Captain, was beginning a slow descent from twenty thousand feet when a sudden tailwind spun the plane.

The calm aviator made a perfect touchdown on the narrow, snow-packed runway, taxiing the aircraft to a gradual halt. Throughout the bone-jarring moments, a ghostly pale Vadim wished that he hadn't said, "I think we should check it out!"

"That was a nail-biting experience," the fifty-year-old geologist exclaimed, scrambling out of the plane. "Have we landed anywhere near the smoke?"

The twenty-three-year-old aviator held back laughter, replying, "No. We have to hike into the forest to get to the source."

Vadim insisted, "Then let's get a move on before it gets dark!" Layered in snug, sub-zero clothing—polar fleece jackets, waterproof pants, woolen caps, gloves, rubber boots, and packs strapped to their backs—the men set off.

The aromatic waft of burning wood met their nostrils. Disbelief cemented their boots into the deep snow at a clearing. Vadim and Poniatowski couldn't believe what they were witnessing. It was as if they had stumbled upon ALFHEIM, the land of elves in Norse mythology.

"Are my old eyes deceiving me?" Vadim exclaimed. "This is not *real*! I know of no one who could survive out here in Koptyaki!" Without another word and not knowing what to expect, the men gingerly made their way toward the dilapidated cabin.

"The door's wide open," Vadim stated. "Hello," Vadim called out. "Is anyone here?" Only the eerie timbers creaking in the icy temperature met their ears. The men entered the cabin.

"Someone for sure lives here," Vadim said. "The woodstove is lit."

Vadim jumped backward at Anatasia's appearance in the doorway. Vadim exclaimed, "*Oh-oh!* You just about frightened the life out of me!"

Both men gaped at the apparition, who stepped in as if there wasn't another human in the room and went straight to the woodstove. Opening the stove, she placed her cold hands near the flames.

"*Co du kurwy nędzy* (what the F!)," blurted Poniatowski, using his native Polish tongue for the first time since setting off from the Moscow airport. "She looks like the walking dead!"

Their astounded eyes were glued to the blood-spattered teenager with matted tresses and several bald spots.

Thinking she couldn't be there alone, he queried, "Where are your parents?"

Anastasia's dirty, thin index finger gestured toward a rustic cot bed.

Anastasia's finger remained extended. Vadim pulled back the bedding and jumped backwards. Staring, unmoving and unblinking, he squawked, "*Oh no!* There's a dead guy under here."

Boris's stiffened body was grotesquely bloated with decomposition gases. They covered their nostrils and mouths.

"How long do you think he's been dead?" Poniatowski probed.

"Not quite sure," Vadim replied. "I'm guessing maybe a couple of days, and he didn't die naturally, that's for sure! Take a good look at his caved-in head." Vadim pointed at the bloodied stone by the bedside, participles of grey brain matter and cranial bone fragments adhering to it.

"That's for sure the murder weapon."

Obviously, something had seriously gone wrong, but who had done it and why?

Vadim observed the girl who hadn't moved a muscle in front of the wood stove.

"Do you think *she* killed him?" he asked Poniatowski.

"Maybe, if there is no one else here to have done it," Vadim replied.

"Or the actual killer is watching us," Poniatowski countered. "We must get back to the plane and alert the police."

"Okay, but I'll try talking to her," Vadim suggested. "Look around and see if you can find anything that will give us a clue as to who either of them are." He lowered himself to the cabin floor, squatted beside her, and reached for her hand. High blood pressure altered her eye color, giving her reddish eyes, like that of a zombie. Anastasia shrunk back against the wall. Vadim had a daughter about her age, and softly said, "Don't be scared. I'm not going to hurt you. But I need some answers. Do you speak, girl? What's your name? Is the dead man your father? Is anyone else living here with you?"

She gave no response.

Vadim sighed.

As he was rising from his squatting position growling, hungry pangs met his ears. "Oh my God, you must be hungry! When last did you eat something?"

Vadim checked around the room to see if there was anything he could give her. Not a morsel of anything edible. He reached into his backpack, finding only a mandarin. "I'm sorry; this is all I have."

A grubby hand snatched the mandarin, and the hungry girl bit into the fruit, devouring both the flesh and the peel.

"Poor thing, she probably hasn't had anything to eat since—"

Poniatowski interrupted, "You are not going to believe what I've just found."

"What?"

"Come over here."

Vadim examined the hollowed-out bible and then the items Poniatowski had placed on a round, wooden table, the only piece of furniture in the abode. The gold brooch studded with emeralds and diamonds, a handful of uncut diamonds, and a gold cross. "What the hell!" Vadim exclaimed.

"That's not all! Look at the inscription," Poniatowski added. "This bible belongs to Princess Anna Sophie and Countess Bronya Poniatowski.

Oh my God, it's your last name," Vadim exclaimed. "Do you know her?"

"She married my father, Count Alfred Poniatowski, sixty-three years ago."

Not taking his eyes off the dazzling gemstones, Vadim said, "I'm a little confused. She's your mother, right? So, this wild girl might be your blood relative?"

"No," Poniatowski replied. "We are not flesh-and-blood related. My mother was one of the Count's many mistresses. The old shitbag left the castle to my mother when he died. I inherited his title."

Vadim scratched his head. "So, you are a *real* Count!" he remarked in a sarcastic tone. "Good for you. I'm not sure what this has to do with me. I'm more interested in these jewels. They must be worth a small fortune, and I'm entitled to a share. Finders, keepers, right?"

His jaws tensed. Poniatowski scowled at Vadim, and then something snapped in the mindset of this meek man who couldn't step on an ant. Poniatowski reached into the braided belt strapped to his waist. With a Beretta handgun aimed at him, Vadim cussed, "What the fuck, Andrzej! Have you gone insane? I was only kidding about the *finders, keepers*. The stuff is yours by right. Put the fucking gun down!"

A single bullet entered his head, forever silencing the shocked man.

The gunshot resonance opened a floodgate for Anastasia. She screamed in terror, "No, no, no! You killed all my family, and you tried to kill me." With the past events devouring her, Anastasia's skinny legs made a beeline for the cabin door. Poniatowski quickly blocked her exit and placed an index finger to his mouth, "*Shhh!* I'm taking you home to Poland, where you belong. You'll be safe with me."

With a firm grip on Anastasia arm, Andrzej returned to the table and put Bronya's handwritten letters and the valuables into his backpack. Anastasia slumped onto the floor and watched Andrzej remove Vadim's warm coat, hat, and boots. "Put these on," Andrzej instructed. "You are going to need them."

The murderer guided the wide-eyed Anastasia, mistaken for the offspring of Princess Anna Sophie Bronya of Poland, out into the cold. Thirty minutes later, the aircraft engine sputtered into action before taking off.

Twists and turns like epic fiction lay ahead for the Grand Duchess Anastasia Romanov. Like a puzzle missing pieces, Princess Anna Sophie, Countess Poniatowski, and the other deceased wilderness inhabitants, would remain a mystery to the outside world. However, rumors spread throughout Russia and Europe that one Romanov child had survived the massacre.

Death in general always brings out the vultures and, in this case, pretenders.

More than a half dozen women came forward claiming to be Anastasia and hoping to cash in on the Romanov fortune held in European banks. They were swiftly exposed as frauds, but then they had yet to meet Anna Anderson, the trickster that fooled nearly everyone.

Born in 1896, Anastasia Tchaikovsky arrived in America on the ocean *Berengaria* on February 6, 1928. She claimed to be the Grand Duchess Anastasia, who had narrowly escaped the execution of her entire Romanov family.

The imposter was warmly welcomed to America by Gleb Botkin, the son of the Romanov family doctor murdered in Ipatiev House. Gleb addressed her as Your Highness. He affirmed at a press conference that she was undoubtedly Grand Duchess Anastasia, who he had played with at the Winter Palace as a child.

The fake Anastasia was treated as a celebrity at society parties held in her honor. She was afforded free accommodation at fashionable hotels, where she had registered under the name Anna Anderson, which became her permanent alias.

Throngs of international journalists swarmed her hotel foyers and often left empty-handed when she refused to come out of her room.

The Grand Duke of Hesse, Anastasia's uncle (Alexandra Romanov's brother, Ernst), wasn't buying her story. He hired a well-known and highly respected private investigator, Robert Vaughan, to look into her claim. The famous sleuth soon uncovered the truth.

Anna Anderson was actually Franziska Schanzkowska, a Polish-German factory worker with a long history of mental instability, such as extreme paranoia and suicidal tendencies, who was often seen exhibiting violent behavior. She was committed to an insane asylum after a factory explosion in 1916, but she escaped from the institution in 1920, turning up in the United States eight years later.

In 1994, American forensic scientists also sought answers at the requests of the surviving Romanov family members. Dr. Greenbaum, using a sample of Anderson's intestine taken after surgery from the Virginia Hospital Center in Arlington, compared Anna's DNA with that of the Romanovs'. It came back conclusive: Anna Anderson was positively *NOT* a Romanov!

DNA testing did not end there. A strand of her hair was a one hundred percent match with Karl Maucher, her great-nephew, positively identifying her as Franziska Schanzkowska. Finally, the trickster's claims of being the Grand Duchess Anastasia were proven false. The "wannabe" Anastasia died from pneumonia in 1984.

Since the discovery of the Romanovs' remains, more than half a dozen women claimed to be the lost heir to the Romanov fortune.

A suicidal woman was pulled from the Landwehr Canal in Berlin in winter of 1920 by a fisherman. The woman refused to disclose her identity to German officials and was committed to the Dalldorf Berlin Asylum. She lived there in anonymity until 1922, when she, out of the blue, announced she was none other than the missing Grand Duchess Anastasia.

At that time, Europe was filled with hundreds of Russian exiles, and many sympathetic czarists rushed to the woman's side. At first glance, the sympathizers were convinced she was the missing Romanov. She was articulate in several languages and had scars that were consistent with gunshot and knife wounds. Fraudulently, she informed her avid supporters: "A kind Bolshevik soldier hid me in his home and helped me to escape to the West."

A loyal supporter, who just happened to be a lawyer, forced her release from the asylum. She took refuge with one of her staunch believers at his luxury home. When her warped web of deceit that had trapped so many gullible persons finally caught up with her, she took her own life by swallowing strychnine.

Following her published death, many other imposters also faded into oblivion.

In the spring of 1998, a group of fur trappers came across the burned cabin Constantin built with its skeletal remains, equine bones, and the undisturbed three graves. Nothing remained of the home which once held unconditional love and dark secrets!

The dead are not giving them up any time soon!

The unsolved enigma of what truly happened to the *real* Anastasia, hidden away in a castle in Poland, would have forever remained an enigma until an investigative reporter dug her teeth into betrayal, lies, and deceit.

PART TWO
The Past and the Present

"You have to know the past to
understand the present."
—Carl Sagan

CHAPTER FIFTEEN
Berlin, Germany
- October 29, 1945 -

In talking about the past, we lie with
every breath we draw.
—William Maxwell, 1908

IN THE SHADOW OF WORLD WAR II, a tall man in his fifties in a formal dress shirt with spear-point collar tips, white and red necktie, brown flannel jacket, and trousers clutched a large duffle bag in his left hand. A sullen, younger woman wrapped in a mustard wool coat and a shawl covering her blond head stumbled alongside him through the heaps of rubble of the bombed buildings in Alexanderplatz to *Rosenstrasse* (Roses Tomatoes Street).

This city thoroughfare was where a bold protest occurred on February 27, 1943. The uprising was like no other seen on a walkway since the war began, and it was initiated by non-Jewish wives—*Mischinge*—of mixed Aryan heritage who were randomly arrested for deportation. This rounding-up of people escalated as a part of Nazi efforts to remove privileged Jewish family members from their spouses and families.

That day in February 1943, the public outcry came from hundreds, then thousands of German women, cramming the street. "Give us back our men," they hollered in unison. "We have rights!"

The protest was halted on the night of March 1, when the British Royal Air Force bombed Berlin on a public holiday held in honor of the German *Luftwaffe* (Air Force). The wife of one of the interned men spoke of her memories after the war:

"On one side, it was fury and hatred against the Nazis, who deserved the bomb attack, and on the other side, hellish fires and screaming people being burned and buried alive."

The protests lasted for seven days until the eighteen hundred men being held were subsequently freed on the orders of Propaganda Minister Joseph Goebbels. Despite his news blackout, the outcry traveled by word of mouth throughout Germany and beyond to other countries. British and American newspapers reported on the protests. As was expected, the crafty Goebbels's spewed lies, claiming the women were just protesting the blitzing of Berlin, the British bombers' primary target.

It was one of over three hundred and fifty air raids that dropped lots of eleven hundred bombs on this major city.

Three months later, Germany ceased to exist as a nation, opening the Gates of Hell for themselves. With the abolition of the Third Reich government, their currency, and their military forces, their cities, towns, and villages were reduced to dust, which was symbolic of the country's defeat. The Third Reich was at the mercy of four Allied Powers—the Soviets, the US, France, and the British.

Sadly, these mighty powers came too little and too late to save the millions of innocent humans deemed unfit by Hitler and sent to their death by Adolf Eichmann's Final Solution—the lethally efficient carnage of Jews. However, the courageous *Rosenstrasse* protesters saved hundreds of Jews of mixed marriages in the Reich living in Berlin after the uprising.

On a fine October day in 1945, amid the debris of many four-hundred-year-old heritage buildings shrouded by fall foliage, there would be no celebratory Oktoberfest (the singing of songs while attired in *dirndl,* traditional Bavarian costumes).

There was no festival of lights as 1.7 million evacuees from rural areas fleeing the Red Army in the east poured into Berlin and other cities. Amongst them were POWs and concentration camp survivors who realized that nothing, not even a front door mat, belonged to them anymore.

And life would never be the same for the strangers approaching a street blockade.

"Halt," ordered the uniformed US military guard. With his M17 raised, Pvt. Perkins demanded, "Identity papers, please."

Andrzej reached into a jacket pocket and handed over Slovakian national ID's, serving as passports. In Pidgin-English, Andrzej said, "We want Staff Sergeant Miller."

The sentry's eyes squinted. "It says that you are a Polish Count and Countess, yet you carry Slovak identification. Explain."

Andrzej quickly responded, "We are Polish. We went to live in Bratislava when Germans occupied our country."

The sentry frowned. "I think you are fishy, so what is your business with Staff Sergeant Miller?"

Andrzej again reached into his jacket pocket and handed over a folded piece of paper, typed in capital letters which read:

YOUR CONTACT IS STAFF SERGEANT HARRY MILLER, ROSENSTRASSE, BERLIN. CODE WORD: "KINDERSICHERERHAFEN." MAY GOD GO WITH YOU TO KEEP YOU SAFE FROM HARM.

Pvt. Perkins called out to his fellow military guard, "Jonas, take over my post. I'm taking them to Harry."

Under escort, the couple entered a bomb-damaged building and climbed two flights up a creaky stairwell. On the top floor, Perkins knocked on the top-quality wooden door with ornate moldings.

"Come in," a baritone voice boomed.

"Morning, Staff Sergeant Miller. These Poles with Slovak identifications have asked to see you."

Harry Miller's wide-set eyes fixed on the pair before gesturing to the two chairs opposite his desk. "Sit down," Harry said. "What can I do for you?"

Seated opposite the balding man with beady eyes, Andrzej guessed him to be in his late fifties. "Sir, I do not speak English well. Bishop Kowalski in Bratislava gave me your name for you to help us. Here," he ended, handing Miller a folded note.

With his forehead wrinkles stretched to the limit, Miller rose from his chair and yelled to persons in an adjacent office, "Any of you speak fucking *Polack!*"

"I do," returned a twenty-five-year-old uniformed soldier holding a large bundle of files. The older son of Polish emigrant parents warmly smiled at Andrzej. "Hi there, my name is Jack Novak. Can you tell me what the purpose of your visit is?"

Andrzej sighed. The language barrier was solved. "Please tell the officer we have come to Berlin for his help to get us out of Europe. Bishop Kowalski said Miller runs an underground organization to help people like us."

The interpreter's forehead creased. "I'm not following," Miller said after Novak relayed Andrzej's reason for being there. Novak repeated the translation.

Miller jumped from his chair, shrieking, "Are you fucking out of your mind, Polack? Get the fuck out of my office before I have you arrested! You are one dumb Polack who obviously doesn't know German because *KinderSichererHafen* means *Safe haven for children*. You two are definitely not fucking kids!"

With Miller's foul and derogatory comments laid aside, Novak relayed his superior's outrage in Polish. Sophie lifted her bowed head. "For God's sake, Andrzej, give this отвратительный (very unpleasant man) what he wants."

Andrzej swallowed hard. "I have what you want," he said, emptying the contents of a velvet pouch onto Miller's counter. Then unzipping the duffle bag, he removed the bundles of one thousand US bills in each strap and piled the money beside the gems.

Miller and Novak of the US 7th armored division mesmerizingly stared at the handful of uncut diamonds, a gemstone-swathed gold brooch, and the wads of money. "Where did you get these?" Miller probed. "Are they stolen?"

Andrzej adamantly countered, "Nothing is stolen! The jewelry belongs to my wife's grandmother, Princess Anna Sophie of Poland, who died in the Russian wilderness, and the money has been legitimately earned. I am a wealthy nobleman with—"

Miller cut in, "Okay, this is beginning to sound like a movie script. Why don't you start at the beginning and tell me without any bullcrap why you want to get out of Europe?"

Andrzej sighed, "It's a long story. I am on the wanted list!"

"I'm listening."

A long, exacerbated sigh washed through Andrzej's lips. Even though he had long suffered an overwhelming emotional anguish for his wrongdoings, revealing the dark secrets to a stranger could backfire.

"Hurry up!" Miller groaned. "I haven't got all day."

The ghastly past, which had been concealed in the cortex of this broken man's brain, spewed forth like a burst water pipe.

CHAPTER SIXTEEN
Past and Present
Memories Come to Light
- 1918 to 1945 -

If you lie down with dogs,
you will get up with fleas.
—JAMES SANFORD, 1573

TWENTY-SEVEN YEARS EARLIER, Andrzej had clutched Anastasia's cold hand as he led her down the snowy trail leading to the airplane he'd nicknamed "Flying Squirrel."

On the runway, she saw the aircraft, and her legs took flight. Andrzej caught up and held the trembling teenager in a firm embrace. "Don't be scared," he soothed. "It's not going to bite you. It's going to take you home where you belong."

With the now silent girl, head on her knees in the passenger seat, Andrzej taxied and effortlessly ascended the plane into clear blue skies. "See, it wasn't that bad," he said. "We will be home soon, and you'll never suffer again."

Three and a half hours later, the aircraft touched down on a snow-laden runway on the Poniatowski castle's grounds. Andrzej helped his pea-green-faced passenger, who had not uttered one word since takeoff. He gestured towards the stone fortress looming in the distance. "Welcome to my home, now yours."

The tired and hungry travelers entered the imposing castle portcullis of steel and heavy-paneled wood. Waiting on the stone steps leading inside the castle, five servants, eyeing up the petite girl dressed in a man's winter jacket and boots, greeted their employer, "Welcome back, Your Excellency."

Andrzej addressed his older servant, Ruth Salomon. "This is Princess Sophie Anna," he introduced. "Take her inside, bathe her, and supply whatever will fit her from my mother's wardrobe."

With disbelieving ears, his servant's eyes transfixed on the girl with cornflower blue irises and unkempt knotted hair.

Andrzej turned to the younger female servant, "Tauba, prepare food for us."

The Count's Jewish servants were sixty-eight-year-old house-keeper, Ruth; a thirty-eight-year-old chef; eighteen-year-old housemaid, Hanna; fifty-eight-year-old groundskeeper, Arek; and twenty-one-year-old stable hand, Efraim.

Ruth, the only daughter of the late Count Alfred's housekeeper, who had grown up with her widowed mother at the castle, brooded with confusion: *A princess! It must be a joke! She's all skin and bones, reeks of foul body odor, and looks like someone who has escaped a mental asylum!*

Ruth's ponderings were dispelled when she saw her employer's tender attachment, a kiss on the girl's cheek.

"Come with me," Ruth said, leading the red-rimmed-eyed teen-ager across the entryway. "Sophie is a lovely Polish name. How old are you? Do you have a family? How did you meet my employer?"

Sophie remained unresponsive.

Ruth sighed.

In the ground-level main bedroom with a bathroom attached, Ruth spoke, "Lift your arms, *moja droga* (my dear), so I can remove your dress—"

An intense gasp escaped through chapped lips, ending her conversation. "Oh, *Elohim*," Ruth muttered in Hebrew. Large sienna-brown eyes scanned the physical imprints of bodily trauma, the raised dark brown scars on the girl's boney chest and abdomen. "What happened to you, child? Who did this? You can talk to me. I won't tell anyone!"

Silence prevailed.

With tears brimming, Ruth helped the emaciated teenager into the warm waters in a cast-iron tub that Andrzej's father, Count Alfred, had installed in 1842. Andrzej had modernized the old castle with indoor plumbing and electricity shortly after his mother died.

Ruth gently washed the layers of grime off Sophie's face and body, leaving the skinny girl soaking while searching for an outfit to fit her. The servant selected a white dress with a high neckline and puffed sleeves from her former mistress's wardrobe. It was Greta's favorite dress. Ruth had tried suggesting that the clothing should be given to the poor after she died, and Andrzej had a tantrum. "Her clothing will remain until I say otherwise!"

Ruth found Sophie sound asleep in the tub. "Oh, my goodness," Ruth exclaimed, holding out her hand. "Come, child. We can't have you drowning in the tub."

Ruth left Sophie slumbering in Andrzej's bed in a room adorned with Catholic icons, images of holy figures, and saints that Greta had acquired. Although Andrzej practiced no faith, he'd kept his mother's religious artifacts in place.

Ruth headed downstairs to find him. "Your Excellency," she addressed Andrzej. "I know it's none of my business. Who is this girl with horrible scars? She seems frightened out of her wits and won't speak to me."

"Ah, it's a long story, and I do not wish to discuss it now. I want you to take good care of my guest until her mind heals." The Count waggled a finger. "And how many times have I told you to call me Andrzej!"

"It's simply habit, *Sir*."

Ruth headed to the kitchen to help Tauba prepare the evening meal.

Ruth woke the princess from her deep sleep as sunset darkened the winter skies. "My dear, dinner is being served. I will take you downstairs."

Clothed in the 1880s fashionable dress Ruth had chosen, Sophie ravenously gulped down the beef and beet borsch, four large pierogies, and a thick slice of gingerbread to the delight of the amused cook. "She has a healthy appetite," Tauba observed. "My cooking will soon put meat on her bones."

With hair and eyes the color of a Raven, Tauba had been sold to a sex trafficker at age fourteen. After her mother died birthing her ninth child, Tauba's unemployed Gentile father, Kasper, handed his eldest child Tauba over to Madam Szafranek, who ran a high-class brothel. "Be a good girl now," the Gentile had said that day. "Make money to feed your brothers and sisters."

The teenager escaped a life of violation with the help of a hero—

Andrzej's mother. The police raided the brothel, and twenty under-age children were rescued, many of them placed in orphanages which Greta supported. She treated Tauba as her daughter. Between them, hands-on cuisine was perfected.

Tauba never forgot Greta's kindness or Kasper's betrayal. Her father was arrested when the police raided Madam Szafranek's establishment. Kasper Bokil languished in a labor camp, where he died of typhus five years after being arrested.

On this crisp winter evening, Andrzej smiled. He recalled how his mother had loved that dress and worn it often up until her death from the Spanish flu six years ago. How she would have reacted to her son bringing an unknown "waif and stray" into her home was another thought. Andrzej truly believed that the young woman wearing Greta's dress was indeed the granddaughter of Countess Bronya Poniatowski.

Sophie wiped her mouth with the cotton napkin, then looked intently at Andrzej and, for the first time since being taken from the wilderness, she spoke in her natural tongue, "Where am I?" she asked with eyes going over the elegant dining room.

His eyebrows arched— *Russian!*

"I'm so happy to hear your lovely, sweet voice. I assumed it would be Polish," Andrzej responded in Russian. "I'm a bit confused. Your grandmother was Polish, right? Was the man in the cabin your father? Was he Russian?"

With tears falling, Sophie whimpered, "Who are you? Where am I?"

"Hush, hush," Andrzej said. "You are safe in Poland. Please tell me your name?"

Sophie exhaled loudly, "I am Grand—"

This short period of lucidity abruptly ended. Anastasia Romanov was voiceless. Was her refrain from speech deliberate or genuine mind blockage?

The following day, anxious to have answers, Andrzej hired a private investigator. "I want you to find out everything you can about Princess Anna Sophie of Warsaw, whom I'm informed subsequently became a Countess by marriage to my father, Alfred."

Ten days later, the investigator returned to the castle. "She was last seen in Wisztyniec in late 1845," he disclosed, "with a young man near the Russian border. The old-timers in the village believe they were in trouble and had crossed over into Russia, but I've been unable to verify that. Princess Anna Sophie's parents have been dead for many years. I presently know of no other relatives still alive. Do you wish me to keep checking?"

"No, thank you," Andrzej replied, handing him an envelope of money.

Two years flew by without the Romanov survivor revealing any past secrets. Instead of spoken words, she expressed herself through sign language. Andrzej was content to have her near, regardless.

"From the moment I saw her," he told friends, "I couldn't think of anything else."

In October 1921, Andrzej and Sophie married in a private ceremony at the castle with friends and servants in attendance. The bride had gained weight with Tauba's healthy cooking and looked radiant in a white silk wedding dress adorned with layers of lace accents. The back of her wedding dress fastened with silk-covered buttons. Atop her head was a delicate, flowing veil, handmade by Hanna's seamstress mother.

Andrzej wore traditional white balloon trousers and a white shirt with puffed sleeves, resembling medieval times. The husband-to-be beamed like a Cheshire cat when the Orthodox priest pronounced them Man and Wife.

But it wasn't the same joyfulness for Andrzej's best man and friends. They thought that Andrzej had abandoned his senses.

The eligible wealthy bachelor, who could have had his pick of nobility partners, wanted to settle down with a mute who had no past they knew of. Notwithstanding her divine beauty, with a smile that could sink ships and hypnotizing blue eyes that melted a heart, they were genuinely concerned. They had learned from Ruth that when Sophie first arrived, she did utter a few words in Russian.

Andrzej's best man, Yanek, pressed Andrzej with his concerned issues:

"Where did you meet her?" "How long have you known her?" "Beware, my friend, Russian women are dangerous!" "You might be getting in a tank with a shark." In the end, Yanek acknowledged,

"You know something, my friend, I'm happy for you, because I have never seen you so weak at the knees."

The newlywed, twenty-year-old Countess enjoyed her new role to the fullest. She was tender-hearted towards Andrzej and his friends, especially Ruth, her "adopted mother," whom she adored. Sophie's sweet nature held a surprise for the people who loved her.

One bright sunny morning, she walked over to the Grand Piano in the main entrance hall, lifted the maple wood lid, sat on the piano stool, and positioned her feet on the pedals. Concerto Number Two by Russian composer Sergei Rachmaninoff filled the stately room with musical notes that could have awed heavenly beings.

The look on Andrzej's face was priceless. When the performance ended, he rushed over and hugged her. "Darling, that was amazing. Where did you learn to play like that?"

"My mother taught me," she replied in perfect Polish speech. Andrzej squinted. She had spoken his language like a native! *Mother!* He hadn't noticed any musical instruments in the cabin and artfully seized the moment, "I wish *my* mother had taught me to play as well as you do. What was your mother's name, darling?" he cunningly probed. "And your Polish is perfect! Is it the language of your mother?"

"I don't know," she answered. "I cannot see her face anymore, and I am bilingual."

Andrzej never asked her again. He loved his partner for her inner self and all the changes and flaws that came with her. However, an abyss resided in Andrzej's heart to cement their love—an heir.

Almost two years into their marriage, Andrzej took Sophie without her consent to be examined by Russian-Polish Dr. Kanjorski, a top gynecologist in Warsaw. His patient was not happy when she learned an examination of her womb, ovaries, cervix, vagina, and fallopian tubes were about to take place. Her screams were heard down hospital hallways, and her erratic heartbeat caused concern, so they sedated her against her will.

The specialist's shocking conclusion was not what a devoted spouse would wish to hear.

With an appropriate high index of suspicion, Dr. Kanjorski made eye contact with Andrzej. "Your wife's infertility may result from heavily scarred fallopian tubes and excessive polyp blockages to the uterus."

Andrzej's forehead wrinkled.

The doctor explained, "She has had blunt force trauma by a sharp object inserted into her vagina."

It had turned his stomach. Andrzej's resonating whack to his chest halted the prognosis.

"I'm going to kill the bastard when I find out who it is."

Dr. Kanjorski exhaled. "Oh, you didn't *know*?" he said. "I'm so sorry." Andrzej's shocked mind had a hard time coping with everything.

Emotionally overcome, Andrzej broke down and confided, "My wife has suffered from memory loss since the day I found her near starvation in Russia's wilderness."

Those outside the doctor's room waited patiently for their

appointments as Andrzej recounted the past. "I'm aware of her injuries. I honestly do not know how they came about, as my wife won't talk about it."

"Oh, I'm sorry. I could refer your wife to Dr. Gorki, a neurologist specializing in brain disorders. I could also give you the address of a sexual assault center to help with post-traumatic stress symptoms that I believe your wife hides well. You did inform me that she doesn't speak. I believe it is selective mutism. If left untreated, her anxiety disorder will worsen."

Of course, he never confessed to murdering the Russian geologist in front of her! Andrzej would have no knowledge that in the future, aided by the money of oligarchs, bone fragments from "hermit" Boris and Russian Vadim would yield positive DNA results. He also wouldn't know that Russian and Polish homicide detectives would seek the last person to have seen the geologist alive. A bullet retrieved from Vadim's body was in evidence storage, as was the weapon, a blood-stained rock, that ended Boris's life.

Would the investigators fail to solve the case?

Maybe, then maybe not!

Andrzej nodded at the physician's suggestions but had no intention of putting Sophie through any more emotional or physical discomfort. He collected her from the Post-Anesthetic Unit and walked away from the hospital resolved. He never wanted to know who she was or how she had gotten her horrific injuries.

"I can't change the wrong done to you," he whispered. "Please don't let it change you. Just tell me who hurt you, and I'll kill the bastard. Then I will dance at his funeral and piss on his grave!"

Sophie sighed. The emotional and physical trauma suffered from being shot, stabbed, raped, and then buried alive was forever imprinted. No one, no matter how caring, could erase her internal torment, and *silence* was her remedy.

Would her dark secrets eventually claw their way through to life?

On the flight home, Andrzej's feelings broke from a tender heart—loving his wife forever and wanting to spend the rest of his life childless was all that mattered to him. *Until death do us part.* And if her memory did return, terrific, but if not, *c'est la vie.*

This man with such a passionate and thoughtful attitude would, in time, reveal his true colors.

Twenty-one years later, at 5:20 on the morning of September 1st, 1939, some 1.5 million German soldiers, accompanied by twenty-five hundred tanks, crossed the Polish border without declaring war. The invasion of Poland marked the start of World War II. France and Britain formally declared war on Germany following the attack, but it would be another eight months before they engaged in a full-scale war with the Nazis. The U.S. didn't join the fight until December 1941, two years later.

Why was the U.S. so slow to stop the ruthless dictator Adolf Hitler and the spread of his evil messages? At this moment in history, the American people and organizations held a range of viewpoints between "isolationism" and "noninterventionism" until the Japanese attack on Pearl Harbor.

On September 1st, 1939, in a dazzling display of might, German troops annexed Poland, stunning the population. The government, without contingency plans, faced monumental tasks. They were not going to be as submissive to the German Reich as the occupiers thought, because they had a "we're not going to be as wilted as you assume" attitude. The brave Polish challengers began to make these unwanted Nazis as miserable as possible. They wrote anti-slogans such as DEATH TO ALL HUNS on subjugated properties, trucks, and cars, on their clothing hanging on washing lines, and they burned swastika flags that draped down buildings.

The Polish army and partisan fighters tried to crush this evil by sabotaging airfields and transport trains and blowing up thousands of railroad engines, petroleum depots, telephones, and electric power lines. Ultimately, their retaliatory measures cost the lives of sixty-two thousand men and women who were captured, tortured, and then shot. Civilian losses are not included in this death toll.

In the first week of the German occupation, political figures, the nobility, and other affluent Poles went underground, but not Andrzej and his friends, who believed that the Americans would enter the war and send the villainous Germans packing in no time.

He was a foolish dreamer!

Sunday, September 10th, 1939, aging legs sprinted across the lush green lawns he had so tenderly nurtured as he bellowed to Efraim, who was training one of the Count's stallions. "Ride like the wind to the castle and tell the Count the Germans are here," Arek ordered.

The stable hand and the stallion reached the castle. Efraim dashed through the back door. "Count, they *are* coming!"

Andrzej, Sophie, and all the servants now stood outside. They watched the German convoy of several three-axle off-road jeeps, motorcycles with sidecars, and a black Mercedes heading toward the castle. The chauffeur-driven Mercedes pulled up to the Portcullis with the motorcade parking behind.

A tubby small man in a black SS uniform with collar patches denoting his rank and shiny jackboots stepped out. The high-ranking Secret Police officer removed his black cap with its *Totenkopf* skull and bones logo (a symbol for death) badge emblazed. "*Guten Morgen*, Count Poniatowski," he greeted.

"I do not understand German," Andrzej responded. Before another word could come out, Sophie glared at the unwanted visitor. "But I do," she stated firmly in German.

Lieutenant Colonel Ricohard Eichenauer beamed. "May I ask who you are?"

"You will address me as Countess Poniatowski," she returned imperiously.

"I see," he flippantly countered. "I'm curious. Are you originally from the Fatherland? I appreciate someone who speaks good German, and you look like our beautiful Aryan ladies."

"I am not German," she snapped. "I am Polish."

Unaware of what had verbally transpired, Andrzej touched his wife's shoulder. "Sophie, ask him why he is here. Want does he want?"

"My husband would like to know the purpose of this visit."

"All is good, feisty *Frau*," the Nazi officer replied with a wry smile. "You can inform him we are requisitioning the castle, and all his assets are being seized. We will be back at dawn to carry out—"

A loud explosion was heard in the background. Eichenauer grinned smugly. "Well, that's one asset we won't be removing. Was the THULIN just a collector's item, or did you pilot it?" he inquired.

Spiraling plumes of thick smoke drifted from the airstrip. A furious pilot, who had recently flown the vintage two-seater in a national airshow, instructed Sophie, "Inform this Nazi maggot that blowing up my flying machine is barbaric behavior. I will not take it lightly."

Without much thought, Sophie repeated it word for word.

Rage reddened the officer's face. "It's our job. Accept it!"

Their terrified facial expressions and high-pitched screams shattered the morning air as they saw firearms aimed at their bodies. They raised their hands in a gesture of surrender. "Easy, easy," Andrzej pleaded. Considering this chilling circumstance, he realized he had to navigate the stormy waters wisely. "Take everything, but please leave my wife and staff alone. Perhaps what I have concealed in the gamekeeper's cottage will make you leave us alone!"

With a satisfied gaze, Eichenauer responded, "Then you and I may do great things together." He ordered his men to lower their weapons. "I'm very interested in what you offer. Show me."

Andrzej exhaled a *What have I done?* self-condemnation breath.

In these uncertain times, the nobleman had little choice but to disclose his significant money-making asset to the enemy. "After my *German*-born mother," he emphasized, "inherited the castle, she was granted exclusive rights to produce and sell the best premium vodka, a significant source of income which was passed down to me—"

Eichenauer, stomping past Andrzej, ended his words. The Nazi forcibly grabbed Ruth's arm. "Well, what do we have here, a filthy Jew!" he sneered. "I'm correct, yes?"

Sophie sunk sharp nails into his arm. "Leave her alone!" she snapped.

Eichenauer chortled like a demented idiot. "Ah, it seems your husband has *no* German blood, and not only is he a bootlegger, but a Jew lover. Your servants are *all* Jews, right? *Fraulein*, translate freely, or I will put a bullet in this Jew bitch's head and yours!"

Five days after Eichenauer and his thugs had arrived at the castle, Ruth, Tauba, Hanna, Arek, and Efraim were arrested. Vicious German attack dogs herded the Count's staff into one of the trailers transporting Andrzej's thoroughbred horses. Parked in front of the horse carriers now hitched to canvas-covered trucks, a half-ton vehicle was packed to the rim with looted antique furniture, artworks, and other priceless valuables owned by various Polish noblemen since the 10th century. The Nazi thieves also seized two milking cows, four goats, and twenty chickens. They shot four ducks in the castle moat, which the dogs had retrieved on command. As the motorcade set off, Sophie's agile legs ran after the trailer like an arrow. "Where are you taking them?" she hysterically hollered. "Fetch them back, I beg you!"

A bullet whizzed past her head in a warning that the next one would end her life. The young woman tripped and fell heavily to the ground. The wind carried the cries of the prisoners and a bereft Sophie.

As the sun slipped behind the horizon, Andrzej returned from working at the distillery to find Sophie nowhere in sight. Frantically, he searched their home, shouting, "Darling, where are you?"

An hour later, he finally found his wife curled up under a mound of leaves about a quarter mile outside the property. "Why? Why?" she cried in Russian.

"Please, my darling, try to understand," said a saddened man lifting her into his arms just as Boris had done. "I had little choice but to give them all up in exchange. I just could not let that pervert Eichenauer take you from me!"

Distancing herself from reality, Sophie returned to her traumatized, silent world. She didn't understand or wish to know about the deal her husband had made with the Devil Incarnate, who intended to take her for his mistress. The cowardly Andrzej had given up five souls in exchange for Sophie. Nonetheless, his faithful servants were not the only humans he had betrayed to keep Sophie safe!

The broken-hearted young woman locked herself in the bedroom. Sophie couldn't stop crying and didn't want to look at the man she had married. Andrzej tried everything to get her to open the door. "I'll find out where they have been taken," he said contritely through the keyhole. "And I'll pay whatever it takes to get Ruth and the others back, I promise."

It was a promise that could not be kept.

Andrzej contacted his former private investigator by telephone: "I need your help again."

Forty-eight hours later, the detective telephoned his client: "Your servants and your Jewish friends are being held in a ghetto in Warsaw." (Warsaw, Poland's largest city at that time, had a population of 1.3 million, thirty percent of whom were Jews).

After the Germans took control, they ordered all Jews to register and identify themselves by wearing white armbands with a centralized blue Star of David. Jewish business storefronts and doors were smeared: "JUDE." Non-Jews were banned from all Jewish premises. If caught, as punishment, they had to pin a large button on their clothing: "JEW LOVER."

On October 12th, 1940, a few weeks before the German's appearance at the castle, a decree compelled all Jewish people to move into an area of 1.3 square miles, with eight to ten persons per room, making it much easier for the Nazis to clear the towns of Jews. The Nazi organizers then sealed off the ghetto from the rest of the city with brick walls over ten feet high, topped with barbed wire, and guarded by armed soldiers.

Many Jewish people hid in their attics or cellars. Among them was thirteen-year-old Abraham Lewents, who lay deathly quiet in a dirt crawl space no larger than an orange crate when the Germans came and seized his father, mother, and five sisters in a raid. A few days later, an SS soldier spotted Abraham rummaging for food in a garbage dump. He joined his family in the ghetto for a very short while before being sent to a labor camp.

The survivor wrote in his memoirs:

Hunger was so great, so bad, that my people were crumpled on ghetto streets dying from starvation, and children as young as two years went around begging.

German documents found after the war state that Jewish prisoners subsisted on less than six hundred calories per day from unsafe, rotting food. They were unaware that the rations contained ground pork from diseased swine!

Among the notes was this heartless comment, "A pig-eating pig. What could be better?"

Even though smuggled food and medicine did get into the ghetto, it did not keep the death rate from increasing. Over four hundred thousand Polish Jews were detained in the Warsaw ghetto. Between 1940 and mid-1942, eighty-three thousand people died of starvation and were left to rot like decayed food outside on the streets. Ruth and Tauba were amongst them.

Hanna was gassed at Auschwitz concentration camp in 1944.

Efraim and Arek did not join the women in the ghetto. Andrzej's loyal workers were transported to a labor camp built along the Lublin-Chelm-Wlodawa railway line, making it far easier for transport trains to offload Jewish prisoners. A dense forest of pine shielded *Sobibór*, a death camp, from view.

Three-quarters of Jewish inmates were exterminated in killing centers across Germany and Poland. Andrzej's best friend, Yanek (the best man at his wedding), and six of the Count's other Jewish friends whom the Count betrayed joined the dead.

After the ghetto liquidation in March 1943, Jews were transported in cattle railroad cars to their deaths. Those who escaped the fortified walls hid on the Aryan side of Warsaw.

On January 17, 1945, Soviet troops liberated Poland, and, according to Russian records, only six percent of incarcerated Poles survived. Of the total number of people who escaped from Sobibór camp and evaded capture, it's estimated that only fifty souls survived. One of them was Efraim, and he had much to say to the liberators.

In July 1945, Russian *militsia* (military police) entered the Poniatowski estate, when they received no response to their knocking, Major Mikhail Stoletov, towering over six feet, ordered, "Break down the damn door."

With a larger version of a fireman's tool, a soldier successfully rammed the door, and Mikhail and his men rushed through the doorway with weapons drawn. "*Militsia*," they yelled. "Come out, or we will start firing!"

The men were met with eerie silence. They searched every inch of the massive dwelling place to no avail. The castle was empty.

An infuriated Mikhail grizzled, "Check roads, trains, and border crossings," he ordered. "I want *him* alive!"

As the Russians were driving from the property, a soldier spotted something. "Look to our right," he uttered. "That's one helluva fire burning."

"Drive over there," Major Mikhail ordered his driver. The game-keeper's property, out of which the distillery operated, was engulfed in flames.

The day before, Andrzej and Sophie snuck out of the castle at midnight. They stuck to the back woods just as the Polish princess and Constantin Vladislav had done in 1845, as they made their way to Główna railway terminal. With one exception: Sophie had not uttered a word since Ruth was taken away.

No amount of Andrzej's sweet-talking: "Darling, we are going to be safe where we are going. We will start a new life, an even better one," made a dent in her sad psyche. Sophie was once more lost in time and space.

The railway platform was crowded with people trying to flee Poland. Attired in peasant knee-length, beige tunics and hats and clutching one small suitcase each, the runaways boarded a train bound for Bratislava, Slovakia with second-class tickets.

After the 688 km trip, nearly eight hours sitting on hard bench-styled seats, the Count and Countess finally arrived in Slovakia. They exchanged their peasant disguises for upper-class attire in the railway terminal's bathroom. Finding something to eat and drink was Andrzej's next plan.

In a small café, Sophie hardly touched the traditional cuisine of potato pancakes but gulped down a mug of hot chocolate. "Please eat, my darling," Andrzej urged. "We still have a long way to go."

In the center of Bratislava, Andrzej and Sophie stayed under the protective custody of Bishop Kowalski until Slovak Roma smugglers transported them in a fishing vessel and into the seaport of Hamburg. From there, a two-hour ride by tram brought them to Berlin. Andrzej again reassured his wife, "Darling, we will pick up the pieces and make a new life in America as soon as possible."

Sophie's small internal voice answered him: *I know you better than you know yourself, because your promises are as empty as your words.*

CHAPTER SEVENTEEN
Rosenstrasse, Berlin
- 1945 -

One's guilt will always,
always live with you!
—LUCIA MANN

AS THE SON OF BAVARIAN IMMIGRANTS, the Staff Sergeant had changed his German name Müller to the American version of Miller before enlisting in the U.S. army. He glared at Andrzej, convinced the man and his wife were wanted Germans with false papers.

"You are paying for my time," he snorted. "I'm not here to hear your confession. However, I'm rather curious how the vodka business worked out with the Krauts."

"Of course, Eichenauer lied to me," Andrzej replied. "He did not intend to share the vodka income he pocketed weekly with me. Eichenauer brought in his own staff and transport vehicles and had me watched day and night. Armed soldiers stood outside the distillery and at my home. One day, I managed to slip out with one of the Jewish workers, but the Nazis could not have known this. His dark hair had been dyed blond and with the aid of a Polish eye doctor, Awszalom wore blue contact lenses. I knew I was risking my life by hiding him, his parents, and two little sisters, Avigal and Asna, in the castle cellar, but it was the right thing to do."

"Did they survive the war?" Miller queried, looking at the man with a soft gaze.

"Unfortunately, I do not know what became of them," Andrzej responded. "I paid a Polish partisan to smuggle them across the border and into Russia, and he informed me that they had successfully crossed onto Russian soil. I got one over on that bastard Eichenauer, which made me feel powerful. It happened before the Sobibór prisoner revolt in 1943. Eichenauer informed me one of his drivers was too sick to make a delivery. Eichenauer ordered me to drive to Sobibór to deliver six cases of vodka to Commandant Karl Burmeister." Andrzej saw Miller's eyes squint and added, "*Honestly*, I had no idea it was a concentration camp."

"Were you living in Cloud-Cuckoo-land?" Miller sniped. "*Everyone* in Poland knew what was going on. Don't tell me you couldn't see the Majdanek concentration camp from the castle windows. I've seen photos of that German hellhole. It was a *huge* complex!"

"*Seriously*, I didn't know such places existed until I drove along the railway tracks and saw the barbed wire fence. But that wasn't unusual, as the Germans fence everything."

Miller wasn't buying the explanation. "Ah, come on! Don't tell me you didn't know about this place and the Warsaw Ghetto. You know, where the servants you betrayed perished. Or is that, too, lost in memory?"

With an overdose of frustration fueling his demeanor, Andrzej rubbed the back of his neck. "Like I told you, Eichenauer had spies watching me twenty-four-seven. I feared for Sophie's safety and mine and did his bidding without question. When I arrived at the labor camp, I saw walking skeletons near the fence and spotted Efraim, my stable hand, among them. I shouted his name, and a rifle bullet fired from a guard tower missing me by an inch. I dove back into the truck, unloaded the cases of vodka for the commandant at his house, and got the hell out of there. Driving away, I spotted a crumpled body by the fence. I prayed that it was not Efraim."

The corners of Miller's mouth curved in an expression of, *I got ya!* "There is something I must tell you before you go further with your wild tales. Efraim escaped from Sobibór and the Russians, whose defeat at Stalingrad irreversibly changed the war's course. The Soviets are handing him over to us as we speak."

"Oh, we will be so happy to see him," Andrzej said.

A knock at Miller's door halted any further conversation. "Enter," Miller shouted.

What happened next was jaw-dropping.

Sophie, who had sat looking at her gloved hands throughout the conversation, suddenly released a yelp that sounded like a wounded animal, leaped from her seat, and squirmed under Miller's legs.

"Holy shit!" he exclaimed, staring at the shaking woman with flared nostrils and arms wrapped firmly around his boots, rocking back and forth. Miller, Andrzej, Novak, Efraim, and Nikitin's mouths gaped.

The astonished onlookers couldn't have guessed Nikitin's Red Army (Bolshevik) uniform had amplified past experiences and brought to life the execution scene at Ipatiev House and the sexual violations in the courtyard. It was Efraim who squatted. "It is okay, Mistress Sophie," he soothed. "Whatever is troubling, you let it go. You *didn't* betray me."

Andrzej's stable hand halted his bitter tirade to shoot his former employer a look of utter contempt. "*You* are the spineless bastard who handed us over to the Nazis as if our lives meant nothing to you or your sweet wife."

Andrzej's stolid expression was unresponsive to the accusations as he squatted. "Darling, what's gotten into you?" he said. "You are making a spectacle of yourself." Andrzej held out his hand. "Come, let me help you up."

"Leave me alone," Sophie screamed, "or I bash your head like I did the *wild* man!"

"Jesus Christ, is your wife deranged?" Miller snorted. "She needs to be seen by a shrink!"

Sophie's sobbing spread through Miller's office. "I don't remember anything," she mumbled. You are all *bad* people!"

"Enough of this crap!" Miller hollered. He looked at Anatoly Nikitin, whose eyebrows had been raised the whole time. "Take them both away. I'm done with this fucking drama."

As Nikitin was escorting Andrzej and Sophie from Miller's office, Efraim, whose sagging facial folds resembled a man much older than his actual age, whispered, "I'm sorry, Mistress, but as I've said, the Count did wrong by us and must pay for this crime. Don't worry. I know someone to help *you* when the Russians are done with the Count."

Sophie was detained for less than an hour. Waiting for her outside the Russian detention center was Efraim.

Andrzej was released four days later and returned to Miller's office to ask for help in locating his missing wife. Novak opened the door. "If Miller finds you here, there will be hell to pay, so wait outside," he said in Polish. "But I'll make a call to the Russian detention center."

A few minutes later, Novak said, "You didn't hear this from me, okay? It seems your wife was seen walking away with your servant. That's all they know."

With tears rolling down his cheeks, Andrzej walked down *Rosenstrasse* when an army vehicle pulled up alongside him. "Get in," a voice bellowed. Andrzej was more than surprised to see Miller sitting in the back seat.

"I underestimated you, Count Poniatowski," Miller admitted. "After you left my office, an eyewitness has testified by affidavit that he witnessed you placing a large quantity of ammonium nitrate, coupled with alcohol from the vodka, you not only blew up millions of dollars of Nazi distillery distribution, but you also *annihilated* the fucking Kraut Eichenauer along with twelve of his Nazi workers and fifteen trucks. But that's not the only reason I have decided to assist you. Rabbi Aryeh Agmon has validated your story of hiding Jews. He is the father of the distillery worker you hid in the cellar."

Andrzej sighed with relief as Miller instructed his German-Jewish driver, "Drive to Muritz, and I'll direct you once we're there."

Three hours later, he was happily reunited with his precious wife, who didn't recognize him.

She frowned. "Who are you?"

Efraim, who had sheltered her at his partially bombed-out apartment, stepped forward. "You don't deserve this kind woman, but she is your wife. Will you promise me that you will get her help? The Countess is so *lost* in mental illness."

"I promise," Andrzej replied. "Please, forgive me, Efraim. I hope you will understand one day."

Efraim fired back angrily, "I'm not likely to ever forget or forgive." He kissed Sophie on the cheek. "May your God go with you, lovely Countess," he said, then slammed the apartment door shut.

Andrzej held Sophie's cold hand in the back seat of Miller's transport. Miller turned his head and made eye contact with the back seat passengers. "You repeat one word of what I am about to tell you, you will be a dead Polack, understood? I presume you still have the uncut diamonds?"

Andrzej nodded.

"Good, then let's get down to business."

The Count and Countess Poniatowski arrived in Tasmania, 240 km south of the Australian mainland, in November 1946. They remained there until surreptitiously receiving Canadian visas in the mail and arrived in Montreal, Quebec, in the spring of 1953. A month later, they took up residence in Arrow Lakes Valley, British Columbia, near Betty Beal's property not far from the luxury homes and businesses in the same rural area owned by German nationals (non-Jewish) with doctored variants to their birth names. Allegedly, eight hundred and one immigrants flooded the Lower and Arrow Lakes Valley region from the early fifties to the late seventies.

This odd Polish couple, now living the dream, kept to themselves, living an idyllic rural life. Andrzej and Sophie embraced the outdoor life and were often seen swimming naked in the nearby lake, skiing in the winter, and foraging in woodlands for edibles. They lived off the grid under "Andrew and Ruth" for the remainder of their lives.

Andrew, the descendant of Count Alfred Poniatowski and Prince Gartoryski, who was known to have courtly manners, especially towards women, died of old age at ninety-two.

Ruth vanished shortly after his death. An eyewitness reported seeing her get into a sleek, black Bentley a couple of days after Andrew's funeral. "She was elegantly dressed from head to toe in white, and I remember clearly the exquisite green, red, and white brooch pinned on her coat lapel."

Many years earlier, a female gas station operator in Tasmania said that Sophie had come into the site, as she usually did, to gas up her Vauxhall-model car and buy her favorite drink, root beer. On this occasion, the attendant watched Sophie rush to a magazine stand and grab a popular read, *Australian Journal*.

On the cover was the last photograph of the Romanovs taken at Ipatiev House. It was captioned: BLOOD-THIRSTY TSAR.

The attendant reported that Sophie had clasped the magazine to her breast, crying, "Mama, Papa, Maria, Olga, Tatiana, and my little brother Alexie." The attendant reported that she didn't know what to make of Sophie's bizarre behavior.

It was well-known that Sophie was an avid reader and had an

extensive collection of history books, especially publications about Imperial Russian rule.

There's no doubt that she had read of her father's incompetent government management, his abdication, her mother's affair with the mad monk, and their extravagant palace lifestyles, which she had taken part of while Russian people starved to death, and her family lived extravagantly. Many Russian people had perished during the Coronation stampede that had been highlighted in the magazine article.

Of course, Sophie had been deeply affected seeing her younger self and her family depicted in the last known photograph.

Was her memory loss just a ploy to conceal the shame she felt by keeping silent about the past? In the waning and waxing of tragedy, had she known who she was all along? It is possible. Or what happened in the past was no longer important, water under the bridge. That is also plausible.

What became of the uncut diamonds and the Romanov brooch is unknown. One guess is that a sizeable chunk of these valuables was used to pay the underground organization for their escape from Germany to Tasmania and then to Canada. As arranged, a German estate agent in Frankfurt who was working with a British Columbian German realtor, found residential and commercial properties in the Arrow Lakes Valley district for their new wealthy clients.

The best place to hide is in plain sight, right?

Do these unconscionable people sleep well at night?

People aren't always what they seem; the first appearance
deceives many; the intelligence of a few perceives
what has been carefully hidden.
—PLATO

PART THREE
The Atrocities

"I swore never to be silent whenever and wherever human beings endure suffering and humiliation, we must always take sides. Neutrality helps the oppressor, never the victim. Silence encourages the tormentor, never the tormented."
—Elie Wiesel Nobel Prize Acceptance Speech, December 10, 1986

CHAPTER EIGHTEEN
Lies, Deceit, and Evil Transgressions

Some people don't change.
They just find new ways to lie.
—LUCIA MANN

LARGE-SCALE BRAINWASHING AND GASLIGHTING under the noses of the public is an ancient practice. Many people worldwide believe that the genocide of Jews is a conspiratorial myth that never happened, especially among eighteen- to thirty-nine-year-olds. A study commissioned in 2021 by Alexis Lerner, an assistant professor of political science at the U.S. Naval Academy in Maryland, found that one in three students surveyed believed that the Holocaust was just fabricated. Unless I'm missing something, I'll set deniers brainwashed on social media platforms straight!

The truth is illustrated clearly with photographic evidence taken of burning corpses in gas ovens and other ghastly human endings. Murdered people, who lived every day of their lives in fear, piled high in pits photographed by "Hun" killers themselves, and they are not photoshopped. This modern technology did not exist in the 1940s.

It's absurd that the authentication of eyewitness accounts accumulated by the Allies, who liberated the thousands upon thousands of death camps, are being refuted by paranoid Holocaust disbelievers.

CHAPTER NINETEEN

Notorious Death Camps
- 1939-1945 -

Now in the light of past and present events, the bitter truth must be spoken. We feared too little, and we hoped too much. We underestimated the bestiality of the enemy, and we overestimated the humanity, wisdom, the sense of justice of our friends.
—CHAIM WEIZMANN
(Former Israeli President, 1949 to 1952)

IN THIS 21ST CENTURY, how many of us are familiar with the names of all Nazi concentration camps, sub-camps, and ghettos established during World War II from 1933 to 1944?

Extensive historical research shockingly reveals that there were *forty-two thousand and five hundred* concentration camps, where millions of the "undesirables" were physically and sexually abused, experimented on, then systematically murdered by the cold-blooded Nazi killers. This figure includes the labor camps, POW camps, and five hundred brothels.

Some prisons had euphemistic names such as, "care facilities for foreign children," where pregnant prisoners underwent forced abortions and experimental sterilizations, and "retirement for the elderly," where lethal injections euthanized seniors.

To Holocaust disbelievers, I pose this question:

Are these evil camps just figments of the imaginations of survivors, Allied liberators, and historians?

Are they all pathological liars, including my mother?

Think again!

I will enlighten idiosyncratic mindsets with a mere handful of the alphabetically listed death camps.

ARBEITSDORF (LABOR VILLAGE), GERMANY

This concentration/labor camp was one of the first to be established in Germany in late April of 1942, after Czech engineer Ferdinand Porsche proposed the manufacture of the "people's car" that would be affordable for *all* Germans. Labor for the expansion of his company brought together Porsche, SS Heinrich Himmler, and Hitler four months earlier.

With their approval, a defunct armaments workshop owned by the wealthy Krupp family was selected for the KDF-Wagen, presently known today as the Volkswagen. Volkswagen and subcontracting companies received his pool of free manpower. Jewish political prisoners worked from six in the morning to eight o'clock at night, with a twenty-minute meal break as their only rest period. Prisoners had to work speedily on the production of this affordable car, dubbed the "Beetle."

"There was no walking, only running. Always running, and

our overseers would cuss and insult us," Arbeitsdorf survivor Willi Leeuwarden testified. "My younger brother was strung up by his wrists from the ceiling for dropping a wrench. It was their way of enforcing discipline in the workplace."

Food distribution was not evenhanded, and extra rations were used as an award, primarily to the privileged prisoners who operated valuable machinery.

Eight hundred undernourished Jewish laborers perished at the factory. Commandant SS Vetter listed their deaths as suicide, heart attack, or work accident! And the number of prisoners tortured is unknown.

In December 1942, the Arbeitsdorf camp was closed, and the remaining factory workers and SS staff were transferred to other camps. As a reward for demonstrating that concentration camp labor could be productive, Vetter was presented with a Volkswagen Beetle.

How many transferred Arbeitsdorf prisoners survived is unknown.

AUSCHWITZ-BIRKENAU, POLAND

This concentration/labor camp, located in a suburb of Oswiecim, Poland, was established in late 1939. The mass arrests of Jews after Germany's invasion of Poland exceeded the capacity of existing prisons.

Sixteen trains, crammed full of prisoners, reached Auschwitz from Tarnów prison on June 14th, 1940. Among the prisoners were many literary figures from Jewish intellectual life, scholars, and artists, including the Polish-Jewish poet and dramatist Itzhak Katzenelson.

Endlösung der Judenfrage "Hitler's Final Solution of Jews" began in Oswiecim in 1941. Along with the sub-camp of "Birkenau," the Auschwitz complex was the largest Nazi center for destroying the Jewish population of European countries. Approximately seven million individuals, including more than two hundred thousand children, teenagers, and infants, were gassed immediately upon, or shortly after, their arrival at Auschwitz.

In the spring of 1942, Jews, arriving in separate transports, were sent directly to their deaths while others, classified before deportation as fit for labor, were placed in the camp. An average of twenty percent of prisoners capable of work were employed chiefly in constructing new buildings in the camp or at German companies involved in maintaining and developing the military potential of the Third Reich.

More than nine out of every ten humans incinerated in the gas ovens were Jews. Poles, Soviet POWs, and people of other nationalities were slaved to death or murdered. But Jewish prisoners suffered the worst mistreatment by Nazi-indoctrinated "handlers," who regarded a Jewish life as the least valuable. They were victims of deliberate starvation, hypothermia, hard labor, constant harassment and abuse, disease, and even human experimentation.

Like all the concentration camps listed in this chapter, Auschwitz-Birkenau symbolized pure evil, utter terror, barbarism, and genocide. There is sufficient photographic evidence, taken by Nazis, to prove that the Holocaust did exist undeniably! Over seven tons of hair from victims also exists as evidence.

I wish I had the courage to write more about this notorious camp, but my heart is heavy. I envision my mother locked behind its razor-sharp fences. I can only imagine fear racing through her thirteen-year-old body. (I wrote about Maria Picasso-Genovese's life experiences in the third publication: *The Sicilian Veil of Shame*, in my four-part "African Freedom" sequels.)

BELZEC, POLAND

This concentration camp was established in November 1942, and was divided into administration sections, inmate barracks, a storage facility for confiscated luggage, and three buildings. The walls were filled with sand, each with airtight doors. One door was for entry, and the other was an exit to remove corpses.

In the first phase of Nazi operations, six-hundred thousand Jews were transported by rail from the ghettos of Radom, Lubin, Lvov, Warsaw, and Eastern Galicia. Eight hundred Polish men, women, and children robbed of their freedom were crammed like sardines into 7.2-foot-wide cattle rail car. (I figure a cow to be at least six feet long, so six cows head to tail would fit the length of this enclosure.)

The prisoners traveled without water, food, or toilet facilities. Shoulder to shoulder and unable to sit, Hitler's "wanted" arrived at the Belzec. Sapped from hours, sometimes days, in inhumane conditions, they were *told* upon arrival that they had to be disinfected before being assigned to labor duties.

The SS separated the men from wives and children and marched them off to a basement room where they were ordered to undress. While the men stood naked, hands covering their privates, women and children had their hair shaven off. They, too, were ordered to undress, then herded like cattle into another concrete-built room disguised as a shower room.

Within minutes, carbon monoxide was piped into an extraction fan from a diesel engine mounted outside. Much to the sick amusement of a chortling Nazi guard, watching through a peephole, the victims screamed and succumbed to their horrific deaths.

After it was safe to open, guards went into the room to verify no one was still alive. They pulled bodies aside looking for gold teeth fillings, wedding rings, and other items before dragging the lifeless bodies to the gas incinerators, where *Sonderkommandos* (assigned Jewish prisoners compelled to take part in the mass killings of their fellow people), waited to perform their gruesome tasks. While this harrowing operation was taking place, another team of inmates was ordered to cleanse the rail trucks of bodily waste and wash the platform clean before the next transport train arrived.

In mid-May 1943, the next year, the transports stopped pending construction of two more gas chambers, each thirteen by sixteen feet. Once the chambers were completed, they enabled the killers to gas hundreds of Jews at a time, but that wasn't enough. Three more gas chambers awaited hapless victims.

In the second phase of Belzec operations, Jews and Roma were shot and thrown into open-air pits. If that *thought* doesn't send chills down your spine, what the Polish locals did after the camp closed down will churn your stomach! Under darkness, armed with spades, men excavated the graves in search of valuables but were driven off by the remaining camp guard, who threatened to shoot if he caught them there again.

Belzec Commandant Hans Goerzen ordered his men to torch the burial pits to deter the ghoulish human scavengers. Gasoline was poured onto the bodies, and flamethrowers torched every trace of human existence.

Or did they?

After the war, a nearby farm was sold to a Ukrainian couple, who, to their horror, found several human skulls adorning mantelpieces and some that had been used as ashtrays! The shocked couple handed over their grisly findings to a Lutheran Church. What became of these human remains is unknown.

Only fifty prisoners survived the Belzec concentration camp.

Unbelievably, a sixteen-year-old Roma girl, who had been shot in the head, survived. Under darkness, she climbed out of the burial pit and hid in the forest until the Allied Forces found her hiding in a tree trunk. The severely emaciated girl named Vadoma died four days later.

BERGEN-BELSEN, GERMANY

This concentration camp, also known as Belsen, was located near two villages. It's located about ten miles northwest of Celle, Germany, and was established in 1943. It was originally intended only to accommodate ten thousand Jewish prisoners, but, by the war's end, with the arrival of prisoners from the evacuated Auschwitz camp and other eastern camps, it imprisoned sixty-thousand humans.

Although Bergen-Belsen had no gassing chambers, over time, thirty-five thousand lice-ridden people perished from starvation and mainly typhus due to the most squalid, fetid living conditions of any of the concentration camps. Thousands of humans painfully succumbed to their untreated typhus.

Anne Frank, whose diary became world famous, died of typhus in March of 1945, a month before liberation by the British Army on April 15th.

To prevent the deadly typhus from spreading even further, the British Army Medical Corps set up a hospital at the site, where they assisted in the physical rehabilitation of the former prisoners. Bergen-Belsen forced the liberators to bury thousands of corpses hastily in mass graves.

Bergen-Belsen became known as the largest displaced-person camp in Germany. Seventeen survivors, whose lives were forever changed, immigrated to Israel. Only one courageous woman is still alive today. SS Commandant Josef Kramer, also known as "The Beast of Belsen," was sentenced to death by a British military court and hanged.

BUCHENWALD, GERMANY

This vast concentration camp was established in Ettersberg, a hilly, forested area near Weimer, in July 1937. *Buchenwald* means "beech forest" in German, and it housed one of the most villainous and sadistic Nazis. *She* didn't make the history books as Adolf Hitler, Josef Mengele, Goebbels, and Heinrich Himmler did.

Ilse Köhler, nicknamed "The Bitch of Buchenwald," was born in Dresden, Germany, on September 22, 1906. She was the daughter of a factory foreman and Gretchen, a housewife. Shortly after her fifteenth birthday, Ilse attended an accounting school, one of the few educational establishments for women at that time. Following graduation, she became a bookkeeping clerk during Germany's collapsing economy, struggling to rebuild itself after the country's defeat in World War I.

Two days shy of her eighteenth birthday, the chubby Ilse, with long blond braids and ice blue eyes, joined the Nazi Party shortly after taking up employment. She met her future husband Karl at a Christmas office party. The short, pudgy SS Colonel and Ilse married two months after their meeting.

In the summer of 1937, the couple was ordered to oversee the Buchenwald concentration camp. Above the entrance, an iron-lettered sign read: *Jedem das Seine*, which means "To Each His Own," an ominous statement to all prisoners. Another emboldened "statement" below read: *Everyone gets what he deserves.*

These profound writings proved more than befitting for a human who was to gain the reputation for being one of the most *feared* Nazis. Ilse was a sadist and nymphomaniac, jumping at every opportunity to become involved in her husband's work. Her first order of business had been to use money stolen from prisoners to construct a $62,500 (approximately one million today) indoor horseback-riding arena, where she could ride horses confiscated from the ranches of arrested Jews. Riding a magnificent steed in her underwear, Ilse would taunt prisoners until they gazed at her. With a twisted smile creasing lipstick-red lips, she would dismount and brutally flog with her riding crop whoever dared to look up at her.

Many of her "don't-you-dare-look at me" victims died of bacterial infections from the untreated flogging lacerations. Hapless inmates were ordered to perform physically exhausting activities while she cackled with sadistic entertainment. And Ilse purposely lay naked in her front garden to snatch anyone who gawked at her nakedness so that she could beat them, sometimes to death.

While humans were starving to death, the evil couple lived a lavish lifestyle in an elegant house within the camp's grounds and had all the food and expensive liquor they desired. The Kochs often held debauched orgies for their SS staff to abuse underage prisoners, who were immediately gassed following the sexual abuse.

During her time at Buchenwald, she birthed a son, Artwin, followed by two daughters, Gisele, and Gudrun. Both died shortly after birth. Who sired them is questionable.

Shortly after Gisele and Gudrun's burials, Karl was suspected of corruption and accused of enriching himself by skimming profits from the camp that should have been handed over to the Nazi Security Police. He was relieved of command at the end of 1941. An SS German judge convicted him of corruption and graft, and he was executed by the Allies in 1945.

Following Karl's execution, Ilse, and her son, Artwin, hid in Ludwigsburg, a suburb of Stuttgart, until the Allies discovered her. Her son was handed over to her parents' custody, who then fled to Switzerland.

In 1947 "The Bitch of Buchenwald" was jailed and was awaiting trial by an Allied military tribunal held at the former Dachau concentration camp. Ilse was convicted and charged with multiple heinous crimes, including ordering prisoners displaying "interesting" tattoos to be killed and their excised skin turned into products such as lampshades, book covers, gloves, and so on.

Buchenwald survivors testified during her trial: "She always seemed particularly excited and was seen jumping up and down and clapping her hands when little children were sent straight to the gas chamber."

Despite several witness testimonies by prisoners who were ordered to make grisly lampshades and trophies, prosecutors could not conclusively prove her involvement in committing these mutilations or other crimes.

Unbelievable!

However, Ilse was convicted of being a part of the "common design" to abuse prisoners physically and sexually, and she was sentenced to life imprisonment. At the Landsberg Prison in Bavaria, Ilse gave birth to another son, Uwe, who was likely fathered by a fellow prisoner, Fritz Schäffer, in October 1947. (This penal facility is where Hitler had penned *Mein Kampf* in July 1925, which chronicled insane ideology, and presented *himself* as leader of the extreme right while serving a sentence for an attempted political overthrow of the government in 1923.)

Baby Uwe was taken away from Ilse and placed in a foster home. In his adult years, Uwe tried to clear his mother's name but was unsuccessful.

The Allies used Landsberg to perform the execution of death sentences meted out by the Nuremberg Trials. Two hundred and fifty-two unrepentant Nazis, who had played critical roles in the execution of one of the most appalling mass genocides in history, were executed by firing squad or hung from the gallows. One of the hanged was General Otto Ohlendorf. (Allegedly, a blood relative of Ohlendorf currently resides in a rural area of Arrow Lakes Valley with an altered last name.)

Ilse's two younger sisters, who had served as camp guards (out of the fifty-thousand concentration camp guards, five thousand were females) at Buchenwald, had taken up residence in Arrow Lakes Valley, B.C., Canada. One sister was deported by ICE (the federal agency in charge of criminal-civil enforcement) in 2001.

Ilse's older sister lived a solitary farming life in the same area until her death five years ago. Why she wasn't deported as well remained a mystery until I learned from a credible source that she had given up her sister in exchange for her own freedom!

Yup, it doesn't make sense. Why would immigration officials allow one sister to remain and remove the other? I *know* that immigration needed informers who were still living in the tight-knit German community of Arrow Lakes Valley.

After Ohlendorf was sentenced to death, this father of five children was asked by his kindhearted attorney, David Ginsberg, if there was anything he could do for the condemned man, such as telling his family that he loved them. The Jewish War Crimes attorney hadn't expected the banality-of-all-evil response: "I hope survivors that I failed to kill *suffer* in America."

The attorney was offended by his client's lack of any inherent human remorse for his evil deeds and the capacity of conscience for evil doing. It seems Ohlendorf regretted nothing. Ginsburg looked him in the eye and addressed him in German, "*Verabschiedung* (Goodbye) Ohlendorf. I hope you get eternal punishment in the quenchless fires of Hell!"

It raises a thought: Does evil exist in all humans?

Here is a potentially debatable answer from a criminal psychologist: "Malevolence hides within all human psyches. It manifests in those without consciences, such as the genocidal killers, mostly sociopaths like Ohlendorf and other Nazis who committed inhuman acts and died without remorse."

In 1951, as political and humanitarian pressures mounted, the others convicted in the subsequent Nuremberg Trials, and by the U.S. Military Commissions, were quietly allowed their freedom. Several industrialists convicted of slave labor abuse, evil doctors who performed medical experiments, SS officials and Wehrmacht officers, and Foreign Ministry officials condemned for massive crimes against humanity were all also released.

On May 5th, 1958, prisoners still detained at War Crimes Prison Number One in Landsberg were released. While these releases may be seen as a perversion of justice, the Nuremberg trials set an enduring precedent that "never again" would crimes against humanity be tolerated.

A German newspaper clipping of a memorial service exposed a large German gathering at Spöttinger prison cemetery, giving SS-Haupsturmführer Otto Ohlendorf a Nazi salute. Earlier, a popular

German TV network recorded the hangings of the Einsatzgruppen defendants.

Prison medical reports show that several minutes elapsed before death was pronounced. A photo of the forty-four-year-old monster, Otto Ohlendorf, neatly dressed in a black suit and lying dead in his coffin before burial, is still obtainable on web browsers.

Thirty-three criminals, who committed capital crimes, were also executed in Landsberg. Unfavorably, Ilse Koch's prison sentence was reduced by the U.S. military to time already served. Why? Because of the *burgeoning* Cold War politics and the growing disgruntlement among some West Germans over ongoing harsh sentences handed out to Nazi war criminals!

After Germany surrendered to the Allies, the former Nazi country was divided into four zones, with the western powers fostering parliamentary democracy, while the Soviet Union opened the door for socialism in the east. And so, the Cold War began.

On May 23, 1949, the newly appointed Lutheran Chancellor Konrad Adenauer of the Federal Republic of Germany put political pressure on the Allies to exercise clemency for Nazi war criminals being held under their watch.

"The Bitch of Buchenwald" was released on October 17, 1949. As she stepped out of the prison compound, she was immediately rearrested and charged with abusing captured German Lutherans during her time at Buchenwald. Ilse was then sentenced to life in prison.

In the winter of 1967, Ilse hung herself using prison bedsheets and was buried in an unmarked grave in the prison cemetery.

Unlike their German counterparts, the Soviets had no scruples about hanging Nazi criminals in their eastern prisons. Only a handful of "Krauts" were found alive in the Soviet-occupied territory after the Berlin wall came down in the November of 1989. The prison where Ilse committed suicide continues to operate today.

DACHAU, GERMANY

Dachau was established soon after Hitler was appointed as Chancellor in January 1933. It was the first and longest running Nazi concentration camp. Dachau was Hitler's prototype for the concentration camps that followed. This prison mostly detained Hitler's political opponents—four thousand communists, two thousand social democrats, and other dissidents.

Dachau was run by *Standartenführer* Hilmar Wäckerle, a former Waffen-SS officer selected by his compatriot Heinrich Himmler. On the first day of his appointment, Wäckerle fired half of the over one hundred Nazi guards at Dachau for being too "soft" with prisoners.

Now under his ruthless watch, countless so-called "Jewish criminals," artists, the physically and mentally disabled, and homosexuals died from malnutrition, dysentery, and other contagious diseases. But only *Jewish* prisoners were singled out for the heinous medical experiments, testing the feasibility of reviving people from freezing waters. One of the experimental subjects was fifty-year-old Titus Bradsma, a Carmelite cleric, historian, and an avowed anti-Nazi. He was forcibly submerged in a tank filled with ice water for hours, succumbing to death shortly after being released from the tank.

They also administered lethal injections to time how long it took for a prisoner to die. Wäckerle insisted on being present during this procedure.

There was a more heinous side to the Dachau Commandant. Boys as young as five were separated in the lineups of transport arrivals. Wäckerle had them isolated in a separate prisoner barrack, where they were sexually abused. His victims were subsequently shot during *alleged* escape attempts. Wäckerle's disgusting, lascivious behavior was eventually reported by an SS guard to higher command. He was immediately discharged and sent to the eastern front.

In February 1942, during the battle of Kharkiv in Russia, the Red Army shot Wäckerle's reconnaissance aircraft down near the village of Mykolaivka, south of Kharkiv. He was buried at a German cemetery in Ukraine. His body lay there until the Soviets defeated the Germans. The Kremlin ordered the graves to be bulldozed. No trace of coffin wood or bone fragment remained after flamethrowers torched every inch of the German graveyard.

Wäckerle's predecessor at Dachau was Waffen-SS officer Eicke. He was killed in action that day, and his remains were blown to smithereens. (Theodor Eicke introduced the blue and white striped pajamas that came to symbolize the Nazi concentration camps across Europe.)

In Germany, Wäckerle's widow, Elfriede, assumed her maiden name of Aeichelle and moved in with another man without a day of mourning for her husband.

An outraged Himmler had Elfriede's lover sent to Dachau, where he was beaten to death by an SS official. The widow fled to Sweden with her three children in fear for her life. Elfriede died in a skiing accident two days before Germany surrendered. A German family in British Columbia adopted her sons, and one is still alive!

In the 1940s, Dachau was overcrowded with over thirty thousand prisoners in a camp designed to house only six thousand. The SS ordered the construction of an on-site crematorium.

The primary victims were Polish-Jewish political and Soviet prisoners of war, who were selected after evening roll calls, separated, and shot. This arduous killing mode was subsequently reverted to lethal injections following complaints by locals of blood and body parts washing up in village streams.

One transport arrived at Dachau in December of 1943, with almost half of the nine hundred forty-eight prisoners dead.

The rate of killings increased during the final months of the camp. The SS "Death Squad" executed high-profile Russians, thirteen Allied secret agents, and seven prominent German anti-Nazis, who had been kept alive for interrogation—the most likely to escape or organize resistance.

On April 10th, 1945, Germany was losing the war and SS Heinrich Himmler ordered camps to be evacuated. "Not a single prisoner must fall alive into enemy hands," he stressed.

When Wäckerle's replacement, Commandant Max Koegel, got Himmler's evacuation notice, he ordered SS families to leave first. Then, he separated Jewish prisoners into an assembly lineup. Dachau inmates were marched in groups of ten out the camp gates, forced to undergo an eighty-six-mile trek to Tegernsee, a town in the Miesbach district of Bavaria. Those unable to maintain a steady marching pace were shot on the spot and thrown into ditches. Many died from starvation, physical exhaustion, and hypothermia along the way.

Nine days later, the United States Infantry entered Dachau, where they found thousands of emaciated Jewish prisoners who couldn't walk lying helpless on the ground. U.S. soldiers also discovered dozens of train cars filled with decomposing corpses and several nearby open pits with half-burned corpses exposed.

Out of three thousand marchers, only one third of the prisoners survived the "Tegernsee Death March." They were freed by American troops on May 2nd, 1945.

FLOSSENBÜRG, SOUTHEASTERN BAVARIA

This concentration camp was constructed for its proximity to a granite mine in May 1938 by the SS Main Economic Office in a remote area of the Fichtel Mountains, adjacent to Flossenbürg, near the German border with Czechoslovakia.

The camp was exclusively established to exploit the forced manual labor of Jewish prisoners to mine good quality blue-gray and yellow-grey granite for Nazi architectural demand. Three quarries were operational by the end of 1938.

Jewish prisoners were woken before dawn, handed their daily ration of a thin slice of *schwarzbrot* (black bread), then assigned to dangerous mining tasks. Many died of starvation and quarry accidents, and mangled bodies remained outside the mine to rot until the Bavarian civilian workers complained about the stench.

A quarry survivor's testimony:

I was fifteen when my father and I were transported to Flossen-bürg. I worked alongside him in the quarry. One day, I heard his cry for help when a large slab of granite pinned his body to the ground. I rushed to help him and was stopped by a Nazi overseer who threatened to shoot me if I took another step.

My father's last words to me were, "I'm good. I am going to join your beautiful mother. You need to be strong and survive, my son. I love you."

After the civilians complained about the foul odor, we were forced to throw the dead, including my father, into a depleted granite mine backfilled with rocks. I had no tears left that day.

According to one survivor:

In 1943, granite production was temporarily halted when two thousand prisoners and a group of German civilians were put to work on the mass production of aircraft wings and tailpieces for Messerschmitt fighter planes and other armaments for the Nazi war effort.

Of course, German laborers were not forced to work long shifts and received "healthy" monthly pay-packets. However, "compas-sionate" German civilians smuggled food into the plant for their wretched "slaves" counterparts, many in the death throes of mal-nutrition and exhaustion.

Although this camp was initially intended for criminal and "asocial" Jews, following Germany's invasion of the Soviet Union it became swamped with captured Russian soldiers. Due to chronic overcrowding of the barracks, prisoner conditions worsened due to a shortage of fresh water and adequate nourishment.

Also, in the frigid mountainous elevation, many prisoners, clad only in their thin pajamas, froze to death during long winter months. Their frozen corpses, packed in ice, were shipped to experimentation laboratories in Munich, Germany. Prominent Nazi doctors likewise toured Flossenbürg, selecting inmates, primarily Russian Jews, to be sent to euthanasia centers such as Auschwitz in Poland.

When the U.S, Infantry liberated Flossenbürg on April 23, 1945, hundreds of prisoners, too ill to be sent on a death march, were discovered by the liberators. Half died in field hospitals.

Investigation of Nazi war criminals at Flossenbürg began on May 6th, 1945. The head of the labor department, SS-Haupsturm-führer Frederick Buerge, who signed the transport lists, received a death sentence. Commandant Max Koegel committed suicide by hanging shortly after being captured by the Americans in 1946.

Thirty-three Flossenbürg guards received death sentences, eleven SS officials received life sentences, and the remainder received varying jail terms. Charges against seven Kapos were dropped, and five were found not guilty.

One witness at the trials, was Emil Fackenheim, the son of the crushed granite worker, who stated that the SS guards joked and laughed as his father lay dying. Emil passed away in Israel in 2002, at age ninety-two.

MAJDANEK, POLAND

This German concentration camp was established in Lubin (now known as Ukraine), in July 1941, after the German invasion in 1939. The camp was intended to supply forced construction labor for permanent German settlements in Poland.

Himmler's chosen site in the suburb of Majan-Tatarski, nick-named *Majdanek*, was primarily to accommodate the arrival of two thousand Soviet prisoners of war. But that didn't work out, and Himmler's Operation Reinhard (a secret German plan to extermi-nate Polish Jews) was enforced. The plan was to implement the mass murder of all Polish Jews and to seize their property. Some Jews were to be spared temporarily for labor.

Jews were seized off the streets of Lubin to become forced labor-ers in Majdanek. The following year, non-Jewish prisoners arrived with only healthy Jews selected from the Lubin ghetto.

Majdanek's Commandant, Karl Otto Magenau, was instructed by the SS Main Office in Oranienburg that approximately seven thousand Slovakian Jews, initially bound for Auschwitz, would be arriving soon. The SS officials also selected German and Austrian Jews off transport trains bound elsewhere.

Between March and June 1942, fourteen thousand Bohemian and Moravian Jews landed in Lubin and were driven into a ghetto. Later, two thousand were picked out for slave labor. The rest were transported to the Sobibór killing center. By December, Majdanek camp had filled beyond capacity. Prisoners slept on the ground outside overflowing barracks until Zyklon B and carbon monoxide gas ended their lives. Jewish men, women, and children, arriving on additional transports, were shot on the railway platform.

In the summer of 1943, Himmler ordered the cleansing of Polish villages, starting with Zamosc, on the outskirts of Lubin. Thousands were held temporarily at Majdanek. In Himmler's deranged mind-set, it was the first step in "Germanizing Poland." Over time, the SS expelled one hundred thousand Poles, deporting half to Auschwitz. The remaining prisoners were transported to labor camps across Germany.

In November 1943, SS death squads carried out Himmler's orders to kill all Polish Jews from the camps and jails in Lubin, including the remaining eight thousand temporally held at Majdanek and ten thousand Sobibór prisoners.

Himmler's "Enterfest" (Operation Harvest Festival) was nefariously implemented a month later. Prisoners were forced to dig deep trenches in preparation for the mass killings of forty-two thousand Jews, the largest killing operation during the Holocaust.

No witness-no crime!

Himmler had received an intelligence report of an imminent, large-scale attack by armed Jewish resistance fighters heading toward Majdanek. But Soviet troops beat them to it. With the Russians approaching the Polish border from the east, panicked Majdanek operators began evacuating prisoners. Thousands of emaciated humans were packed into transport trains bearing Nazi logos. Unfortunately, the trains were bombed by Russian aircraft after the pilots spotted the Nazi logos painted on the tops. No one survived

In July 1944, the Soviet forces liberated Majdanek. Just five hundred surviving prisoners, almost at death's door, cried while greeting rescuers. In the short span of Majdanek's three-year operation, one hundred thirty thousand people were killed. The majority of which were Jews.

Later, the Polish-Soviet Nazi Crimes Investigation Commission, established to document Nazi atrocities committed during the German occupation of Poland, ordered exhumations at Majdanek to investigate the mass killings in the camp. The Crimes Commission later published its alarming findings in Moscow on September 16th, 1944, in Polish, Russian, English, and French.

Two Majdanek prisoners, Kula and Volanski, will forever remain alive through their relatives, who now reside in the Kootenays, British Columbia.

MAUTHAUSEN-GUSEN, UPPER AUSTRIA

This camp was established in August 1938, several months after the German annexation of Austria. Albert Sauer was appointed Commandant until February 1939. Franz Ziereis assumed control of Mauthausen from 1939 onwards, until the camp was liberated by the American forces in 1945.

The SS-Totenkopfverbände, headed by SS Herbert Blöttnig, oversaw the workforce. Unfortunately, most records of camp leadership were destroyed by Nazi officials to cover up war atrocities and those who were involved.

By 1940, Mauthausen was packed with socialists, communists, anarchists, homosexuals, Boy Scouts, teachers, university professors, and religious groups such as Jehovah's Witnesses, who refused to participate in Nazi military service, rejecting loyalty to Hitler.

In September 1940, four hundred captured Spanish Republican activists were handed over to the Gestapo after fleeing from Franco's regime. Following the outbreak of the Soviet-German war in 1941, Mauthausen received Soviet POWs. Retained in separate barracks, the soldiers were first in line to be killed in the newly built gas chambers.

After the Nazi invasion of Yugoslavia in April of 1941, fifteen hundred people suspected of aiding the partisan resistance were transported to Mauthausen, along with eight thousand Dutch Jews. The first transport from Auschwitz of Hungarian male Jews arrived in February 1942.

Overcrowded in bunks, prisoners weighing around forty kilograms (88 pounds) resulting from reduced rations and were put to work in the Mauthausen rock quarry, also known as the "Stairs of Death." Prisoners were forced to carry boulders of stone as heavy as 50 kilograms (110 pounds) up the one hundred and eighty stairs, back-to-back, in unbearable heat or frigid temperatures as low as minus thirty degrees, from morning to night. If an exhausted prisoner collapsed in front of the other prisoners in the line, it created a domino effect: the first prisoner would fall onto the next, and so on, all the way down the stairs, and Nazi guards brutally whipped those responsible for the disruption.

A Mauthausen survivor, Edward Mosberg, stated:

If you stopped to catch your breath, you were taken to a cliff known as Parachutists Wall. At gunpoint, a prisoner was given a choice: Be shot or have a fellow prisoner push him off the cliff. Most chose to be shot.

Another survivor stated that the guards often brutally forced exhausted prisoners to race up the stairs, carrying blocks of stone.

Those deemed unfit for further labor by the SS overseers would be thrown onto a 380-volt electric barbed wire fence. Or forced outside the camp perimeter and shot on the pretense of attempted escape. Some three thousand were killed by hypothermia after being forced to take ice cold showers and then compelled to stand on frozen ground in frigid weather.

Other prisoners, mostly women, too feeble to struggle, were drowned in barrels of water. Their bodies were removed and flung to the ground. On command, Kapos piled the deceased into wheelbarrows bound for the crematorium.

As if this dreadfulness wasn't sadistic enough, doctors Sigbert Groenhysen and Karl Josef Bergner performed pseudo-scientific experiments on the dead and dying victims.

On May 5th, 1945, U.S. Army soldiers of the 41st Reconnaissance Squadron of the U.S. 11th Armored Division, and of the 3rd U.S. Army, broke through the Mauthausen's reinforced steel gates. Most of the SS bigwigs had fled to parts unknown, but thirty guards who were left behind were killed by the prisoners after the American soldiers entered the gates.

Lieutenant Jack Taylor, an officer in the U.S. Office of Strategic Services, was among the inmates rescued.

Another of the camp's survivors was Simon Wiesenthal, a Jewish architectural engineer. This undaunted man vowed that, for the rest of his life, he would hunt down Nazi war criminals, and he did. Wiesenthal died in his sleep at age ninety-six in Vienna on September 20th, 2005. He is buried in the city of Herzliya in Israel.

The Simon Wiesenthal Center, headquartered in Los Angeles, is named in his honor. (I visited this center in 2012 and started weeping after the first exhibit. The sadness and madness of their suffering still live deep inside my heart. To Holocaust deniers, the evidence of what another human can do to another is waiting for you in the Wiesenthal Center.)

Tibor Rubin, a Hungarian Jew who was incarcerated at Mauthausen at age fourteen, subsequently joined the US Army upon his liberation. He became a corporal in the Eighth Cavalry Regiment, First Cavalry Division.

Francesc Boix, a photographer and veteran of the Spanish Civil War, was imprisoned there for four years. He worked at the camp's photography lab and smuggled several negatives out of the camp. The proof was later used as evidence at the Nuremberg trials.

The trial of personnel from Mauthausen-Gusen took place between March 29th and May 13th, 1946. Among the accused there were seventy former members of the camp's administration: August Eigruber-Gauleiter of Upper Austria; Viktor Zoller, the former Commander of the SS-Totenkopfverbände guard battalion; doctors Friedrich Entress, an SS member and a medic who killed prisoners with phenol injections; Eduard Krebsbach and Erich Wasicky, who were responsible for the Zyklon B gassings.

Commandant Franz Ziereis was shot several weeks later following the liberation of the Mauthausen by an unknown assailant.

The defendants were criminally charged with violations of the laws and usages of war, murder, torture, beating, and starving the inmates. After six weeks, all were found guilty. Fifty-eight were sentenced to death by hanging. Nine had life imprisonment sentences but were later paroled. Three Kapos were sentenced to life imprisonment. All but one of the death sentences were carried out. SS Otto Striegel won a last-minute stay of execution. He was eventually hanged on June 20th, 1947.

An additional fifty-six trials took place between March and November of 1947, within the framework of the Mauthausen cases against specific individuals, such as the *Kapos*. (The origin of this title "Kapo" remains a mystery. Speculation is that the word derives from the Italian "capo," meaning "boss.")

Jewish prisoner functionaries were called Kapos and assigned to forced labor by the Schutzstaffel guards. They received extra food and privileges to supervise the labor and to minimize costs by allowing camps to run with fewer SS personnel. These Jewish inmates, blurring the lines between collaborator, perpetrator, and victim, faced many moral-ethical dilemmas for their choices. In existing Nazi documents, it seems that Kapos were often more feared than the Nazi overseers.

In the making of these concentration centers, Heinrich Himmler ran the Kapos' functions by Hitler:

We have organized our system of control over these sub-humans. If you like, one prisoner will be the overseer of others, with the responsibility for thirty, forty, or even more than a hundred other prisoners. He will then be responsible for meeting the work target, preventing any sabotage, and seeing they are all clean and the bunks are set up. A recruit in any German army barrack could not be more spick and span.

Following the capitulation of Germany, Mauthausen fell within the Soviet sector of occupation of Austria. Initially, the Soviet system used the Mauthausen camp as barracks for the Red Army. The underground factories' spoils were dismantled and sent to the USSR as reparations. In 1946, the camp was shut down. But before leaving, the Red Army blew up the underground tunnels and handed the fifty-acre property to the Austrian civilian authorities, and Mauthausen was declared a national memorial site ten years later.

MITTLEBAU-DORA, GERMANY

This concentration camp was established in October 1944 as a subcamp of Buchenwald near the town of Nordhausen, Germany in the Harz Mountains.

Retired Wehrmacht Captain Manfred Hans Hornharten was appointed Commandant but later removed after a camp guard reported seeing his superior stash a considerable wad of money and jewelry items in his pockets. According to the snitch, a Jewish prisoner had handed over his valuables as a bribe to turn a blind eye to his planned escape.

Hornharten's replacement, Otto Försh, was a Jew hater who shot prisoners on the spot for not lowering their heads when he passed by. Försh sent one hundred inmates to the Mittelwerk tunnels in the Harz Mountains, tasked with converting coal into hydrocarbon deposits, an explosive material used to fuel A-4 ballistic missiles that were christened the "Vengeance Weapon." When irreversible lung damage from the highly toxic fumes afflicted the first set of workers, the dying were left outside, and a new batch of workers were brought from the camp to replace them.

An Allied bombing raid on April 8th, 1945, destroyed not only the top secret Mittelwerk underground factory but the six Nazi overseers inside. The shelling also collaterally killed all the Jewish laborers.

On April 11th, 1945, the U.S. 3rd Armored and 104th Infantry Divisions entered Nordhausen. Before reaching the camp, the soldiers found in the tunnel hundreds of corpses that were burned by fire in the air raid. They also discovered large quantities of intact missile parts. The devices were later shipped to a U.S. Army base in New Mexico.

On that day, an enraged American general ordered his men to round up German civilians from the town and commanded them to dig mass graves for the victims in the tunnel and those piled outside the tunnel.

Operation Paperclip, tunnel operations designed to exploit German technology, began its origins in the Mittlebau region. Discovery by the U.S. of another previously unknown mountain tunnel, which housed nuclear weapons components, sent shockwaves down the grapevine of allied liberators.

But America was not the only allied country interested in German science! Soviet powers were also eager to grab the fruits of German rocket and missile technology to assemble and refurbish some V-2s. The Soviets sent their prisoners of war—German engineers and technicians—to the USSR. (Yikes! Vladimir Putin comes to mind because we know he has "Doomsday" weapons technology, probably designed by the former captured German nuclear physicists.)

Following the liberation of Mittlebau-Dora, the first wave of the SS functionaries was charged by the British in the fall of 1945. All were hung.

Five Kapos received prison sentences for their mistreatment of prisoners. In the Soviet-occupied zone, a Mittlebau SS officer was sentenced to twenty years in a Soviet jail, where he was beaten to death by a Russian-Jewish inmate.

Further investigations of war crimes by an establishment in West Germany led to another "Mittlebau-Dora" trial in Essen. SS Richard Baer was at the top of their list. He was discovered living under an assumed name. He committed suicide shortly after being arrested in 1967.

Helmut Bischoff, security chief of the Mittlebau region, was eventually released on the grounds of poor health, and yet, he lived to age ninety-one!

Erwin Edmunds, an infamous SS guard, escaped prison and was rumored to be seen in British Columbia, Canada in 1969.

The name Dora has lived on because of its connection to German rocket engineers like Wernher von Braun, who was given sanctuary by the U.S. government to aid their space program. The U.S rocket program continues to advance today as NASA (National Aeronautics and Space Administration).

A French prisoner who survived the bombing was able to take with him photographic proof of the underground rocket plant.

Declassification of these photos ensured the tragic stories of the Mittlebau-Dora concentration camp lived on in history. Only eight hundred and fifty inmates survived Mittlebau-Dora. Many of them later died from various lung diseases.

NATZWEITER-STRUTHOF, ALSACE, FRANCE

This remote camp, surrounded by dense forest, was established on French soil in 1941. Heinrich Himmler selected this site as a perfect location of strategic interest to the Third Reich, as pink granite was in abundance. The granite was favored building material for Nazi monuments.

Natzweiter was also a sinister reminder of the Nazi occupation of France. For the local Alsatian people, this picturesque area was used for picnics during summer and skiing in winter. The German invasion of France abruptly ended all recreational pursuits.

From 1941 to 1944, the Natzweiter housed fifty-two thousand captured political figures, including resistance leaders Andree Borrell and Charles Delestraint. Natzweiter also captured British spies including Vera Leigh, Diana Rowden, and Sonia Olschanezky. They were known as *Nacht und Nebel* ("Night and Fog") because they would "vanish into the night and fog" without their families ever knowing their whereabouts.

To prevent resistance figures from being made into martyrs and gaining popular support from the resistance, prisoners, especially the Jews, were immediately gassed.

Men and women transported from the overflowing Auschwitz camp were killed. "Warm" corpses were shipped to Nazi doctor SS-Haupsturmführer August Hirt, a Swiss-German head of the

Department of Anatomy at the Reich University in Strasburg, France. His research was funded by the Ahnenerbe Foundation—Heinrich Himmler's think tank to explore the reality of religions and myths around the world. Himmler believed modern Germans are descended from an ancient Aryan race, which he considered to be biologically superior to others, and assigned the 1603-built Renaissance Wewelsburg Castle in the village of Wewelsburg, for secret meetings. Within the fortress's forbidding stone walls, dubbed "Himmler's Camelot," the most malevolent of blueprints for world domination and genocide were designed. This castle also operated as a non-military training center, where only the purest of selected Aryans propagandized Germany's evil history and culture.

The Nazi treasury handed a vast fortune to Himmler's medieval fantasies to restore the castle to the best Nazi symbolic grandeur. In time, swastikas, occult symbols, and Nazi-approved artwork and artifacts adorned walls. An added feature was the crypt chamber with a statuesque eternal flame surrounded by twelve seats, where Pagan ritualism was freely embraced.

Of course, Jewish slave labor was used. Many construction workers died from hunger and exhaustion. A survivor testified that they were ordered to bury the bodies—some still alive, but barely—under the foundations.

After the castle was restored to its former glory, Himmler sent his occult cronies to seek mythological artifacts and antiquities to imbue the crypt with magical powers. They engaged in depraved rituals in the crypt. Donned in white ceremonial robes, they took their sexual proclivities with Jewish girls and boys, prisoners as young as eight, to heinous carnal levels. Petrified victims were ordered to remove their striped pajamas and, with their wrists tied, drink the semen of the "purest" Aryans before being raped.

Furthermore, boiling wax was their rapists' final act of depravity, laughing at these little humans charred skin and exposed bones.

A quote from Albert Einstein: *Two things are infinite, the universe and humans' stupidly.*

With the tide of World War II turning, Himmler ordered SS Major Gutsche to destroy the castle. However, the fortified crypt survived being reduced to ashes, like the cremated souls who had unwillingly entered its dark doors. SS Major Gutsche and two high-ranking officials from Natzweiter evaded capture. It is rumored they were disguised as displaced Jewish inmates and smuggled into Canada using forged IDs.

It seems it was easier for German forgers to make *female* identification. Immigration Canada didn't examine "fake" females closely!

Wewelsburg castle is a moving *"aide-mémoire"* of how a civilized country can collapse at any given moment into genocidal savagery when lunatic despots take control. After major renovations, Wewelsburg castle is now a youth hostel for schoolchildren and boasts an impressive museum that features ceremonial robes, barrels of hardened wax, and other depraved artifacts.

When the U.S. Infantry entered Alsace, they discovered hundreds of dismembered body parts preserved in formalin in the basement of the Anatomy Institute. It sent nauseous shock waves through the most hardened of soldiers. Some tattooed numbers were visible on corpses, enabling war crime researchers to identify some of them. Sadly, many victims found in the basement will continue to remain nameless.

With Allied troops on the doorstep, the Natzweiter was evacuated, forcing all inmates to march two hundred miles under brutal conditions to the Dachau camp in southern Germany.

One of the death march survivors was Boris Pahor, a Slovenian-Italian writer, who wrote poignantly of his experiences in his autobiographical novel, *Necropolis*, published in 1967.

Pahor died at his home in Trieste, Italy, on May 30th, 2022, at age one hundred and eight. At his funeral, a family member stated that he was a broken man, with frozen blood of hatred for the Germans in his veins.

The U.S. Infantry entered Natzweiter on September 4th, 1944. Fewer than one thousand souls survived this camp.

NEUENGAMME, HAMBURG, GERMANY

This concentration camp was established in Hamburg, Northeastern Germany, shortly after the invasion of Poland in 1938.

Under Himmler's directive, the abandoned *Deutsche Erd-und-Steinwerke* (German Earth & Stone Works) was selected as a prison camp. It naturally required slave laborers to rebuild the defunct brick factory. Healthy Jewish men, boys, and women were selected. Abuse and hunger reigned supreme during the backbreaking rebuild without adequate tools. Many workers died within three months and were systematically replaced.

When the factory was finally completed and operational, the SS camp authorities selected the healthiest inmates to reconstruct a canal on the offshoot of the Elbe River, which was needed to transport raw materials for the up-and-running brick production. Prisoners excavated the heavy, peaty soil, regardless of weather conditions. Then, armament production became a priority until the war ended.

Private businesses profited from *free* labor. "Merchants of Death" producers, like Messap, Jastram, Walter-Werke, and Deutsche Ausrüstungswerke, wanted to share this success and jumped on the "free labor" bandwagon.

While conditions for prisoners slaving fourteen hours per day in these privately owned facilities were a little better than the harsher brick factory and canal digging, men and women continued to work under the constant threat of beatings, starvation, and rapes perpetrated by the non-Jewish civilian coworkers.

Wilhelm Bahr, a German medical prison orderly at Neuengamme, testified that Bruno Tesch, the owner of Testa, a company that had supplied hydrogen cyanide (Zyklon-B) gas to the Neuengamme SS officials, bragged about killing countless people with his lethal product. After the war, a British military court condemned Tesch to death, along with his business partner Joachim Hans Driedger, for knowingly supplying Zyklon-B to commit murder.

Three crematoriums were built at Neuengamme to handle the mountains of decomposing bodies resulting from the gassings of the forty thousand Jews and two hundred Russian POWs.

For Hitler's so-called "undesirables," life in the Neuengamme camp was a constant struggle for survival, and one of the few possession's inmates were allowed was their rusty food bowls. Half of the inmates slept on the floors of the overflowing barracks. As large prison transports arrived daily, three-tier bunk beds were installed and shared by four to six people each. After the fourteen-hour workday, sleep was almost impossible. Nevertheless, the imprisoned clung to their friendships, relationships, and distracting activities. Literature, poetry, and songs helped them maintain the will to survive. Approximately one thousand prisoners died each month, and the death toll reached catastrophic proportions before the Allies entered Hamburg.

In early April of 1945, Himmler ordered Neuengamme's evacuation. The newly appointed Commandant Kaufmann immediately rounded up the prisoners for evacuation. He instructed five SS functionaries to remain behind, destroy the camp's internal documents, and blow up the barracks and the crematorium after he got all the prisoners out.

Nine thousand prisoners were marched to waterfront docks to board German naval ships, the DEUTSCHLAND and CAP AR-CONA, and two steamers, SS THIELBEK and ATHEN, anchored in the Baltic Sea off the coast of Neustadt in Schleswig-Holstein. (Northernmost German federal State bordered by Denmark to the north, and the German state of Lower Saxony to the south, with two seacoasts: the North Sea to the west and the Baltic Sea to the east.) The prisoners were packed into cargo holds for several days without food or water.

In London's War Office, British Intelligence learned these vessels were Norway-bound, with fleeing high-ranking Nazi officials. They were also informed about the thousands of prisoners onboard these vessels. And so, on April 20th, 1945, the Royal Air Force Hawker Typhoon aircraft attacked with an incendiary bomb decimating the convoy. Survivors jumped into frigid waters and were subsequently machine-gunned. Survivors not peppered with bullets eventually died of hypothermia. Within hours, thousands of dead bodies were washed ashore.

British occupiers now ordered German POWs and civilians to dig mass graves for the dead Neuengamme souls. Incredibly, four hundred Neuengamme boat prisoners survived!

One month later, British soldiers arrived at the concentration camp to find it deserted except for a fourteen-year-old and his brother. The Jewish teenagers, with puncture wounds from rodent bites, crawled out from under a latrine sewer tunnel after hearing English accents. Jacob ran to a soldier and hugged him. His brother, Levi, handed the soldier a hardcover book titled *Death Register*. It survived the fire that the Nazi guard had set to destroy evidence.

The detailed ledger shockingly revealed that over two thousand sick prisoners were given a bowl of turnip soup laced with sodium cyanide on the day the camp emptied.

The Commandant's last instruction to a couple of remaining guards, "Make sure the dead are doused with gasoline and burned and burn everything in my office."

"I heard piercing screams and prayed it wasn't my father, but I knew in my heart that one of the screams had to be him," Jacob tearfully told the British soldier. "An overseer broke his leg when he didn't run fast enough to the bastard's side. It was my father who told us about the tunnel under the latrines."

On March 18th, 1946, the trial of fourteen Neuengamme guards began before a British military tribunal in Hamburg, Germany. It was the first of thirty-three such trials.

Twenty ship-bombing survivors, including the "latrine" teenagers, testified under oath to the medical experiments, poisonings, gassings, beatings, and other appalling inhumane treatments. Sixteen defendants were found guilty of war crimes in May 1946. In addition, five high-ranking SS officials were sentenced to death, and twenty SS guards to prison terms ranging from ten to twenty years.

On October 8th, 1946, five Nazi camp operators, Tesch (Zyklon-B manufacturer) and his partner, Joachim Hans Driedger, were led to the gallows and hung by Albert Pierrepoint, an English hangman who had executed a substantial number of the condemned persons over his twenty-five year career. Albert's father and uncle had been the official hangmen before him.

Neuengamme's Commandant Kaufman escaped Albert's rope! Allegedly, his body was found among the drowned. (I can't find any record of his burial.)

Albert Pierrepoint died on July 10th, 1992, at the age of eighty-seven. On his deathbed, he said to his wife, "I'm haunted by the hundreds of "drops" (hangings) that I have been a willing part of. May God forgive me."

In the post-war months, Neuengamme concentration camp was used as a Soviet displaced persons camp, with German POWs held separately. Then British forces used this site, renamed to Civil Internment Camp, for turncoat SS Nazi witnesses who were hoping to get out of being prosecuted, but many were sentenced to death.

This facility was closed on August 13th, 1948, and the grounds were transferred to the Free and Hanseatic City of Hamburg, which was then rebuilt to be used as a women's prison.

NIEDERHAGEN, GERMANY

This concentration camp was established in 1941, on the outskirts of Wewelsburg in Germany. It accommodated newly arrived prisoners to replace the dead workers assigned to Himmler's "Camelot" castle. Though it was a smaller prison than other camps, Niederhagen housed the largest crematoriums. Over one thousand Jehovah's Witnesses of all ages were put to death in its crematoriums.

The U.S. army liberated the camp on April 2nd, 1945, and fifty emaciated people were in their death throes. Only ten survivors lived to give testimony to the evils of Niederhagen. Purportedly, Niederhagen's brutal Commandant Adolf Schultz was among those who perished in the British bombard. I couldn't find his burial record, but after months of research, I finally tracked down a survivor who claims that Niederhagen is still alive. This is the ninety-year-old Jehovah's Witness' account:

> *That's hogwash. I saw him walking down Sainte-Catherine Street in downtown Montreal, where I live now. He was with a tall, slim blond woman and five children. Yes, his blonde hair had been dyed black, but the pink scar along his left cheek left no doubt to whom he was because I knew how he got it. Kaufmann was beating a prisoner with a club, and the brave man grabbed a knife from the Nazi's belt and slashed him. Kaufmann took out his pistol and shot him. I do remember the evil German bleeding profusely, and later seeing the healed facial scar.*
>
> *Lucia, it was Kaufmann. I was shaking when I walked into the police station. The officer behind the glass partition told me*

they could do nothing, and I was to call immigration if I had a problem!

I tried to report this witness's revelation to the immigration authorities and was placed on hold for fifty-five minutes. I even wrote a letter; I never got a response. It was seventy-eight years too late!

Will this elderly man, whose life meant nothing to Kaufmann, ever see justice before he dies? Tragically, the answer is NO.

Today, an extensive housing estate with two-family homes, a fire station, and an ambulance station screens the historical tragedy of humans gone forever at Niederhagen.

Several homeowners have reported hearing mysterious moans and cries filtering up from their foundations. A newlywed homeowner complained to the housing developer, "Nearly every day, I find dead birds on my deck. Is there something I should know, like gas leaks or whatever?" She was too young to know what really happened on the grounds she called home.

RAVENSBRÜCK, NORTHERN GERMANY

This concentration camp was exclusively established to intern so-called deviants—sex workers, lesbians, abortionists, and Roma. It was in dense woodland in the village of Ravensbrück, fifty-six miles north of Berlin. By early 1940, eight hundred and sixty-seven so-called "aberrant females" were brutally whipped by bestial Aryan female guards, spurred by hate, through Ravensbrück's bricked gateway. Many non-deviants, mainly Jewish people, were to follow.

SS Colonel Gunther Tamaschke was the first commandant. Captain Max Koegel replaced Tamaschke in January 1940. Captain Zobel (sable fur) was the *last* Nazi official to hold this position until the end of April 1945.

The concentration camp billeted eighteen barracks, twelve for prisoners, two as hospital sickbays, one as a penal block, and three warehouses for confiscated belongings. As prisoner transports arrived, SS Johanna Lagerfeld, an overseer, and her right-hand, Herta Bothe, separated prisoners who were fatigued, injured, mentally and physically disabled, mute, and deaf and marched them to the camp's infirmary, where Doctors Herta Oberheuser and Erika Diebolt awaited with their nursing staff.

These female medical personnel came to work at Ravensbrück for a variety of reasons. Some volunteered, and some were sent under compulsion. One of the German nurses was posted to the camp as punishment for sharing her meals with a French male prisoner with whom she was in love. This nurse remained at the Ravensbrück Infirmary until liberation. Under a fake identity, she is in an assisted living residence in Arrow Lakes Valley. She is in her nineties, in poor health, and is not expected to live much longer. Good riddance!

In May of 1940, an advert in a German newspaper advertised:
**HEALTHY FEMALE WORKERS BETWEEN THE
AGES OF 20 AND 40 ARE WANTED IN MILITARY SITES.
GOOD WAGES, FREE BOARDING, AND
CLOTHING ARE PROVIDED.**

Of course, the newspaper did not disclose the "military site" was a concentration camp!

Siemens & Halske, a major producer of heavy equipment and telephones, was only a tiny part of their manufacturing range. Operating in Berlin, the company was in the right place and at the right time when the Nazis came into power.

Hitler's cronies compelled the company's owners to produce other electrical components for the war effort, supplying free labor from Ravensbrück prisoners.

"We will need more workers," the company said.

"Not a problem. We can supply as many workers as needed at *no* cost," the Nazis replied.

Siemen & Halske's cooperation with the Third Reich remains a dark chapter in this company's history, because Ravensbrück prisoners slaved in their factories from dawn to dusk with little food and water.

The worst for these enslaved workers was the fear!

At each roll call, big-boned muscular prisoners, mostly Polish Jews, were pulled aside and viciously beaten before being marched off to the factory.

In the spring of 1941, the SS established an adjacent camp for male inmates to build and manage the camp's gas chambers. The SS built brothels to reward the male prisoners who surpassed production quotas. Former arrested prostitutes, Jews, Catholics, and Jehovah's Witnesses were singled out to "service" male prisoners and visiting SS personnel with fetishes such as acrotomophilia (sexual interest in amputees), algolagnia (sadism, inflicting pain), and, in some instances "getting off" while women die by strangulation. Many women, girls, and boys forced into prostitution had life-threatening complications of their untreated sexually transmitted diseases.

With the Red Army's rapid approach, the SS began evacuating Ravensbrück. Prisoners marched on foot toward northern Mecklenburg, on the coast of the Baltic Sea, a four-and-a-half-mile trek. Before evacuation, camp records left behind specify that forty thousand females and five thousand males transported from Nazi satellite camps were gassed.

On the day of the march, the Soviet Army spotted the columns of prisoners and shot the SS guards, freeing the exhausted prisoners. Ravensbrück's remaining SS officials and female guards had fled the day before the Soviets entered the camp.

Thirty-five hundred women worked as concentration camp guards, and some with children were allotted cottages. From balconies, they could overlook the old-growth forest and a lake, and from their windows, their children could watch prisoner chain gangs go by and see the belching chimneys of the gas chambers.

The adult daughter of a Ravensbrück guard remarked decades later. "Living there was the most beautiful time of my life. I miss being treated like a queen. But I don't miss the *filthy* Jews." If I had been the reporter interviewing this insulting woman, I would have hit her—and hard! These women, former housewives, some professionals, portrayed themselves as "ignorant" helpers, so *easily* rationalizing in the post-war that they were NOT exploited!

They were nothing more than sadists, who had danced to the beat of Satan's drum over helpless others.

I interviewed ninety-seven-year-old Mira Serchuk, a Polish-Jew resistance fighter, from her home in London. "The female guards were awful," she told me. "I didn't think women could be that cruel. I was eighteen when I was captured and sent to Ravensbrück as a political prisoner—"

"Hello, you still there? I asked.

"Yes, I'm still here," a tearful voice replied. "I still don't like to talk about it. You see, I was forced to work in the brothel. I never married because I couldn't live with the shame of what had been done to me by so many men."

Only seventy-seven Ravensbrück guards were held to account for their roles after the war. Most were unrepentant, changed their names, married, and then faded into society. There are exceptions: A handful left Ravensbrück's recruiting office when they realized what the job actually involved. They refused to talk about it after the war.

SS overseer, Herta Bothe, was jailed for horrendous acts of violence. She was pardoned by the British after just a few years in prison, and I haven't been able to find out why.

In a rare interview recorded in 1999, before she died, the evil Herta Bothe remained apathetic: "Did I make a mistake? No. The mistake was that it was a concentration camp, but I had to attend. Otherwise, I would have been put into it myself. That was my mistake." That was an excuse former guards often gave. But it was not true. They were allowed to go without consequences.

In October of 1945, the U.S. military arrested the nurses. They were all found guilty of willingly assisting Ravensbrück's "Doctors of Death" in their inhumane experimentation on inmates. Some were immediately executed; others were imprisoned. Some got off relatively scot-free, like the nurse in the earlier paragraph.

The Ravensbrück doctors were arrested a month later. One of the doctor's preposterous statements dumbfounded legal minds in the Nuremberg doctors' trial conducted by the U.S. military tribunal in December 1946. Unmoved by the criminal charges, Herta Oberheuser exclaimed, "I just wanted to improve my financial situation, that's all!" She went on to tell a packed courtroom that she obtained her medical degree at Bonn University in early May of 1937. She specialized in dermatology and had practiced at several clinics in Düsseldorf before responding to a newspaper advertisement:

DOCTORS AT A RE-EDUCATION CENTER
IN RAVENSBRÜCK REQUIRED.

No one in the court was buying her sob story, so her German defense lawyer argued in litigation: "Given the heavy expenses and general restrictions brought about by Hitler's war, it was impossible for my client to set up her own practice."

Did this Doctor of Medicine *really* believe that her own absurd excuse could justify simply wanting a paycheck? Herta was convicted and sentenced to only twenty years in prison. And the unremorseful doctor served only five years! A reduced sentence for good behavior let this abominable killer walk free, and, within weeks, she was practicing again in Germany, but not for long. Under pressure from Ravensbrück survivors, the German College of Physicians and Surgeons formally revoked her license in 1958.

Throughout the war, this doctor, who had taken the Hippocratic Oath to "...*abstain from all intentional wrongdoing and harm*," instead subjected prisoners to mutilations without anesthetics. Some of the procedures included amputations, bone-grafting, muscle and nerve regeneration, sterilization (to develop a more efficient method), and administration of sulfonamides (synthetic bacteriostatic antibiotics) into wounds that were deliberately infected with dirt and glass to test for gangrene cures.

One hundred and eight women, mostly Jews and Roma, died as a result. Survivors of these procedures suffered permanent damage. (In my opinion, historians have been slow to acknowledge the role of female medical personnel in crimes committed during the Third Reich.)

Today, Ravensbrück prisoner barracks, camp guard quarters, the infamous infirmary, and the additional Ravensbrück buildings are long gone, demolished by the Red Army liberators.

All that remains of this infamous camp is an unnervingly empty, rocky field 80 km (50 miles) north of Berlin. In 2013, a Dutch tourist visiting the historic site used her iPhone to take photos of the old forest. When she scrolled through the pictures later, she noticed something perplexing in one of her images. She sent a copy of the blurry image of a woman holding a baby in her arms to Gaurav Tiwari, a paranormal investigator, who validated the snapshot to be authentic.

What are those, so withered, and so wild in their attire,
that look not like th' inhabitants o'th' earth, And yet are on't?
—WILLIAM SHAKESPEARE

SACHSENHAUSEN, GERMANY

This model concentration/labor camp was established after Hitler appointed Heinrich Himmler chief of the German police in July of 1936. It was designed to provide more efficient methods of execution.

During the earlier stages, executions were carried out in a windowless room, known as *Genickschussbaracke*, where loud music was used to mask the sounds of shooting. Prisoners believed they were there to have their height and weight measured. One at a time, they were shot in the back of the neck while standing on scales. When this extermination method was found to be far too time-consuming, Zyklon-B replaced the scales.

By September 1941, five showers were operational.

Sachsenhausen housed sixteen hundred prisoners, which included Jews arrested during *Kristallnacht*. Also imprisoned were Soviet civilians:

- Expatriate, who shot German diplomat Ernst Vom Rath in Paris. (Herschel's reprisal essentially "launched" the *Kristallnacht* riot).
- Paul Reynaud, the Prime Minister of France, who had vowed to bring the Nazi regime down.
- Francisco Largo Caballero, Prime Minister during the Spanish Civil War.
- Bavarian Prince Adalbert, his wife, Marie, and their six young children, who Hitler believed to be a threat to his leadership.

Also interned was Ukrainian freedom fighter Stepan Bandera. Bandera was recruited by a German Military commander as a Russian-Ukrainian translator in preparation for their attack on the USSR. This post was beneficial as Bandera hoped to free Ukraine from Soviet rule and establish his *own* government there. The delusional Ukrainian freedom fighter was unaware that the Germans intended to keep Ukraine for themselves. The Nazi collaborator was arrested for his intransigence on the issue of independence but released when it appeared that his popularity with Ukrainians might help stem the Soviet advance. However, Bandera and the Nazis had shared a key obsession—blaming Jews for Communism and Stalinist imperialism. "The Jews of the Soviet Union are the most loyal supporters of the Bolshevik Regime and the vanguard of Muscovite imperialism in Ukraine," Bandera preached to his Nazi commander comrade.

When the Nazis invaded the USSR in June 1941, they captured the East Galician capital of Lvov. Bandera declared independence in his name and the triumphant militant promised to work closely with Hitler, and he did. Four thousand Lviv Jews were shot. "We will lay your heads at Hitler's feet," Bandera crowed.

Though the murders and his shameful speech didn't go unpunished. On October 14th, 1959, the KGB (*Komitet Gosundarstvennoy Bezopasnosti*, Russia's Security Agency) assassinated Bandera in his Munich apartment building.

The KGB was disbanded in 1991 with the collapse of the Soviet Union. (Vladimir Putin was a KGB officer in Soviet times).

My two pennies' worth: Bandera should have been eliminated sooner, because what is despicably outrageous is the large bronze statue erected in a park in the east Galician town of Drohobych. The park stands on the site of a former Jewish ghetto, where fifteen thousand Jews were murdered. It saddens me to think he was declared a "hero" in Ukraine when he aided in the Holocaust killings.

Another prominent prisoner was Lt. Yakov Dzhugashvili, Joseph Stalin's eldest son. He died in the camp on April 14th, 1943. Commandant Johann Lippert stated Yakov committed suicide by running into an electrified fence. Though a photograph of Stalin's son's bullet-ridden body taken by Johann Lippert exists today!

Following Yakov's death, Sachsenhausen became the site for the infamous "Operation Bernhard," created by Chief Reinhard Heydrich. At the time, it was the most extensive currency counterfeiting operation ever recorded. Inmate artisans, under threat of death, were forced to produce fake American and British currency to undermine the British and American economies. The fake British £5-, £10-, £20-, and £50-pound notes were to be dropped over London by plane, but it didn't come to fruition. The Bank of England failed to discover them before or after the war. Today, these notes are very valuable to collectors.

Heinkel, the German aircraft manufacturer, was the primary user and abuser of Sachsenhausen prisoner labor. Timesheets found after the war showed Heinkel had enslaved approximately eight thousand prisoners to construct their bombers.

Although German reports claimed the prisoners were "working without fault," it was far from the truth. Many aircraft crashed by sabotage. In reprisal, they were all shot, and a new batch of workers was brought into the factory.

The bomber projects ended on April 20th, 1945, after an evacuation order was received. The first group of marchers received minimal food rations. Prisoners departing later received no food at all. Those who were debilitated from hunger and unable to keep up were shot on the spot. Prisoners were selected to throw the bodies into ditches along the way. As the sounds of Allied tanks neared, the chicken-livered guards turned tail and ran, leaving behind their disoriented captives. The prisoners ambled down the road until they were spotted by American tank commanders near the town of Schwerin.

The soldiers surrounded the Nazis and shot them. Prisoners, many with bleeding feet, cheered. Even the most hardened of battlefield medics were shocked to find how many of the prisoners were literally walking on the bones in their feet, disabled for life.

Their compassionate American rescuers, some with tears in their eyes, handed out chocolates and bottled water and then buried the dead in surrounding woodlands before moving on.

On April 22nd, the Polish 1st and 47th divisions that were under Soviet command entered Sachsenhausen. From the initial prisoner count of one hundred forty thousand, only two thousand skeletal bodies rejoiced their arrival. One female survivor dropped on her boney knees and kissed a soldier's boot. "I will never forget you for as long as I live," she cried. "May *Yahweh* (God) bless you."

From behind her, another woman sacrilegiously sniped, "Are you crazy? The *scnuk* (jerk) didn't give a shit about us, now did he?"

Later, the Soviet Investigative Commission estimated that two hundred thousand perished in Sachsenhausen concentration camp. (A more realistic figure, considering the thousands of unregistered prisoners would make it a helluva lot more!)

The Russian directive collected volumes of the crimes committed at Sachsenhausen, and the evil perpetrators who hadn't vanished were brought to trial. Camp officials, including Commandant Anton Kaindle, all the guards, and Kapos were tried on October 23rd, 1947, before a Soviet Military Tribunal.

Sixteen were found guilty. Fourteen defendants, including Commandant Kaindl, were given life sentences with hard labor. The criminals served their time under harsh conditions in Siberian labor camps. Six of them, including Kaindl, died from frostbite and hypothermia within a few months. In early 1956, those still alive were released and sent back to Germany.

One of Sachsenhausen's survivors was Antonín Zápotocký. In April 1939, following the German invasion of Czechoslovakia, Zápotocký was arrested for trying to cross into Poland illegally and was transported to Sachsenhausen. The Dutch government sought his extradition to face charges for participating in the execution of Dutch citizens, while he was appointed as *Kapo,* though it was unsuccessful.

Born in December 1884, Zápotocký was a Czech communist politician who became the Prime Minister in 1953. He stayed in office until his untimely death in Prague in 1957. Zápotocký's death certificate stated that, at the age of seventy-two, he died of a heart attack.

Unofficially, however, he possibly succumbed to poisoning by the KGB. Why? Zápotocký's treasonous actions of aiding the Nazis during the war had not been pushed to one side. The saying about elephants having long-term memories was aptly pertinent for Nikita Khrushchev. His hate for Zápotocký was well known.

Zápotocký was the second Czechoslovakian president to die suspiciously while in office. Zápotocký predecessor was Klement Gottwald. His death certificate also stated he died of a heart attack.

In March 2009, eighty-three-year-old Josias Kompt, a former high-ranking Sachsenhausen guard, was deported from Wisconsin, U.S., back to Austria and was found guilty of his crimes. He never spent *one* day in jail!

In May 2022, the sensational trial of SS Josef Schuetz began. The adage: *When you have done something wrong, it will bite you where it hurts* wasn't taken seriously by the one hundred and one-year-old former Sachsenhausen guard, who claimed he was just a local farmhand working on a friend's farm during that timeframe. But, unbeknownst to Schuetz, prosecutors had already built the case against him with evidence provided by another SS guard at the time of his own arrest. The oath-taker swore that Schuetz was a fellow guard. Schuetz's backstabbing former friend emphatically said that Schuetz *had* participated in the executions of prisoners. The notebook keeper had described in graphic detail how Schuetz castrated Jews of all ages by cutting off the blood supply to their testicles with rubber bands.

The most incriminating evidence against the former Nazi Schuetz included the material presented by concentration camp expert historian Dr. Stefan Hoerdler, who provided a file he received from the German Central Immigration Office, revealing that the entire Schuetz family were Lithuanians. The file's contents verified Joseph's date of birth, precise details, and passport photo, an identical copy of which appeared on an SS identification card.

The Nazi records also proved that Schuetz had served in six SS guard positions from October 23rd, 1941, to February 18th, 1945. He was promoted from Private to SS-Rottenführer (Corporal) and appointed to Sachsenhausen. In August 2022, the German Landgerict Neuruppin Court found Josef Schuetz guilty. He was convicted of thirty-five hundred counts of accessory to murder and mutilations.

The Sachsenhausen murderer was sentenced to serve only *five* years in prison. His shyster's lawyer appealed his client's convictions! Due to his advanced age, Schuetz was released and returned to his apartment to sleep in a comfy bed, enjoy morning coffee, and never to see prison walls! There is something not *kosher* about that!

Thomas Walther, a lawyer representing several camp survivors and victims' relatives, was outraged, "What can be a fitting punishment when the leading SS officers in the Reich Security Main Office were indicted for the murder of hundreds of thousands of people but were able to get off scot-free because of the lapse in time and their incapacity to stand trial."

Present in the courtroom was hundred-year-old Holocaust survivor Leon Schwarzbaum. Tears cascaded down his wrinkled face as he held up a photograph of his family. "He killed them all, and you think it is alright that this *shedim* (demon) lives!"

Leon spoke to the foreign press representatives gathered outside the court, waiting for the verdict. "This will probably be the *last* trial attendance for my friends, acquaintances, and loved ones murdered in Sachsenhausen. I pray for them that he will be convicted." Leon passed away in his sleep the day after Schuetz was released.

Josef Schuetz kept up the façade: "I was *never* in Sachsenhausen camp. You have me mistaken."

A week later, the Schuetz's homecare nurse reported, "I heard screaming and rushed into his bedroom. He was naked and clawing at his *privates*, and then he took his last breath." Schuetz's testicles were rubber banded. Although the Koblenz Federal Archives, the Stasi (East German secret service) archives, and Sachsenhausen residual archives have since refuted his involvement, Schuetz undoubtedly carried out gruesome crimes at Sachsenhausen. Schuetz's informer was stabbed and died on the pavement outside his German residence on the day his former boss was released. The Nazi torturer's assailant is unknown!

A year after Schuetz's sensational trial, a German government official investigating Nazi crimes, Thomas Will, stated, "We go by the simple principle that murder does not have a statute of limitations. It is what's right, and, of course, it should have been so many years ago."

It was a welcomed verdict by the president of the Central Council of Jews in Germany today. A spokesperson said, "Thousands of remorseless persons who worked in the concentration camps kept the murder machinery running. Without them, it could not have been possible."

Why were so many Nazi monsters given clemency, sent home to live out their lives when they obliterated the lives of so many innocent people? Hopefully, dark justice awaits them on the spiritual "other side."

SOBIBÓR, POLAND

It was an *extermination* camp, slyly hidden behind double barbed-wired fences, thatched with thick pine branches to block the view inside. Sobibór was established to annihilate the Jewish population of Poland.

Before Sobibór became operational, SS-Haupsturmführer Richard Thomalla, a civil engineer by profession and the manager of the SS Central Building Administration at Lublin reservation in occupied Poland, designed this camp in 1942. His "brainchild" was handed to the six-foot-two, blond, blue-eyed Austrian-born Franz Stangl, who had participated in the T-4 program for the killing of disabled adults at the Hartheim and Bernburg euthanasia centers.

With the camp up and running, the newly appointed Nazi whippersnapper presided over operations wearing an over-starched white linen jacket that smelled like rotten vinegar according to a survivor's report after the war.

As transports to the camp arrived, Stangl ordered SS officers to comfort the terrified people with promises that they would soon be transported to live and work in a Jewish state in Ukraine, adding a sick and twisted ploy. He handed out beautiful, picturesque post-cards to prisoners, telling them to write to loved ones and reassure them they are being treated well. Within hours, the starving and dehydrated humans were gassed. Those not killed were forced to bury the dead in pits.

After the war, Sobibór records revealed that two hundred and fifty thousand Jews were murdered during this camp's operation.

As expected, Stangl, SS officers, and guards lived in homely cottages with lush lawns, flower and vegetable gardens, outdoor terraces, and gravel-lined paths. Bold signs with ludicrous headings such as *Lustiger Floh* (Merry Flea), *Schwalbennest* (Swallow's Nest), and *Gottes Heimat* (God's Own Home) adorned cabin frontages. They even had a cafeteria, a bowling alley, a hairdresser, and a dentist, all staffed by Jewish prisoners. These idyllic charades, of course, hid the true nature of the camp.

A ninety-nine-year-old survivor from his home in Israel attested, "After seeing the Tyrolean cottages, with their bright little curtains, geraniums on the windowsills, and rose beds out front, my wife assured our fearful children, 'See, it can't be bad. Look at those beautiful flowers.' That same day, my whole family was taken from me and killed in the gas chamber."

Sobibór was buttressed with escape-proof, deep trenches surrounding prisoner barracks. It had workshops for tailors, carpenters, mechanics, sign painters, and a bakery where a Jewish baker toiled from dawn to dusk, making bread, rolls, muffins, pies, cakes, and cookies only for the camp officials. Several animal pens held chickens, pigs, and geese and were maintained by prisoners who never got to taste the livestock. There was an out-of-bounds area unknown to most of these assigned prison workers.

Tucked away at the far end of the camp in the thick forest were two wooden structures—a log-cabin office station previously operated by the local Polish forestry services that at one time had held equipment but now stored items such as food, children's toys, male and female apparels, furs, gold jewelry, and other valuables emptied from suitcases. Kapos combed through piles of possessions, sorting, and readying them for shipment to Germany.

The second, much larger building with enormous cellars was darkly more ominous. Only the SS and Sonderkommandos knew of its heinous existence.

Unsuspecting prisoner arrivals walked the *Himmelstrasse* (Road to Heaven), along magnificent flower beds lining the well-trodden pathway, and into the big building's bowels. They were ordered to undress, and then as many as three thousand naked people were herded into Sobibór death chambers disguised as shower rooms. After approximately seven minutes of inhaling the deadly gas, they died.

Sonderkommandos (Jewish prisoners who worked at the camp) dragged out the bodies, and chopped and bagged their hair before the camp's SS dentist supervised the removal of gold teeth and fillings. The corpses were flung into twelve blazing ovens. The ashes were removed daily and scattered in the woods.

Due to the lack of eyewitness testimony, little is known about separate housing assigned to the *Sonderkommandos*, or how many survived Sobibór. And most did not want to speak about their experiences, but one former crematorium worker did state, "I want to forget those gruesome horrors."

Also hidden in this heavily wooded area not far from the crematoriums was a munitions depot that processed arms. Inmates who had specialized skills in jewelry-making and artists were spared to satisfy Commandant Stangl's obsession with unaffordable "finery."

Among them was renowned Dutch-Jewish painter Max van Dam, whom Stangl ordered to paint Sobibór landscapes and hagiographic images of his hero, Adolf Hitler.

In January 1941, when compulsory registration came into force for anyone with Jewish blood, Max van Dam hid in the town of Blaricum, a small village in the Netherlands. When the village became dangerously overrun by Nazis, Max fled to Switzerland, but he was ultimately betrayed by a non-Jewish Swiss wannabe-artist.

A Sobibór guard captured by the Allies stated that Max had received preferential treatment like not having to attend roll calls and having his food delivered to his workshop by other prisoners. The artist was often seen by inmates drinking schnapps at Commandant Stangl's residence. With mounting pressure from Stangl's superiors for fraternizing with a prisoner, Max van Dam was gassed in Sobibór in September 1943.

In May 1944, an overloaded transport train of two thousand Jews from the Opole Ghetto arrived in Sobibór. Among them was fifteen-year-old Stanislaw (Shlomo) Szmajzner, who had come with his entire family. That day, prisoners were ordered from the boxcars. Whips reigned down as the transportees scrambled from the train. While men were being separated from women and children, Shlomo, clutching a wooden box containing an assortment of hand tools, stepped forward. "I am an apprentice goldsmith," the teenager hastily confirmed. "I can be of use to you." Shlomo showed the SS officer a golden monogram as proof of his skill. SS guard Kulaowski had him open the toolbox and examined its contents. Smiling, the guard ordered Shlomo to step to the right side, as his disabled father (whose left arm had been amputated after a welding accident at work), mother, and five brothers and sisters were marched away. Shlomo glibly pleaded, "My father is the best goldsmith ever."

SS Kulaowski smirked.

It was the last time Shlomo saw his family alive. They were gassed that same day.

The teenager worked long hours crafting golden rings from extracted gold teeth and wedding bands with SS monograms for the handles of the Nazi whips.

The now sixteen-year-old became a member of an underground organization that was planning an escape. Polish Jews played a dominant role in the committee that did not include Jews from Europe, especially German Jews, because a German Kapo, known as *Berliner*, turned out to be a spy for the Nazis.

Betrayed, all the committee members were hanged. Their bodies were left dangling on a platform for days to remind inmates not to try and outsmart German intelligence.

Before a new underground plan could be conceived, *Berliner* was beaten by Shlomo and the foreman of the tailor shop. He was then given a lethal injection stolen from the Nazi infirmary.

Under the new leadership of a Russian Jew, Petsjerski and Polish Jew, Feldhender, it was agreed that Shlomo was ideal for helping in a follow-up to a further uprising because the boy's work allowed him unlimited freedom of movement, and he knew the layout of the barracks like the back of his hand. It was very risky, but the heroic boy didn't hesitate to steal the weapons required for a large-scale retaliation.

With a stovepipe in his hands, he headed for the Ukrainian barracks. "I have come to fix your broken stove," he glibly announced to the Ukrainian Kapo. "Everyone must leave so that toxic fumes are not inhaled." When the barracks emptied, Shlomo headed for the gun rack. Using a pair of snippers, he cut the chain that held three rifles together, wrapped them in a blanket snatched from a bunk, and threw the bundle out of a side window where Petsjerski and Feldhender awaited.

On October 14th, 1942, prisoners carried out the planned revolt. They shot several Sobibór officials and Trawniki-trained guards (Soviet prisoners of war were offered a way out of captivity by cooperating with the SS), and several sentinels in the watchtowers.

With clothing wrapped around their hands, prisoners, including Shlomo, Petsjerski, and Feldhender, scaled the sharp barbed wire fencing. Unknown to the escapees, minefields instantly ended some of their lives. Others got stuck in the metal fencing and were shot by the remaining SS. The lucky ones—Shlomo, Petsjerski and

Feldhender—made it safely into the forest.

The SS and Polish farmers were bribed with rewards for killing runaways. Only twenty prisoners, including Shlomo, managed to evade the SS and corrupt farmers. Unforeseeably, the escapees encountered a different foe—heavily armed non-Jewish Polish bandits near the village of Izdebno, twenty-one miles west of Warsaw. These heartless thieves took their weapons and ordered them to undress and remove their footwear. Shlomo's gold rings sewn into his shoe heels brought jubilation. "Look what I found comrades," the leader said.

The bandits opened fire.

Astoundingly, Shlomo was not fatally wounded but played dead for an hour or so, until he was sure they had gone. Bleeding from the gunshot wound that had miraculously missed his heart, he stealthily made his way out of the forest.

Shlomo found refuge with a sympathetic farmer and his wife in Tarnawa, in southern Poland. This courageous young man, who had lost his entire family in the mass killings at Sobibór, remained under loving protection until the end of the war.

SS Heinrich Himmler ordered the camp dismantled immediately after the revolt. Sobibór was the last of the German Operation Reinhard camps to be shut down. The Red Army liberated the fifty remaining, emaciated Sobibór prisoners five months after Shlomo escaped the forest.

Shlomo, whose appearance had aged far beyond his years, eventually immigrated to Brazil, where he continued working as a goldsmith. He kept two rifles in a blanket under his bed in his lodgings.

In 1967, Shlomo recognized Stangl in a public bar. Without accosting the beast who had murdered his family, he headed straight to the nearest police station. Stangl was arrested and extradited to the Federal Republic of Germany and later sentenced to just life imprisonment. It makes one wonder: Why were German judges so feeble on crime?

Did contemptible criminals strike deals?

It seems that way because Stangl escaped from jail two weeks after he was imprisoned. His whereabouts remained unknown until a bizarre encounter with an elderly woman in the Arrow Lakes Valley, British Columbia, Canada, disclosed his actual hideout!

Before his death on March 3rd, 1989, in Goiania, Brazil, the Sobibór survivor, Stanislav (Shlomo) Szmajzner, penned a memoir: *Hell in Sobibór—The Tragedy of a Jewish Teenager.*

In 2007, a Polish excavation project unearthed thousands of items: disintegrated scraps of clothing, eyeglasses, false teeth, leg braces, children identification tags, toys, baby bottles, keepsakes such as photo albums, and tons of suitcase keys.

In 2009, the second excavation determined the exact placement of the double-row, barbed-wire fencing posts around the camp.

In 2012, mass graves were discovered.

In 2013, Israeli and Polish archaeologists unearthed a collapsed tunnel 33-feet long located under the Sonderkommando barracks. Twenty skeletal remains were found under the rubble. Of course, camp records do not mention the blowing up of the tunnel.

Outside a museum building located near the former camp's railway station, a cast-iron martyrology statue of a woman with child on the "Road to Heaven" sculpted by Mieczysław Welter (a Polish postwar and contemporary artist) was erected in memory of the thousands of people murdered at Sobibór.

TREBLINKA, NORTHEASTERN POLAND

This extermination camp was established November 15th, 1941, and, with intent, hidden in a remote forest. It was one of the last remaining primeval wetlands (nicknamed the "Wild West") on the European continent. Treblinka was yet another Operation Reinhard and the shortest operating death camp, lasting only three years. In the relatively short time of its existence, approximately eight hundred thousand Jews: Polish, Austrians, Czechs, French, Greek, German, and Russians, were incarcerated at Treblinka.

The camp commandant Sturmbannführer, Theodor Eger, was a short, broad-shouldered, balding, pudgy man who wore sunglasses day and night because of very poor vision. He claimed to be a German-Dutch aristocrat, which was inaccurate. Even though Eger was nearly visually impaired, he was trigger-happy. "Eger shot prisoners at random and laughed as they fell to the ground, some still alive," Franciszek Ząbecki, a Polish Railway stationmaster, testified after the war.

Eger was even feared by his SS subordinates, whom he threatened to send to the Eastern Front for even the slightest infraction.

On his watch, transportees who were not killed upon arrival were assigned to three units:

Unit One was allocated for Nazi residential homes, all equipped with high-quality items taken from Jewish ghettos. To top that, a miniature zoo next to Eger's residence contained two foxes, two peacocks, and several roe deer. Adjacent to the zoo, several barracks housed non-Jewish Polish and Ukrainian kitchen workers and other Nazi enslaved workers. At the end of the compound, prisoners worked twelve-to-fourteen-hour shifts in gravel pits and irrigation ditches dragging wood from the forest to fuel Nazi woodstoves.

Unlike the well-fed kitchen and cleaning workers of Unit One, Jewish workers were given watery soup for breakfast, their only meal of the day. On a rare occasion, they would receive a loaf of stale rye bread for supper that was shared among other workers.

Unit Two was allocated housing for the hundreds of Kapo and Sonderkommando workers at the "beck and call" of their Nazi handlers. Most of the Unit Two Sonderkommandos had arrived from other concentration camps without footwear or warm clothing and had to scavenge for needed items from dead prisoners.

Unit Three was allocated for Jewish women who repaired and cleaned Nazi military clothing that was delivered by freight trains.

As Treblinka became overcrowded with transport trains arriving every hour from other camps, water and food were rationed. Punishments for minor infractions were administered by their overseer, Franz Schwart, who attacked prisoners with a hammer at roll calls for not standing to attention. He killed an average of five prisoners a day.

In early May of 1943, Commandant Eger received orders from Himmler to exhume and cremate corpses. Eger ordered Unit Two to carry out the job. Decomposed remains were thrown into open-air pyres, along with the recently gassed victims—mostly pubescent children and babies.

A year later, on August 23rd, 1944, as the Red Army neared, Himmler instructed Eger to kill *all* prisoners ahead of the Soviet advance.

Following the mass execution of prisoners, Eger hired one hundred Treblinka locals to dismantle the camp, haul truck construction waste, plow burial grounds, plant grass, and build a farmhouse to make it appear that nothing sinister had occurred on the land.

Eger and the SS staff fled the camp and returned to Germany. Unbeknownst to Eger, the hired workers had pocketed the money without performing their job of destroying the evidence. The Soviets ultimately discovered Treblinka's sinister secrets, including the names of the prisoners who survived Himmler's genocide plans.

Holocaust nonbelievers have stated through social platforms

that Treblinka was merely a transit camp that moved Jews across Europe. Incorrect!

Samuel Willenberg was a Treblinka survivor who died on February 21st, 2016, in Israel at the age of ninety-three. The apprentice builder arrived on one of the first transports in 1942 at age nineteen. Samuel's trade allowed him to live, but he was nearly worked to death by the Nazis.

Samuel and three hundred other prisoners escaped from the camp in early August of 1943. Although he had been shot in the leg, the injured twenty-year-old managed to evade the massive SS search and made it to Warsaw. He was thrilled to find his father alive and well. Samuel joined his father in the underground resistance movement. Sadly, Samuel's father died of pneumonia shortly before Warsaw was liberated.

In January 2012, British forensic archaeologist Caroline Colls discovered the mass Treblinka graves by using ground-penetrating radar to avoid displeasing Jewish laws, which forbid any inference with Jewish graves. Caroline's discovery finally proved Treblinka's existence.

In mid-December 1944, Commandant Eger was ambushed on the road near Jędrzejów. He jumped out of his car and fled toward Lipówka Village, to a farm where he crawled under a haystack. Polish partisans with tracker dogs located and shot him.

The avengers found incriminating documents in Eger's briefcase. The tracker dogs also sniffed out eight Treblinka guards hiding nearby in barns. They were shot on the spot, and their bodies were dumped next to the Treblinka sadist.

In retributive justice, with "you got what you deserve" expressions, the partisans watched while crows pecked out their eyes and tore out their tongues.

Unbeknownst to the avenging partisans, a large German reconnaissance unit transported to Lipówka found the crow-mauled dead.

In reprisal, the Nazis selected nine local villagers, including a five-year-old child, and shot them. After the war, the heartless killers tried to convince the world that the massacre was the work of Russian paratroopers and not their doing. That blatant lie backfired because one of the German shooters had photographed the dead lying on the road. His camera was found on his body after he was shot by a Russian soldier.

In late December 1944, the SS launched Operation "Schneesturm," the codename for German, Croat, and Bulgarian partisan forces led by Marshall Josip Tito and operating within Bosnia during the occupation of Yugoslavia in 1943. Tito's goal was the implication of an Axis attempt known as the *Sixth Enemy Offensive* to flush out, trap and destroy Polish and Soviet partisans hiding in the Sancygniów forest in central Poland, not far from the village of Lipówka, where the German assassinations of the locals had taken place. The "Schneesturm" operation cost over two thousand lives on both sides.

Today, the village of Treblinka is deserted. Yet, nestled in Treblinka's pinewoods are a few rural dwellings so humble that no one would suspect that humans live there if it were not for the lace curtains hung in windows.

In memory of the eight hundred and fifty-thousand souls who perished, endless stone memorials stretch on and on. Some of the stones are engraved with the names of towns and villages, and of lost residents or notable people murdered at Treblinka, but most present a blank face to the world.

A tourist wrote in her blog:

During the visit, this place was empty and silent. Not even the birds sang. The silence was eerie but really added to the somber atmosphere of Treblinka. This place is haunting but so important if we are ever to learn to avoid these horrific events happening again.

Only two Treblinka survivors in their late nineties, living in Israel, are alive. One told me via telephone, "I just want the pain to go away, Lucia."

I cried for this poor soul who didn't ask for his life to be emotionally and physically mutilated by heartless snakes. Nothing can change the past, nor can one truly understand what it must have been like to be unwanted and hated by another race unless one can relate to their dreadful suffering.

VAIVARA, POLAND

This concentration/labor camp was established in early August 1943 in proximity to the Vaivara train terminal. It was also one of the last labor camps to be built. Three months earlier, Heinrich Himmler ordered the liquidation of all the ghettos in the Baltic States, so Vaivara was born to accommodate over twenty thousand Jewish ghetto prisoners.

Vaivara served as a forced labor camp throughout Estonia primarily for the oil-shale extraction operations produced by a German chemical and pharmaceutical conglomerate—IG FARBEN.

In 1925, IG merged with six other chemical companies—BASF, Bayer, Hoechst, Agfa, Chemische Fabrik Griesheim-Elektron, and Chemische Fabrik Vorm. The board members joined the Nazi Party, employing economic and political blackmail, which became the decisive factor in the constructing of labor camps such as Vaivara.

Why? Because the costly initiatives of synthetic rubber (Buna) from coal or gasoline were hit hard after the economic crisis of the 1920s and 1930s. With bankruptcy around the corner, these greedy corporate mongers established close ties to Hitler, who knew this potential opportunity to make Germany independent of imported raw materials was necessary.

The CEOs clapped their complicit hands after Hitler personally guaranteed the purchase of their products and promised to provide "free" labor. Like ducks to water, struggling German companies came on board. With the Führer's "green light," Commandant Helmut Schnabel exploited the Vaivara prisoners, young and old, without a break in the oil-shale extraction in numerous quarries, until many workers dropped dead from exhaustion.

The tall, slim Nazi official, with wolfish eyes and cold sores dotting his mouth, also ordered prisoners to harvest wood from the nearby forest to keep the SS woodstoves burning. Schnabel's records, found after the war, stated that the prison population ranged from almost seven thousand in October of 1943 to ninety-two hundred in November, and eighty-two hundred by February of 1944.

The slave driver's operation stopped when a typhoid epidemic claimed the lives of forty percent of the camp's population, putting a big dent in the available labor. They then had little choice but to employ local civilians who would not work for free. Prisoners too old or sick to work in quarries were killed in *Selektionen* (selections), as were all children. One thousand and five hundred aging Jewish men and women were lined up and shot in nearby woods. The next day, one thousand and fifty more transportees—men, women, children, and newborns—were executed.

In 1944, with the Allies approaching Poland, Himmler ordered Schnabel to evacuate and dismantle the camp. Prisoners were marched to Kiviõli, a town twenty-nine miles from Vaivara. Captives limped for three days in bitterly cold winter weather wearing ragged, blue-striped pajamas, most with no footwear. As the prisoners with SS escorts neared Kiviõli, a Soviet pilot spotted the Nazi columns and attacked, but with unintentional collateral damage. Approximately five hundred prisoners were killed in the military attack.

A year later, the Soviets brought many Vaivara SS guards and Estonian collaborators to trial and gave them various prison sentences.

Why didn't they get comparable capital punishment that was dished out by other Allies? The answer could be because it was politically opportunistic!

The Soviet Union abolished the death penalty two years after World War II ended due to contemporary debates regarding the "place" of Russia's criminal justice in their legal system. In 1954, the death penalty for non-political crimes became legalized, overturning a Stalin-era decree that abolished the death penalty in times of peace. Over the next thirty-seven years, courts across the Soviet Union sentenced thirty-three thousand plus people to death, who were then executed by hanging. These killings transformed the lives of their mothers, fathers, wives, husbands, children, co-workers, friends, and members of their communities.

Most of the Russian public still has little to no knowledge of Soviet laws or the legal system that administers them. A *classified* collection of one hundred and nine death penalty case files spanning the 1945 to 1991 period are locked away in the Central Archive of the Moscow Region.

Vaivara's Commandant Helmut Schnabel hung himself in his jail cell in May 1945 before being tried, and Karl Boettiger, a brutal overseer, evaded capture.

In the early 1960s, survivor Zvi Berkowicz was visiting a relative living in British Columbia, Canada, when he spotted the man who had whipped him nearly to death for not answering quickly enough when his name was called out during a roll call. Zvi approached his attacker in the coffeehouse, "Do you remember me, Karl?"

Boettiger glared. "My name is not Karl," he replied.

Zvi unbuttoned his shirt, exposing the scars that dotted on his chest. "Oh, there is no mistake." Zvi sneered. "You *are* Karl Boettiger, and *you* did this to me!"

Patrons in the coffee shop stared at the men. Karl got up from the booth, pushed Zvi aside, and stormed out the door, never to be seen again.

Zvi reported his encounter with Karl to Immigration Canada, but many incidents like this were never followed up on. Zvi Berkowitz died in London in 1990 at the age of ninety-one.

Unbelievably, most of the Vaivara SS personnel had their sentences commuted and were set *free*!

A stone memorial to the Holocaust victims of Vaivara's forced-labor camp was erected in the forest by the Estonian Jewish community in the small borough of *Klooga*, northern Estonia, in 1951.

PART FOUR
Arrow Lakes Valley Connections

"That so many were complicit in such barbarity could live happily ever after in Canada is a searing indictment of our justice system and the lack of political will to prosecute them. Their continued presence here over the past 75 years is an affront to our values as Canadians."
—Michael Levitt, the CEO and president of the Toronto Friends of the Simon Wiesenthal Center for Holocaust Studies

CHAPTER TWENTY

The Holocaust Is Forever Etched in History

*Regardless of lack of understanding, disbelief,
or pure ignorance, the truth will always be actual.*
—LUCIA MANN

Are concentration camp survivors a myth?

Are the trials of war criminals also a myth?

Are deportations of Nazis killers again a myth?

Are persons such as the renowned Simon Wiesenthal, a Holocaust survivor and Nazi hunter, a figment of misinformation?

I will leave it up to you to decide whether the heartbreaking stories of people, who had little hope of being treated humanely and were victims of perverse entertainment for Nazis, are validated by my research!

In the late nineties, I received an invitation to a birthday party from one of my book fans. She won't be enthralled with *this* publication!

Frankly, I did not wish to attend, as I have never been a party-goer, and oops, wrong thing to say, but I'm not keen on German company either. I gave way when she pleaded, "Please, I want to introduce you to my daughter. She has read your books and wants to meet you."

I arrived at the opulent lakeside property at 4:30 p.m. and was the only non-German among the party host's closest friends.

Of course, I didn't reveal my fluency in their language. I smirked at the sign on the gate to the luxury lakeside home: FOBOTEN DER EIGANG-NACHHUNDS (Entry Forbidden—Guard Dogs). The strange thing—there wasn't a vicious hound in sight!

The hosts (who have since returned to Germany) were dressed to the nines, as were the guests, unlike me, who decided that a pair of jeans and a T-shirt would be acceptable attire.

The party snacks were to die for, and the company was tolerable until the daughter came out of a back room carrying a garment bag, which she unzipped in front of the guests. I nearly choked on apple strudel. An authentic black Gestapo uniform proudly displayed, with a skull-and-crossbones symbol, a swastika sewn onto a red armband, and several pinned valor medals brought oohs and ahhs from the admirers.

"Isn't my Opa's uniform cool?" the smiling daughter heralded, unzipping the garment bag. I didn't wait to see if she was going to try it on and bolted out the door to my car and sped all the way home.

I recall throwing up and the telephone ringing at the same time when I got home. I did not answer but listened to the recorded message:

"Lucia, you left so suddenly without saying goodbye. Call me back."

Of course, I never did. I have not spoken to the party host since that frightful event. A few days later, the host's German neighbor confronted me in a supermarket. "Hildegard is upset because you won't take her calls."

"Oh, do me a favor," I said. "Tell Hildegard something for me. I'm *Jewish*, and she can stick the offensive Gestapo uniform up her arse."

The next unpleasant happening came when what I believed to be a nice German asked me if I knew someone to help clean his home while he was recovering from knee surgery. "I can help with that," I offered. In hindsight, I wish I hadn't been so accommodating.

I'll call him *Rolf*. His home contained some imposing antique furniture to dust and polish. A magnificently carved sideboard caught my attention. I was a little envious since I *love* antiques. Polishing the underside, I saw an engraved Star of David, bearing an inscription: **MADE BY DAVID STEIN, 1940**, and my neck hairs bristled. I checked other pieces of furniture. Many had the same logos.

I found Rolf in his bedroom and cagily asked, "Where did you obtain the beautiful furniture pieces?"

"They belonged to my grandfather," he replied. "I got them after he died."

"Just curious," I said. "Was your grandfather Jewish by any chance?"

"Definitely *not!*" he returned smarmily.

I continued to bait Rolf, "Well then, he must have favored Jewish-made furniture because most of your pieces have the name David Stein on them."

"Yes, I know," he answered. "The man was arrested. I don't know why. My grandfather said he purchased the stuff to help the money-strapped man's family."

"Are you shitting me!" were my last words as I stormed out of the home.

Another German name was added to my list.

A further encounter with a "baddie" came when I was at the local hot springs. I spotted an older man, I guessed to be in his nineties, with the most piercing blue eyes. What got my attention was a serial numbered tattoo on his upper left chest.

I hit my computer and Googled. I learned that single-needle devices were used to pierce serial-number digits on the inner side of the left upper forearms. Before that, the Nazis used a metal stamping device with interchangeable numbers only one centimeter long to allow the whole serial number to be punched on skin. Black ink was then rubbed into the bleeding wounds. When this method proved too time-consuming, the single-needle method was used.

My heart beat happily. Had I found a *Jewish* survivor among these "tainted" Germans? Besides me, only three other persons in the valley are Jewish.

That day in the pool, without engaging the man in conversation, I memorized his inked numbers. When I got home, I texted an Israeli intelligence friend. "Can you check this tattoo number for me?"

The following day, my phone rang. "Are you sure you memorized the numbers correctly? Because the number two is missing in 128232, which incidentally adds up to eighteen, the Jewish mystical symbol of life. Hang on, I have someone on the other line. He's been checking into this tattoo as well."

A few minutes later, Aaron reported, "Well, he must have paid to do that because the number 128232 belonged to Jacob Radoszynski. He was fourteen years old when he was arrested with his family in the Warsaw Ghetto in 1939. Jacob survived Sobibór and died here almost twenty years ago. The guy you saw in the hot springs is probably an erroneous Nazi, who has faked his way into Canada, pretending to be a Holocaust survivor, and he won't be the first to use this type of deception!"

Deep down, I regret not engaging him in conversation, not because I am a Nazi hunter, but because he had to be scared to put that very painful inking on his flesh.

I frequent the hot springs often and have not seen the fraudster again.

That encounter, just knowing this person was hiding something, left a bitter taste until his *real* identity came to light later. The bizarre incident continues to attack my ethical conscience today. Strange things happen, but boy, oh boy, I was absolutely *not* prepared for this one!

In the spring of 2021, I spotted an elderly lady, who reminded me of Betty Beals, at a bake sale to raise money for the local Animal Rescue Center. She made eye contact. "I just love chocolate cake," she commented in a deep masculine nasal tone. But there was no mistaking her nationality.

She had a very thick German accent and was tall— I guessed her to be about six feet. Her shoulder-length hair was as white as snow, and she had an infectious smile.

I have no idea why I warmed to her, but I did.

I learned that day she was ninety-seven, which surprised me. She definitely did not look her age. She also disclosed that she lived near my home in the senior citizen rental property.

Strange! I had resided in the valley for over twenty-seven years and hadn't seen her.

"You are remarkable," I flattered. "I'm much younger and not wearing it as well as you. What's your name?"

"I'm Heidi Magenauski," she replied. "And what's your name?"

"My name is Lucia Mann. It is a pleasure to meet you."

After many years of practice, what I'm good at followed, "Are you Polish?" I asked, hiding trickery in my tone.

"No, my dear, I'm German," she replied. "My husband was Polish-German. He died in 2019."

"Oh, I'm sorry to hear that," I responded. "Do you have any children?"

"No, I do *not!*" Heidi snapped. "I can *never* have children!"

Wow! My mind went haywire. Not only was her tone bitter in context, but her angry facial expression prompted me: *Okay, time to read her whole-body language!*

From her gestures, I professionally determined that Heidi undeniably *oozed* deception.

Intrigued by my analysis, I prompted, "I live only a block away.

I have Dresden *teekanne* (black tea)," I lied. I'm not too fond of the strong taste of this German beverage. "Please pop in anytime."

"I would love that," she smiled and then frowned. "You said your last name is Mann. *Sind Sie Deutsche?*" (Are you German?)

Yikes! (Actually, Mann is a Jewish Ashkenazi name of German origin.)

"Not sure what you have just said. Sorry, I don't speak German," I said poker-faced. "I'm a writer and use Mann as a pen name."

"Oh, what do you write?"

I bit my tongue and left.

A visibly flustered Heidi with puffy eyelids appeared on my doorstep five days later. "Can I come in?" she asked in a barely auditable tone.

"Of course, please do. Heidi, you don't look well. What's the matter? Are you okay?"

"Nothing is the matter. Honestly, I'm fine. I've come to enjoy the cup of German tea you offered."

Oh, poop. No German tea. I gestured to a leather recliner. "Make yourself comfortable, and I will be put the kettle on."

I have a habit I can't shrug off. I read *everyone* who comes into my presence, and Heidi's body posture revealed a "dark shadow" I wasn't comfortable with. Yorkshire tea was served with home-baked Sicilian lemon cheesecake.

"This is delicious," she praised. "You must give me the recipe."

My thought: *I hope to make my Sicilian yummy when I reach her age.*

We chatted about this and that. There was little doubt that Heidi was highly intelligent. Her articulation was as sharp as an eagle's claw. I was just about to enquire about her former profession when she exclaimed, "I hardly know you, but I'm a good judge of character."

My self-assured internal voice instantly disputed—*No, you are not! I am!*

"Lucia, I feel that you are a good person, very sincere, with a big tender heart, someone trustworthy. I will tell you something, but please promise you won't tell anyone else. I must get it off my chest before I pass on to be with my beloved Carl."

Okay, he must be her husband, my mind silently deduced.

I noted her hands twitching (the body language of extreme anxiety) as she divulged, "I have been diagnosed with terminal cancer and do not have much longer."

"Oh, I'm so sorry, Heidi, but it comes to all of us," I genuinely uttered.

Heidi reached into her handbag, removed a Kleenex to wipe her tears, and handed me a photograph. "This is my beloved Carl."

Holy crap! My brain felt like it was going to explode out of my skull. The hot springs man was posing in a swimsuit with the machine-inked tattoo on his chest. My mind scrambled. *Was he a Holocaust survivor?* A feeling in my bones that something wasn't *Kosher* prompted my trick question, "Did Carl belong to a motorcycle gang because he has a rather peculiar tattoo on his chest."

"No," she laughed. Her mirth instantly dissipated as she rolled up her sleeve, revealing a faint tattoo, "I have one, too. But not as painful as Carl's was."

There was no mistaking *that* one. My mother had one that was similar. So much for my training that failed to detect her deceptiveness. My Jewish blood flowed with compassion. I hugged Heidi.

"Thank you," she said, "but my tattoo is *not* real, Lucia. I'm not who you think I am. I'm a dreadful person. I have done horrible things and will burn in Hell."

What the heck! Her critical characterization was tantalizing. "Something is eating you alive, Heidi. Let it go. I'm listening, my friend."

Halfway through Heidi's outpourings, I shrieked. "Leave my home *now*! I never wish to see you again!" I slammed the door behind her. I was so numb-brained that I thought I would pass out. I have never felt surprised, or shocked, or even fazed before, but this one had bushwhacked me!

This seemingly delightful little old lady was, in fact, born Sigmund Friedrich Grusen and had transitioned to become a woman out of dire necessity.

In the quiet of my office, I weighed up Heidi's shocking revelations. In 1943, SS medical officer Sigmund Grusen was assigned to the infamous Block-10 of Auschwitz camp, where the "Angel of Death," Dr. Josef Mengele, committed the most heinous medical procedures on prisoners, mostly twins, during the war. When the trains transporting prisoners arrived at Auschwitz, Grusen selected those with deformities, which he classified as "hereditary persons," for his experimentation.

How did these tortuous experiments come about? In 1933, a unanimous declaration from the Prussian Chamber of Physicians declared its readiness to place all its energies and experience at the service of the Nazis: "We salute with joy and gratitude, and none of us will likely shed a tear for the former democratic Weimar Republic."

Dr. Alfons Stauber, president of the German Medical Association, wrote to Hitler:

The Association welcomes with the greatest joy the determination of the Reich government with the promise to faithfully fulfill our duty as servants of the people's health.

It was Nazi doctrine that called for physicians to shift from an individual doctor to the nation's doctor.

Fifty percent of medical professionals became members of the Nazi party—the highest of any profession. Nazi doctors had no moral qualms about taking over the practices of their Jewish colleagues, who lost their licenses due to enforced Nazi racial policies. It is estimated that forty percent of medical practitioners in Germany were Jewish. Taking over the practices of Jewish doctors was a huge financial windfall for German doctors.

I telephoned my Israeli contact. What Aaron revealed was beyond shocking:

"Sigmund Grusen performed hundreds of repugnant experiments on prisoners, including children. Some of his victims were strapped onto tables and had their organs removed without anesthesia. Some people had petrol injected into their hearts to determine time to organ failure."

Sick to my stomach, I couldn't eat or sleep. Disturbing emotions of hate, anger, revulsion and even murder flooded my psyche. I so wanted to kick myself for being tenderhearted. Why had I not sensed the pure evil lurking in Heidi from the moment I laid eyes on her?

Sigmund Grusen was arrested after the war and sentenced to death in two separate trials. Implausibly, his sentence was commuted to life in prison. But guess what? Grusen, alias Heidi, who had sat opposite me at my dining table, served only *three* years of his life sentence. He escaped from the Berlin jail with five other prisoners.

It is alleged these dregs of society paid a huge amount of cash and gold to a German security guard for their freedom. And by "Heidi's" admission, Grusen had fled to Egypt, where genital reconstructive surgery, followed by a cosmetic facial reconstruction, made him Heidi.

I can recall shifting my eyes to Heidi's neck, looking for the telltale Adam's Apple, but a colorful scarf had thwarted that natural laryngeal protrusion in males.

Heidi disclosed, "I recognized Carl at a restaurant. He was a German political prisoner assigned as a Kapo to the hospital to remove the dead. We became good friends, and eventually, we married."

I recall my mind churning with repugnance. How I kept my cool, I do not know.

Heidi disclosed, "We decided we didn't want to live in Egypt. Carl came up with a plan to have Jewish identification tattoos done. They were very painful."

Really! Nothing like the pain your "patients "suffered, my thoughts screamed. I wanted to strangle her! I held back my murderous thoughts.

"Carl found a Dutch forger living in Cairo who was also in hiding. He produced our new identities. We emptied our Swiss and Egyptian bank accounts and purchased plane tickets to Toronto. We entered Canada as displaced Jews with no problem. The Dutchman had also given Carl the name of a German realtor who was one of us. He helped us buy a lakeside ten-acre property in Arrow Lakes Valley in 1959.

"We loved the isolation of our home, but, after a while, Carl became restless. He didn't like being reclusive, so he purchased several properties in Arrow Lakes Valley. Unfortunately, none of his business ventures were successful. All were sold at a loss. But Carl was still restless. He bought a pub with three German acquaintances our realtor introduced, and *that* business was successful." Heidi wept. "I miss him."

That's when I decided enough was enough and kicked Heidi out!

This human without a conscience reviled me. Heidi did not forgive herself because evil people think they have done nothing wrong!   Not once did I hear a remorseful word. But then, most Nazis didn't show any remorse at their trials. Instead, "I was just doing my job, following orders" was their lame excuse.

That day, after I had ousted Heidi, I became conscious that I had inadvertently become an accessory to crimes. I was at a crossroads—turn right, turn left, turn right—with internal torment to do the right thing. Should I report Heidi? But to whom? The local RCMP detachment? ICE? Canadian Immigration? Canadian Intelligence? German Intelligence? Contact the Mossad and let them deal with it?

Would my report change anything?

Nope, since ongoing efforts to pursue the ever-shrinking numbers of Nazis who are still alive to be prosecuted for war crimes seem fruitless. They typically do not spend a day in prison because they are too old or sickly.

My conscience still pricks me today since I let a Holocaust murderer walk free, not with compassion, but just knowing there would be no jail time for Heidi! She died three days after her unwelcomed visit.

EPILOGUE
Crimes Against Humanity

"Justice for crimes against humanity
must have no limitations."
—Simon Wiesenthal, founder and head of the
Jewish Documentation Center in Vienna

CHAPTER TWENTY-ONE

Those Who Escaped the Prosecution Net

Nazi murderers are being discovered, but far too late.
We should ask ourselves why.
—LUCIA MANN

The following information raises questions:
Countries didn't thoroughly check out the hundreds, if not thousands, of imposters entering their domains after the war.

The answers to these questions lie in these alarming facts:
Following the Second World War, over twenty thousand Nazi war criminals slipped surreptitiously into Canada after concealing from Canadian officials their participation in the genocide of innocent people. Their presence, sometimes suspected, was *ignored* by the Canadian government until 1985.

Prime Minister Brian Mulroney requested an independent body of inquiry to investigate the worldwide accusations that Canada was giving safe havens to Nazi war criminals, including Joseph Mengele. Jules Deschênes, a Justice of the Court of Appeal of Quebec, was placed in charge of what came to be known as the Deschênes Commission.

The Commission members were asked to determine how many Nazi war criminals were residing in Canada and what legal procedures should be pursued regarding their presence. It was recommended that the Canadian Criminal Code, the Canadian Citizenship and Immigration Act, and the Canadian Extradition Act be amended to simplify bringing these individuals criminally or civilly to justice.

The Deschênes Commission passed legislation in 1987 to prosecute Nazi war criminals residing in Canada. This legislation was expanded in 2000 to become "The Crimes against Humanity and War Crimes Act." This law permitted courts with jurisdiction to prosecute war criminals in Canada. And yet not a single criminal conviction was carried out. "Operation Last Chance," a Simon Wiesenthal Center project, presents a yearly report on their efforts to investigate and prosecute Nazi war criminals. The group's first report, written in 2002, granted Canada a B-minus. The United States, on the other hand, had expressed adamant political will in the prosecution of Nazi war criminals and was duly awarded an A-plus. The lack of Canada's efforts is emphasized by contrasting numbers with those of the United States, the only country that relies on civil proceedings to prosecute WWII criminals.

Canada has convicted only *three* Nazi war criminals, while the United States has convicted *thirty-four*. Canada has filed *four* new cases, while the United States has filed *thirty*.

Canada opted to seek justice through civil remedies, supposedly stripping eight citizenships instead of deportation.

Absurd!

It makes one wonder if it was worthwhile.

As Canadians, we must ask ourselves if we are prepared to share buses, playgrounds, offices, or community centers with mass murderers. They may not threaten one's safety, but they indeed threaten the morals and values held by this country.

War crimes are never prosecuted to the fullness of the law when criminals can get away with their crimes because they are wealthy or have the right connections. The scales are so tipped that justice loses its purpose. In my opinion governments that are silent and do nothing shirk their duty in bringing justice to humanity.

Vile Nazis, who went along with Hitler's insanity, wear crimes like proud tattoos and often walk free. Imagine the pain of seeing your baby's fragile head being bashed against a wall or a loved one being dunked in iced water for German scientific studies. Or being forced to watch your mother, father, brother, or sister shot, hanged, beaten to death, or burned alive!

Here are some prime examples of how some Nazis escaped the prosecution net.

FRIEDRICH KARL BERGER

 He was a ninety-five-year-old Nazi living in Tennessee who was arrested and eventually deported to stand trial. He arrived in Frankfurt on a special flight from the U.S. on January 22nd, 2021. The German Hesse state police detectives met the uncuffed Nazi at the airport. Berger glared at them, "I will

not talk without legal representation."

The well-educated deportee played his hand. He knew that bringing his counsel up to speed on the facts of his case would take time, and lots of it. But his shrewd tactic failed because his trial began one week after his return to Germany.

The jury heard that Berger had illegally resided in the U.S. since 1959 and was a Nazi overseer at Meppen concentration camp in Germany, near the Dutch border. Three survivors testified how inmates were used for outdoor forced labor, worked to death from exhaustion or freezing temperatures. With overwhelming evidence stacked high against him, Berger finally admitted to working in Meppen, but he argued it was only for a few weeks near the war's end and brazenly added that he had not witnessed any abuse or killings. *Yeah right!*

The prosecutor argued that Frederick Berger also assisted in guarding prisoners during a forced evacuation that claimed the lives of seventy people.

Unbelievably, jurors debated whether enough evidence could be brought against him to bring charges.

In December 2021, Berger was freed due to insufficient evidence.

Outside the courthouse, his lawyer announced to the press, "Nothing has changed, except my client was wrongfully charged and found not guilty." The legal audacity is beyond comprehension!

I learned from my Israeli contact that Berger was born in the tiny northern town of Bargen in 1925. At the age of eighteen, he enlisted in the German Navy. Two years later, he was transferred to guard prisoners in Meppen and served as overseer from January 28th, 1945, to April 4th, 1945. Soviet liberators discovered Berger's registration ID when they entered the prison.

Berger's taste of freedom lasted for five days. He died from a heart attack at his sister's home. His sister was also a Meppen guard. Interestingly, a mountain of ice blocks was found scattered at the bottom of his bed without any explanation!

HELMUT OBERLANDER:

Helmut was a Nazi death squad member responsible for the murder of one million civilians in Russia during the German occupation. He waded through the Canadian justice system from 1995 until his citizenship was revoked for a second time on May 24th, 2007.

In November of 2009, Oberlander's lawyer filed a motion to the Immigration and Refugee Board of Canada to dismiss his client's case on the grounds that his citizenship was never expunged, and immigration authorities lacked the jurisdiction to issue another deportation order.

The plea was refuted, "The case will proceed to an admissibility hearing to determine whether Oberlander is inadmissible and should be removed from Canada," a government spokesperson stated. "The case will be scheduled in due course."

From my research, I learned Helmut Oberlander was Ukrainian. He became a German citizen during the Second World War and arrived in Canada as a refugee in 1955 before becoming a citizen in 1960.

The federal government first began to investigate expelling Oberlander in 1995. Oberlander claimed he was *forced* into joining the Nazis' Einsatzkommando mobile killing squads at the age of seventeen and did not participate in any atrocities. In 2008, he was stripped of his citizenship and continued to fight deportation. In December 2009, Canada's Supreme Court rejected an appeal to restore his citizenship.

A survivor in the U.S. recognized SS Oberlander on the front page of a Canadian magazine and called the Russian consulate. Russia's Investigation Committee demanded Canada's legal files on Oberlander be handed to the committee to check his possible involvement in a massacre at an orphanage in the Soviet town of Yeysk.

In a detailed statement to the Canadian government, the Russian committee stated that several trucks equipped with mobile gas chambers were deployed to the German-occupied Krasnodar region in southern Russia, where two hundred fourteen children and the staff were murdered. The Russian investigator stated German translators and death squad members in the Krasnodar area were captured in 1942 and pointed the finger at Oberlander for ordering the orphanage massacre.

"Oberlander escaped criminal responsibility by hiding from preliminary investigative organs immediately after Germany's capitulation and, it seems, by America's capitulation! We want him deported to us!" a Russian prosecutor demanded.

The child killer lived as free as a bird in Waterloo, Ontario and died there on September 20, 2021.

OSKAR GROENIG

After former SS Unterscharführer (junior squad leader) Oskar Groenig was released from a British prison following World War II, he began an everyday life working at a glass-making factory in Lower Saxony, Germany.

Decades later, Groenig was recognized by a British camp survivor. Of course, he denied the Holocaust ever happened and said he had just heard rumors! Then, during a German press interview, Groenig described the gas chambers and the selection process in detail, which contradicted his lies.

In July 2015, a court in northern Germany convicted Groenig—dubbed, "Bookkeeper of Auschwitz" for his alleged responsibility of keeping track of the money and possessions taken from the prisoners upon their arrival—with three hundred thousand counts of accessory to murder, the ninety-four-year-old was sentenced to *only* four years in prison.

JOHN DEMJANJUK

Born in Ukraine, Demjanjuk immigrated to the United States after World War II. He became a naturalized U.S. citizen in the 1950s, working for many years in a Ford automotive plant in Ohio. Based on eyewitness testimony by Holocaust survivors in Israel, he was identified as the notorious Treblinka extermination camp guard known as "Ivan the Terrible." He was arrested and found guilty to stand trial.

In 2011, after lengthy court proceedings in the United States, Israel, and Germany, a German court convicted him of being an accessory to more than 28,000 counts of murder while serving as a guard at the Sobibór concentration camp in Poland in 1943.

Though Demjanjuk was released pending appeal and died in a German nursing home in 2012, the landmark ruling set an important precedent to charge guards who worked at Nazi death camps as accessories to the murders that occurred there, even when—as in Demjanjuk's case—there was no evidence linking the defendant to a specific crime.

LASZLO CSATARY

Csatary was a Hungarian police officer and Nazi. In 1944, he organized the deportation of more than fifteen thousand Jews to Auschwitz.

A Czechoslovak court convicted Csatary in absentia and sentenced him to death in 1948. He fled to Canada and worked as an art dealer until 1997. After a Canadian Immigration Agency discovered he had lied on his passport application, Csatary's citizenship was revoked. He disappeared for another decade until he was recognized in Budapest in 2012 and arrested. The ninety-eight-year-old Csatary died while awaiting trial under house arrest in 2013.

HANS LIPSCHIS

Following the precedent of Demjanjuk's 2011 conviction, German consultants launched a renewed campaign to bring in some fifty

suspected former guards at Auschwitz-Birkenau, where 1.5 million people were murdered between 1941 and 1945.

The first to face charges in 2013 was ninety-three-year-old Hans Lipschis, who resided in Chicago for three decades after World War II before being deported for lying about his Nazi past. Prosecutors alleged that Lipschis worked as a guard at Auschwitz from 1941 to 1943, even though Hans maintained he was only a cook.

In February 2014, a German court ruled that Lipschis, who suffered from dementia, was mentally unfit to stand trial.

VLADIMIR KATRIUK

A platoon commander in a Ukrainian battalion of elite Nazi Stormtroopers of the SS from 1942 to 1944, Katriuk had immigrated to Canada by the 1950s. In 1999, a Canadian court found that he had lied about his past to enter the country, but the Canadian government later decided not to strip him of his citizenship.

After a new study surfaced alleging that Katriuk was an active participant in a massacre of more than one hundred and fifty people, mostly women and children, in the village of Khatyn in Belorussia (now named Belarus) in 1943, the Simon Wiesenthal Center had placed him second on their annual list of the SWC "Most Wanted" list of former Nazis.

In May 2015, even as Russian powers attempted to extradite

Katriuk to try him for his alleged war crimes, the ninety-three-year-old beekeeper died in Quebec after a long illness.

GERHARD SOMMER

 Of the ever-shrinking number of former Nazis still alive to be prosecuted, Gerhard Sommer currently heads the Simon Wiesenthal Center's (SWC) list of "Most Wanted."

In 1944, Sommer was a soldier in the 16th SS-Panzer Division who helped massacre five hundred and sixty civilians, including one hundred and nineteen children, in the Tuscan town of Sant-Anna di Stazzema. Though an Italian court convicted ten former SS officers, including Sommer, in absentia in 2005, Germany never extradited any of them. In 2012, German prosecutors dropped Sommer's case due to a lack of evidence.

After the case was reopened in 2014, the investigator found the ninety-three-year-old in a nursing home north of Hamburg, suffering from severe dementia, and they deemed him unfit for trial.

ALFRED STARK

A former corporal of the Gebirgsjäger division, the ninety-two-year-old Stark stands accused of ordering the execution of one hundred and seventeen Italian prisoners of war on the Italian-occupied island of Kefalonia, Greece, in 1943.

Germany and Italy broke their alliance in September of that year. In the aftermath of the break, the Germans killed nearly ninety-five hundred officers of the Acqui Division, including the POWs on Kefalonia. In 2012, a military court in Rome sentenced Stark in absentia to life in prison, but Germany also refused to extradite him to face justice. Stark, who died recently, occupied the second position on the SWC "Most Wanted" list.

JOHANN ROBERT RISS

Italian resistance fighters shot *two* German soldiers, wounding them. Then, under SS Riss's command, the Nazis retaliated and shot one hundred and eighty-four civilians, including twenty-seven children in Padule di Fucecchio, Tuscany, in 1944.

In 1945, British sergeant Charles Edmonson took statements from the villagers about the massacre to bring the Nazis responsible to justice. Based on the collected accounts, a military court in Rome sentenced Riss and two other former Nazis to life in prison in absentia for their roles in the killings. The British military court demanded the German government pay fourteen million euros to compensate the victims' relatives.

Naturally, the German government refused to extradite Riss and the shooters or pay a dime to the Italian families. The ninety-two-year-old Riss remained "protected" in a village south of Munich. He died recently and was third on the SWC "Most Wanted" list.

Of course, Riss *denied* the charges against him.

ALGUMANTAS DAILIDE

An officer in the Lithuanian Security Police, sponsored by the Nazis, Dailide, arrested twelve Jews during their attempt to escape from a Jewish ghetto in Vilnius, the capital of Lithuania, in the early 1940s. Dailide immediately handed them over to the Nazis.

The Jews, a rabbi, and their family members were shot and beheaded. Their heads were vertically impaled for display on the ghetto fence. The leader of the Jewish Council pleaded with the Nazis to allow the dead to be buried, but the request was denied. Their mutilated bodies were collected by a local Lithuanian pig farmer.

With false identities, Dailide and his wife entered the United States after the war. He obtained U.S. citizenship and became a licensed realtor in Florida. In May 1990, he was recognized by a ghetto survivor. With his Nazi past revealed, Dailide was stripped of his citizenship and was ordered to leave the U.S.

The "butcher" and his wife settled in the small town of Kirchberg in western Germany.

The Lithuanian government made only half-hearted extradition attempts to bring him to Vilnius to stand trial. In 2008, the Vilnius high court ruled Dailide's health was too poor for him to serve time in prison.

The ninety-eight-year-old died in 2011.

As this book goes to print, I'm elated to learn a steady stream of *new* prosecutions and trials are occurring in German courts. In December 2022, a one-hundred-year-old man was arrested and charged on over thirty-five hundred counts of accessory to murder on allegations he was a high-ranking SS guard in Sachsenhausen concentration camp. A ninety-five-year-old woman, Liesl Mueller, was arrested and charged with ten thousand counts of accessory to murder on the allegation she had served as the secretary to the SS Commandant of Stutthof concentration camp and witnessed his signature for the killings.

If the depravity of Nazism isn't enough to change hate-filled hearts, then think again because a new generation of hate-filled hearts has replaced them. The Canadian Armed Forces released a statement about a soldier with alleged links to a neo-Nazi group. "Master Cpl. Mathews has been relieved of his duties," stated the Department of National Defense spokesperson. "This action was necessary considering the seriousness of the allegations and the risk to unit morale and cohesion."

The RCMP executed a search warrant at Mathew's home in Beausejour, Manitoba, where they seized many firearms. The military stated Mathews had requested for voluntary release from the Canadian Armed Forces, which had been in progress since April 2019.

Major-General Boisneau stated, "It is incumbent on our leaders to know their soldiers, and to take measures when they have acted in a manner that is not aligned with our beliefs and culture of respect for all people. We have taken decisive action and continue to exert full energy in removing those from our ranks who harbor extremist ideologies."

Mathews was released from military detention after only four weeks. He obtained employment as a security guard in a mall but quit after two weeks and was last seen in Dawson City in the Yukon.

The German underground organization *KinderSichererHafen* was abandoned in 1958, when Staff Sergeant Miller and accomplices Novak and Perkins were arrested in the U.S. for trying to fence uncut diamonds and gold ingots. Among the recovered treasure was a priceless Fabergé egg, stolen from the Romanov Winter Palace during the Russian revolution. It was sold to an undercover DIA agent (the Pentagon's intelligence agency) for safe passage to South America.

The disgraced U.S. military soldiers only served two years in the Army Regional Confinement Facility at Fort Carson, Colorado. They remained silent and never spoke about aiding Nazi offspring or other German escapees with fat wallets or disclosed their association with a "real" Polish Count and a Princess in post-war German times.

Miller died from liver failure at age eighty. Novak lived the remainder of his life in a veteran's hospital after being diagnosed with Alzheimer's. The last sighting of the Rosenstasse sentry, Perkins, was in Mexico City twenty years ago.

Afterword

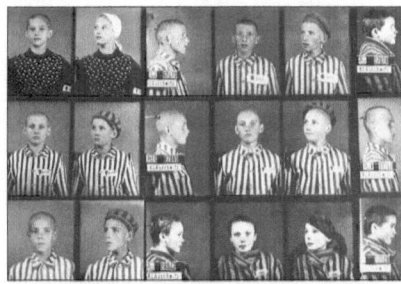

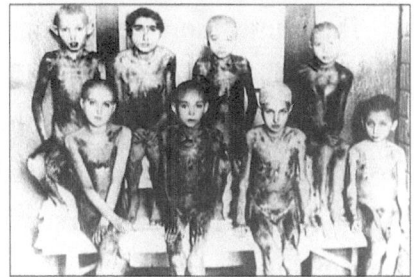

SELECTIONS SOMETIMES TOOK PLACE at the point of departure, often well before people were forced to board the trains, but there were also reports of selections from trains already en route to the camps. In his June 20th, 1942, report, Revier-Leutnant der Schutzpolizei Josef Frischmann, in charge of the guard unit on the train, wrote that "fifty-one Jews capable of work" were removed from the transport at Lublin depot. The train had departed Vienna on June 14th, 1942, ostensibly for Izbica. The remaining prisoners were delivered to their final destination in Sobibór.

The precise number of prisoners who were spared upon arrival in the Sobibór extermination camp is unknown. Still, there were occasional selections for forced labor in other camps and factories, amounting to several thousand people. Many of those selected subsequently perished due to the appalling conditions in the slave-labor details. A number of them were murdered after internal selections following transfers to Majdanek and Auschwitz, where people were also routinely murdered by hanging or shooting for arbitrary offenses.

Thousands of Jews were selected for slave labor. They were all executed in the Lublin district during *Aktion "Erntefest"* (Operation "Harvest Festival").

Thousands more were shot or succumbed to exhaustion while on the death marches in the closing stages of the Nazi regime. However, several Jews at Sobibór ultimately survived beyond the total defeat and unconditional surrender of the Nazis in May 1945.

On August 17th, 1943, a survivor from Sabinov in Slovakia, who has remained anonymous, wrote a report in which he described his selection in Sobibór, together with approximately one hundred men and fifty women, upon arrival.

Luka, a watchmaker, was transported to Sobibór after the violent clearance of deported Slovakian Jews, along with the remaining Polish Jews from the Rejowiec ghetto on August 9th, 1942. He testified to skilled workers, technicians, blacksmiths, and watchmakers being separated upon arrival in Sobibór. He was singled out to repair Nazi watches, clocks, and mantle pieces. Luka further testified to the plumes of smoke visible in the night sky around the Sobibór camp and the stench of burning bodies permeating the air.

One thousand selected from the thirty-four thousand deportees from the Netherlands via Westerbork to Sobibór died between March 2nd and July 20th, 1943.

The last fourteen Nazi trains transporting prisoners from various evacuated camps across Poland with Nazi markings on them were blown up by the Allies. No one survived.

Despite Poland's efforts to continue to bring Nazi murderers to justice, many have died. Those who were discovered were too old to be prosecuted for their role in the Holocaust and other wartime atrocities, the Polish government concluded.

But the Soviets haven't given up that easily. Too many unexplained deaths of elderly Nazis have not made headlines.

And let us not forget, the three great Allied Powers—Great Britain, the United States, and the Soviet Union—who risked their lives to save Europe and other countries from the world domination plans of history's most villainous, insane German. They will always be heroes in my heart, too.

Through DNA testing, I learned Polish-Jewish blood also runs through my Ashkenazi ancestry. I want now to respectfully honor the Polish souls who survived Adolf Hitler's anti-Semitism.

As existing records allow, I have selected the Sobibór death camp in Poland to list those not shot or gassed upon arrival in the appendix.

> **This author's last note**
> Before I kick the bucket, leave this troubled world in a coffin, I hope that one day the people in the world will find genuine empathy in their hearts for the millions of Jews who lost their lives to racism.

Prejudice must cease *now* because the annihilation of humans could happen anywhere, anytime, all over again!

-The End-

Appendix

THE SOBIBÓR CAMP ESCAPE

On October 14th, 1943, members of the Sobibór camp's underground resistance succeeded in covertly killing eleven German SS officers and several guards. Of the six hundred inmates in the camp, roughly three hundred escaped, although all but fifty to seventy were later re-captured and killed. After the escape, SS Chief Heinrich Himmler ordered the death camp closed. It was dismantled, bulldozed under the earth, and planted over with trees to cover it up.

The details of the resistance and final escape began with a train-load of Polish Jews who arrived for processing at Sobibór camp. The

German Commandant immediately gave them a welcome speech, assuring the new arrivals that the place they have just arrived was a work camp. Other SS officers selected a small number who had trade skills (such as goldsmiths, seamstresses, shoemakers, and tailors). The remaining prisoners were sent to a different part of the camp from which a pillar of smoke rose day and night. After some time, the new prisoners realized that Sobibór was actually a death camp; it was a devastating realization.

A small number of prisoners that were kept alive in the other parts of the camp were charged with sorting belongings taken from those who were murdered, and then repaired the shoes, recycled the clothing, and melted down any silver or gold to make jewelry for the SS officers. Despite their usefulness, these surviving prisoners' existence was very precarious, since beatings and murders would occur at any time.

The leader of the prisoners, Leon Feldhendler, realized that when the trains eventually stopped coming, the camp would outlive its usefulness and all the remaining Jews would be murdered. He devised a plan for every prisoner to escape by luring the officers and guards into the prisoners' barracks and work huts, one by one, and killing them as quietly as possible. The plan was that once the Germans were dead, the prisoners would assemble into columns and simply march out of the camp as if they had been ordered to, and it was hoped that the remaining guards, not knowing what was going on, and with no Germans left alive to give orders or raise the alarm, would not interfere.

During the planning of the escape, a new group of prisoners arrived: Russian Jews who were soldiers with the Soviet army. Their leader, Sasha Pechersky, and his men willingly joined the revolt and their military skills proved invaluable.

On October 14th, 1943, the plan went into action. One by one, SS officers and NCOs were lured into traps set by groups of prisoners armed with knives and clubs. Eleven Germans were killed, but one officer, Karl Frenzel, unwittingly evaded his killers, discovered the corpse of one of his colleagues, and raised an alarm. At that point, the prisoners had assembled on the parade ground. They soon realized that their plan had been compromised, yet Pechersky and Feldhendler urged the prisoners to continue their revolt and flee the camp. Most of the six hundred prisoners stampeded the perimeter fences. Some of the Jews used captured rifles to shoot their way through the guards. Other guards opened fire with machine guns from observation towers, cutting many of the fleeing prisoners down, and many would-be escapees were killed on the minefield surrounding the camp. But over three hundred Jews reached the forest and escaped. It would turn out to be the largest escape of the war.

Sobibór Concentration Camp
Listed below are a fraction of the
people who suffered in Sobibór.

Name	Birth	Death	Age of Death	From	Eth-nicity	Arrived	Other Name/ Spelling
Schlom Alster	12/1/ 1908	? after 1926	-	Chelm, Poland	Jewish	11/ 1942	-
Notes: Worked as a carpenter and served on the *Bahnhofskommando*. Emigrated to Rehovot, Israel.							
Moshe Bachir	7/19/ 1927	2002	75	Plock, Poland	Jewish	5/24/ 1942 from Zamosc	Changed to Moshe Szklare
Notes: Worked in provisions barracks, in the *Bahnhofskommando*, and as a barber. He immigrated to Israel, where he wrote a testimony for the Ghetto Fighter's House and testified at the Eichmann Trial.							
Antonius Bardach	5/16/ 1909	1995	50	Lemberg, Poland	Jewish	3/30/ 1943 from Drancy, France.	-
Notes: Later settled in Belgium.							
Philip Bialowitz	12/ 25/ 1925	8/6/ 2012	90	Izbica, Poland	Jewish	1/1943 or 4/28/ 1943	Surname also "Białowicz". First name sometimes "Fishel" or "Fiszel."
Notes: Brother of Symcha Bialowitz. Worked in sorting barracks and provisions barracks, and as a barber and Bahnhofskommando member. Immigrated to the US and co-authored the memoir *A Promise At Sobibór* with his son Joseph.							
Symcha Bialowitz	12/6/ 1912	2/ 2012	101	Izbica, Poland	Jewish	4/28/ 1943	-
Notes: Brother of Philip Bialowitz. Worked in the Waldkommando and in the camp pharmacy. Participated in the revolt at Sobinor. Married a survivor from Zamość and settled in Israel.							
Jakob Biskubicz	3/17/ 1926	3/ 2002	75 or 76	Hru-bieszów, Poland	Jewish	5/1942 or 6/194	-
Notes: Was unloading a truck full of vodka for SS Erich Bauer when the revolt began. Hid in Camp IV and escaped that night. Joined the Parczew partisans and later settled in Israel, where he gave testimony in the Eichmann trial.							

Name	Birth	Death	Age of Death	From	Ethnicity	Arrived	Other Name/ Spelling
Thomas "Toivi" Blat	4/15/ 1927	10/31/ 2015	88	Izbica, Poland	Jewish	4/23/ 1943	Name also rendered as Toivi Blatt and Tomasz Blatt. Used the Polish name Bolesław Stankiewicz for a short period after the war.
Notes: Escaped over the fence in the Vorlager. Witness in post-war trials. Wrote Sobibór memoir *From the Ashes of Sobibór* and history Sobibór: The Forgotten Revolt. Worked as an assistant to Richard Rashke in writing *Escape from Sobibór* and acted as a consultant on the movie adaptation. Interviewed Karl Frenzel.							
Herschel Cuckierman	4/15/ 1893	7/15/ 1979	86	Kurów, Poland	Jewish	5/ 1942	Hershel Zuckerman, including in *Escape from Sobibór*.
Notes: Father of Josef Cukierman. Arrived with his wife and daughters who were gassed upon arrival. Worked as a gardener before the war, but told the SS that he was a cook so he could be selected for work. Had an excellent memory which helped him identify SS officers in postwar trials.							
Josef Cuckierman	5/26/ 1930	6/15/ 1963	33	Kurów, Poland	Jewish	5/ 1942 from Opole Lubelski Ghetto	Joseph Zuckerman
Notes: Son of Herschel Cukierman. Worked with his father in the kitchens. After the war, lived in Stuttgart before moving to Karlsruhe.							
Josef Duniec	12/21/ 1912	12/1/ 1965	52	Równo, Poland	Jewish	3/25/ 1943	-
Notes: Sent to Sobibór from Drancy, having immigrated to France in 1932 in order to study chemistry. Moved to Israel after the war, where he died of a heart attack the day before he was expected to testify at the Sobibór trial.							
Leon Cymiel	2/20/ 1924	1997	73	Chełm, Poland	Jewish	Spring/ 1943	Leon Szymiel
Notes: Stayed in Poland after the war. Testimony available at ushmm.org							

Name	Birth	Death	Age of Death	From	Eth-nicity	Arrived	Other Name/ Spelling
Chaim Engel	1/10/ 1916	7/4/ 2003	87	Brudzew, Poland	Jewish	11/6/ 1942	-
Notes: Killed SS-Oberscharführer Rudolf Beckmann during the revolt. Escaped with Selma Wijnberg-Engel and survived the rest of the war in hiding. The two later married and moved to Connecticut.							
Selma Engel-Wijnberg	5/15/ 1922	12/4/ 2018	96	Zwolle, Nether-lands	Jewish	4/9/ 1943	Saartje Engel, Selma Engel, Saartje Wijnberg, Selma Wijnberg, Selma Wynberg
Notes: Worked in the sorting barracks and Waldkommando. Escaped with Chaim Engel during the revolt. They survived the rest of the war in hiding together. The two later married.							
Leon Feldhendler	1910	4/6/ 1945	34 or 35	Żółkiewka, Poland	Jewish	Early 1943	First name sometimes Lejb or Lej-ba. Surname sometimes Feldhend-ler.
Notes: One of the co-organizers of the revolt. After fighting as a partisan, made his way back to Lublin, where he was murdered under disputed circumstances.							
Dov Freiberg	5/15/ 1927	2008	80	Warsaw, Poland	Jewish	5/15/ 1942	First name also Berek.
Note: Deported to Sobibór from Krasnystaw, where he had been sent from the Warsaw Ghetto. After the revolt, hid with Simeon Rosenfeld after the revolt. Gave testimony at the Eichmann trial. Author of memoir, "*To Survive Sobibór.*"							
Catharina Gokkes	9/1/ 1923	6/22/ 1944	21	Nether-lands	Jewish	4/9/ 1943	First name also Kitty, Katty
Notes: Was shot in the leg by Karl Frenzel during the escape. Joined Parczew partisans but was killed before liberation.							
Mordechai Goldfarb	3/15/ 1920	6/8/ 1984	64	Piaski, Poland	Jewish	11/6/ 1942	First name also Moshe.
Notes: Worked as a sign painter in Sobibór. Joined the Parczew partisans after the revolt and later settled in Israel.							

Name	Birth	Death	Age of Death	From	Eth-nicity	Arrived	Other Name/ Spelling
Josef Herszman	1925	2005	80	Żółkiewka, Poland	Jewish	1942	-
Notes: Worked in the sorting barracks. Later moved to Israel. Gave testimony at war crime trials.							
Moshe Hochman	3/15/ 1935	6/8/ 1993	58	Żółkiewka, Poland	Jewish	4/ 1942	-
Notes: Worked as the foreman in the tailor's shop. He hid Niemann's body after getting him to try on a new jacket. Escaped from Sobibór October 14, 1943 and hid in farmer's barn in Papierzyn until liberation by the Red Army in 1944.							
Zyndel Honigman	4/10/ 1910	7/ 1989	79	Kiev, Ukraine	Jewish	11/ 1942	-
Notes: Escaped from the camp twice. Taken to Sobibór in November 1942 from Gorzków, near Izbica, he escaped by crawling under a fence. Was captured and sent back in April 1943, where he worked in the kitchen and in the forest brigade. Escaped from the forest brigade and joined the Parczew partisans.							
Abram Kohn	7/25/ 1910	1/19/ 1986	75	Łódź, Poland	Jewish	5/ 1942	Abraham Kohn
Notes: Worked in the kitchens, the sorting barracks, and forest brigade. Later moved to Australia.							
Josef Kopp	1944 or 1945	-	-	Biłgoraj, Poland	Jewish	-	-
Notes: Allegedly escaped by killing a Ukrainian guard on July 27, 1943 while on duties outside of the camp in the nearby village of Zlobek; did not survive World War II.							
Chaim Korenfeld	5/15/ 1923	8/13/ 2002	79	Izbica, Poland	Jewish	-	-
Notes: Worked in the forest brigade. Unclear whether he escaped with the forest brigade or in the ultimate revolt. Later moved to Italy, then Brazil.							
Chaim Powroznik	-	-	-	Polish	Jewish	-	-
Notes: Testimony available.							
Chaim Leist	-	10/ 2005	-	Żółkiewka, Poland	Jewish	4/23/ 1943	Lajst
Notes: Little is known about him except that he worked in Sobibór as a gardener and that he settled in Israel after the war.							

Name	Birth	Death	Age of Death	From	Eth-nicity	Arrived	Other Name/ Spelling
Samuel Lerer	10/1/ 1922	3/3/ 2016	93	Żółkiewka, Poland	Jewish	5/ 1942	Szmuel
Notes: Worked in the stables and later in the Erbhof, taking care of chickens and ducks. During the revolt, he escaped with Ester Raab and hid with a friend of her family. In 1949, he and Raab encountered Sobibór "gasmeister" Hermann Erich Bauer in Berlin, leading to his arrest. Moved to New York City and became a cab driver.							
Yehuda Lerner	7/22/ 1926	2007	81	Warsaw, Poland	Jewish	9/ 1943	Jehuda Lerner, sometimes went by "Leon"
Notes: He and Arkady Wajspapir killed two guards, SS-Oberscharführer Siegfried Graetschus and Volksdeutscher Ivan Klatt during the revolt. Joined the Parczew partisans and later settled in Israel. Interviewed extensively in the documentary *Sobibór*,							
Ada Lichtman	1/1 1915	1993	78	Jarosław, Poland	Jewish	6/ 1943	Eda Fisher, Eda Lichtman
Notes: Worked in the laundry and was regarded as a "surrogate mother" to other prisoners. Joined the Parczew partisans. Moved to Israel, married another survivor, and gave testimony at the Eichmann trial.							
Jitschak Lichtman	12/10/ 1908	1992	83 or 84	Żółkiewka, Poland	Jewish	5/15/ 1942	Itzhak Lichtman
Notes: Joined the Parczew partisans. Married Ada Lichtman (Fischer).							
Yefim Litwinowski	5/25/ 1921	1/29/ 1993	71	Soviet	Jewish	9/22/ 1943	
Notes: Red Army soldier in Pechersky's group. Was a participant of the uprising and subsequently rejoined the Red Army.							
Abraham Margulies	1/25/ 1921	1984	62 or 63	Żyrardów, Poland	Jewish	Late May 1942	-
Notes: Worked in the Bahnhofskommando, as well as kitchens and sorting barracks. Joined the Parczew partisans with Hella Weiss, and then immigrated to Israel, where he worked as a printer.							
Chaskiel Menche	1/7/ 1910	1984	73 or 74	Koło, Poland	Jewish	June 1942	-
Notes: Worked in sorting barracks, then as a shoe shiner and hat maker. Immigrated to Australia after the war.							
Mojzesz Merenstein	1/15/ 1899	12/ 1985	86	Polish	Jewish	-	-
Notes: Worked with Feldhendler to plan revolt.							

Appendix

Name	Birth	Death	Age of Death	From	Eth-nicity	Arrived	Other Name/ Spelling
Zelda Metz	5/1/ 1925	1980	54 or 55	Siedliszc-ze, Poland	Jewish	12/20/ 1942	
Notes: Cousin of Regina Zielinski. Worked in the laundry. Went to Lviv after the escape, where pretended to be Catholic and worked as a nanny. Immigrated to the US in 1946.							
Alexander Pechersk	2/22/ 1909	1/19 1990	80	Ukrainian	Jewish	9/22/ 1943	Sasha Pechersky
Notes: Chief organizer and leader of the revolt. Red Army soldier who joined the Parczew partisans.							
Nachum Platnitzky	1913	-	-	Belorus-sian	Jewish	-	Surname also listed as Plotnikow
Notes: Lived in Pinsk, Belarus after the war.							
Shlomo Podchlebnik	2/15/ 1907	2/ 1973	66	Polish	Jewish	4/28/ 1943	-
Notes: He and Josef Kopp escaped by killing a Ukrainian guard on July 27, 1943 while on duties outside of the camp in the nearby village of Zlobek.							
Gertrud Poppert–Schönborn	6/29/ 1914	11/ 1943	29	German	Jewish	-	Luka, Loeka
Notes: Identified by Jules Schelvis as likely identity of "Luka." Presumed dead following mass escape.							
Esther Raab	6/11/ 1922	4/13/ 2015	92	Polish	Jewish	12/20/ 1942	Née Terner, she became known as Esther Raab after her 1946 marriage to Irving Raab.
Notes: She identified gas chamber executioner Erich Bauer after the war in Berlin, leading to his arrest.							
Simjon Rosenfeld	10/10/ 1922	6/3/ 2019	96	Soviet	Jewish	9/22/ 1943	Semion Rosenfeld, Semyon Rosenfeld, Semion Rozenfeld.
Notes: Red Army soldier under Pechersky's command. Was separated from the other Russians and survived in hiding. Rejoined the Red Army and fought in the Battle of Berlin, where he carved the name "Sobibór" into the wall of the Reich Chancellery. Returned to the Soviet Union, but eventually immigrated to Israel.							

Name	Birth	Death	Age of Death	From	Ethnicity	Arrived	Other Name/ Spelling
Ajzik Rotenberg	1925	1994	69	Polish	Jewish	5/12/1943	-
Notes: Joined the Parczew partisans. Murdered in 1994 in Israel by two Palestinian terrorists.							
Joseph Serchuk	1919	11/6/1993	74	Polish	Jewish	-	Surname also spelled Serczuk.
Notes: Joseph and his brother David escaped the day after arriving when on forest duty.							
David Serchuk	1948	-	-	Polish	Jewish	-	Surname also spelled Serczuk.
Notes: David and his brother Joseph escaped the day after arriving when on forest duty.							
Alexander Shubayev	1945	-	-	Belorussian	Jewish	-	Often referred to in accounts by the nickname "Kali Mali."
Notes: Red Army soldier. Killed deputy commandant Johann Niemann with an axe to his head. Joined the Parczew partisans after escaping the camp, but was killed.							
Ursula Stern	8/28/1926	1985	58 or 59	German	Jewish	4/9/1943	Changed her name to Ilana Safran after the war.
Notes: Joined the Parczew partisans. Witness at Hagen trial.							
Stanisław Szmajzner	3/13/1927	3/3/1989	61	Polish	Jewish	5/12/1942	Shlomo Smajzner, Szlomo Smajzner
Notes: Goldsmith and machinist in Sobibór made the knives used in the revolt, and also stole rifles. Shot a guard in one of the guard towers. After escaping, joined the Parczew partisans and eventually immigrated to Brazil where he worked as an executive in a paper factory. Testified against Franz Stangl, and identified Gustav Wagner at a police station in Goiana.							
Boris Tabarinsky	1917	-	-	Belorussian	Jewish	9/22/1943	-
Notes: Job was to cut the barbed wire fence as a backup exit.							

Name	Birth	Death	Age of Death	From	Eth-nicity	Arrived	Other Name/ Spelling
Kurt Ticho	4/11/ 1914	6/8/ 2009	95	Czech	Jewish	11/6/ 1942	Kurt Thomas
Notes: Worked as a nurse in Sobibór. After the war, he brought charges against SS officers Hubert Gomerski and Johann Klier.							
Israel Trager	3/5/ 1906	9/1/ 1969	63	Polish	Jewish	3/1943	Shrulke
Notes: Camp bricklayer and Bahnhofkommando train station worker. After the war moved to Israel.							
Aleksej Waizen	5/30/ 1922	1/14/ 2015	92	Ukrainian	Jewish	Autumn 1943	-
Notes: Worked in sorting room.							
Arkady Wajspapir	1921	1/11/ 2018	96	Russian	Jewish	9/22/ 1943	-
Notes: He and Jehuda Lerner killed two guards with axe blows, SS-Oberscharführer Siegfried Graetschus and Volksdeutscher Ivan Klatt, during the revolt. A Red Army soldier, he joined the Parczew partisans.							
Abraham Wang	1/2/ 1921	1978	57	Polish	Jewish	4/23/ 1943	-
Notes: Escaped on July 27, 1943, along with four other prisoners.							
Hella Weiss	11/25/ 1925	12/ 1988	63	Polish	Jewish	12/20/ 1942	-
Notes: Joined the Parczew partisans; later joined the Red Army.[5]							
Kalmen Wewryk	6/25/ 1906	-	-	Polish	Jewish	11/ 1942	-
Notes: Joined partisans after the revolt.							
Regina Zielinski	9/2/ 1924	9/ 2014	-	Polish	Jewish	12/20/ 1942	Née Feldman
Notes: Worked as a knitter in Sobibór. After the war, married a Polish Catholic army officer and settled in Australia. Her son wrote a book *"Conversations with Regina"* which recounts her experiences, as well as his own later-in-life discovery of his Jewish origins and his mother's status as a Holocaust survivor.							
Meier Ziss	11/15/ 1927	2003	-	Żółkiewka, Poland	Jewish	5/ 1942	-
Notes: Arrived on one of the first transports. After the war, he moved to Venezuela and then to Israel, where he worked in electronics.							

Estimated Number of Jews Killed in the Final Solution

The two most reliable sources for Holocaust data are the U.S. Holocaust Memorial Museum and Yad Vashem. Though this is the best information available, it is based on estimates and cannot riot take into the unknown number of victims whose bodies were never recovered or for whom there were no records. The Nazis kept detailed records of the people who passed through the camps; nevertheless, we do not know how many Jews may still have been unaccounted for in the many places where they were murdered. In addition, as the Allies began to close in on Germany, the Nazis began to destroy their records.

We also don't know the precise number of Jews in any of these areas. The population data ranges from 1937-1941 so, for example, the countries where the figures came from 1937 may not accurately reflect the number of Jews at the time the war began. Though the two institutions have different estimates, if you average the total number of Jews each says were murdered, the result is the commonly used figure of six million.

USHMM

County	Pre-War Jewish Population*	Number of Jews Killed	% of Jewish Population Murdered
Albania	200		
Austria	185,026	65,459	35%
Belgium	90,000	24,387	27%
Bulgaria	550,000		
Czechoslovakia	354,000	260,000	73%
Bohemia & Moravia	117,551	77,297	66%
Slovenia	90,000	75,000	83%
Sudeterland	2,363	360	15%
Denmark	7,500	52-116	2%
Estonia	4,500	963	21%
Finland			
France	300,000-330,000	72,900-74,000	22%
Germany	237,723	165,200	69%
Great Britain - Channel Islands			
Greece	71,611	58,800-65,000	91%
Thrace		4,221	
Hungary**	825,007	564,507	68%
Italy	58,412	7,858	13%
Latvia	93,479	70,000	75%
Lithuania	153,000	130,000	85%
Luxembourg	3,500-5,000	1,200	24%

USHMM (Continued)

County	Pre-War Jewish Population*	Number of Jews Killed	% of Jewish Population Murdered
Netherlands	140,245	102,000	73%
Norway	1,800	758	42%
Poland	3,350,000	2,770,000-3,000,000	90%
Romania	756,930	211,214-260,000	34%
Bessarabia and Bukovina	314,000	103,919-130,000	
Transylvania		90,295	
Soviet Union	3,028,538	1,340,000	44%
Yugoslavia	82,242	67,228	82%
Slovenia	1,500	1,300	87%
Serbia with Banat and Sandžak	17,200	15,060	88%
Macedonia	7,762	6,982	90%
Pirot, Serbia		140	
Albanian-annexed Kosovo	550	210	38%
Croatia with Dalmatia and Bosnia-Herzegovina	39,400	30,148	77%
Montenegro	30	28	93%
Backa and Baranja	16,000	13,500	84%
TOTAL	10,431,569	6,636,235	63%

Appendix

Yad Vashem

County	Pre-War Jewish Population*	Number of Jews Killed	% of Jewish Population Murdered
Albania			
Austria	185,000	50,000	27%
Belgium	65,700	28,900	44%
Bulgaria	50,000		
Czechoslovakia			
Bohemia & Moravia	118,310	78,150	75%
Slovenia	88,950	68,000-71,000	75%
Sudeterland			
Denmark	7,800	60	1%
Estonia	4,500	963	21%
Finland	2,000	7	
France	350,000	77,320	22%
Germany	566,000	134,500	24%
Great Britain - Channel Islands			
Greece	77,380	60,000-67,000	87%
Thrace			
Hungary**	825,000	550,000-569,000	69%
Italy	44,500	7,680	17%
Latvia	91,500	70,000-71,500	
Lithuania	168,000	140,000-143,000	
Luxembourg	3,500	1,950	20%
Netherlands	1,700	102,000	73%
Norway	1,800	762	50%
Poland	3,300,000	290,000-3,000,000	90%
Romania	609,000	271,000-287,000	50%
Bessarabia and Bukovina			
Transylvania			

Yad Vashem (Continued)

County	Pre-War Jewish Population*	Number of Jews Killed	% of Jewish Population Murdered
Soviet Union	3,020,000	1,000,000-1,100,00	33-36%
Yugoslavia	78,000	56,200	60%
Slovenia			
Serbia with Banat and Sandžak			
Macedonia			
Pirot, Serbia			
Albanian-annexed Kosovo			
Croatia with Dalmatia and Bosnia-Herzegovina			
Montenegro			
Backa and Baranja			
TOTAL	9,798,840	5,846,032	60%

Prewar estimates for the latest year available (1937-1941). The two institutions also divided the occupied areas slightly differently.

*When a range of figures appears, the higher numbers wereuse to estimated percentages.
**Borders of 1941

Sources: U.S. Holocaust Memorial Museum.

Mourner's Kaddish

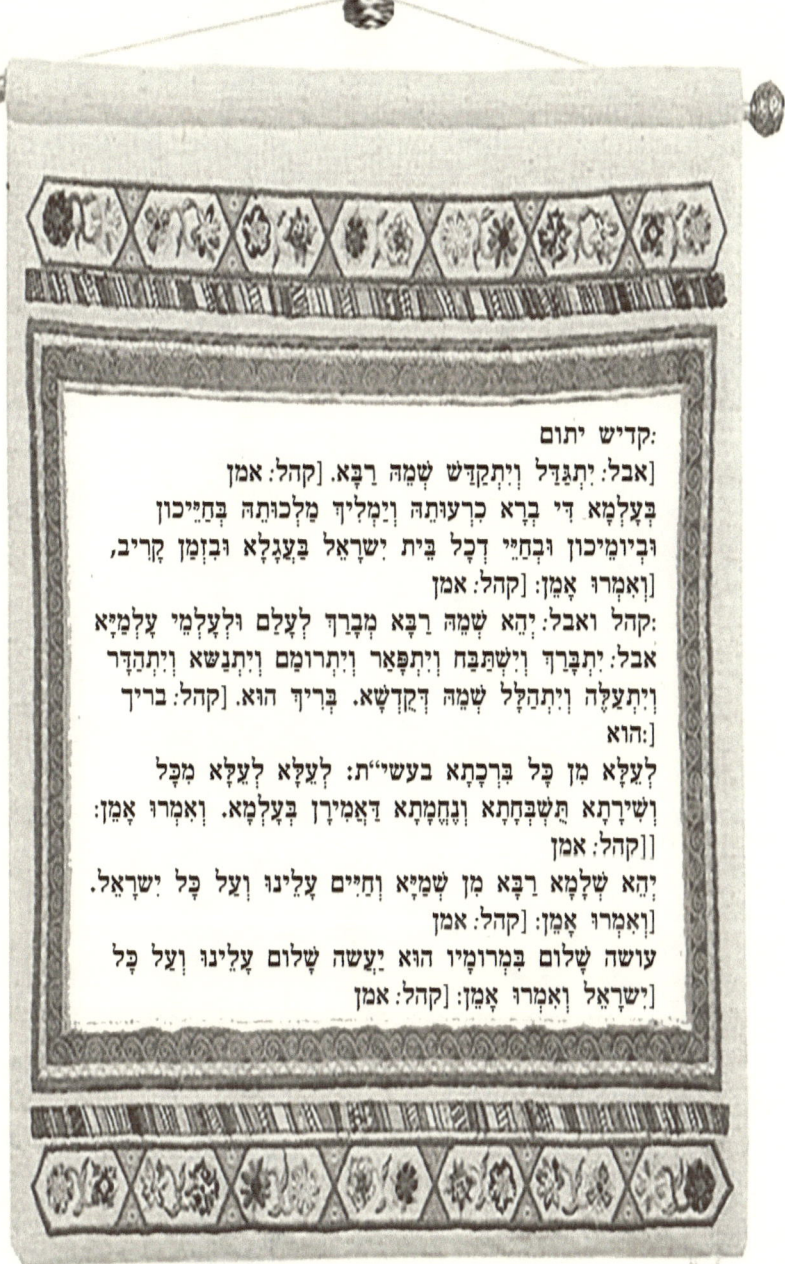

קַדִּישׁ יָתוֹם:

[אבל: יִתְגַּדַּל וְיִתְקַדַּשׁ שְׁמֵהּ רַבָּא. [קהל: אמן

בְּעָלְמָא דִּי בְרָא כִרְעוּתֵהּ וְיַמְלִיךְ מַלְכוּתֵהּ בְּחַיֵּיכוֹן

וּבְיוֹמֵיכוֹן וּבְחַיֵּי דְכָל בֵּית יִשְׂרָאֵל בַּעֲגָלָא וּבִזְמַן קָרִיב,

[וְאָמְרוּ אָמֵן: [קהל: אמן

קהל ואבל: יְהֵא שְׁמֵהּ רַבָּא מְבָרַךְ לְעָלַם וּלְעָלְמֵי עָלְמַיָּא:

אבל: יִתְבָּרַךְ וְיִשְׁתַּבַּח וְיִתְפָּאַר וְיִתְרוֹמַם וְיִתְנַשֵּׂא וְיִתְהַדָּר

וְיִתְעַלֶּה וְיִתְהַלָּל שְׁמֵהּ דְּקֻדְשָׁא. בְּרִיךְ הוּא. [קהל: בריך

[הוא:

לְעֵלָּא מִן כָּל בִּרְכָתָא בעשי"ת: לְעֵלָּא לְעֵלָּא מִכָּל

וְשִׁירָתָא תֻּשְׁבְּחָתָא וְנֶחֱמָתָא דַּאֲמִירָן בְּעָלְמָא. וְאִמְרוּ אָמֵן:

[[קהל: אמן

יְהֵא שְׁלָמָא רַבָּא מִן שְׁמַיָּא וְחַיִּים עָלֵינוּ וְעַל כָּל יִשְׂרָאֵל.

[וְאָמְרוּ אָמֵן: [קהל: אמן

עוֹשֶׂה שָׁלוֹם בִּמְרוֹמָיו הוּא יַעֲשֶׂה שָׁלוֹם עָלֵינוּ וְעַל כָּל

[יִשְׂרָאֵל וְאִמְרוּ אָמֵן: [קהל: אמן

About the Author

Lucia Mann is a respected humanitarian, activist, and author based in British Columbia, Canada. She was born in British colonial South Africa after World War II. After retiring from a successful career in freelance journalism, Ms. Mann dedicated herself to giving voice to the silenced and oppressed. Her dedication to uncovering hidden stories of suffering and injustice has garnered international acclaim. *Hidden Behind the Mist of Arrow Lakes* is Mann's ninth book and serves as a poignant exploration of a dark period in history that demands to be remembered.

BOOKS BY LUCIA MANN

WEEPING GOES UNHEARD
Sacred Tears for Indigenous Victims of Racial Genocide
   NYC Big Book Award 2021

THE LITTLE BREADWINNER
War and Survival in the Salvador Heartland
   Literary Titan Award Winner, Independent Press Award, Royal
   Dragonfly Award, Book Excellence Literary Award

ENDLESS INCARNATION SORROWS

A Spiritual Odyssey of Mortal Imprints on Earth
Literary Titan Award Winner, Book Excellence
Literary Award Winner

ADDICTED TO HATE

Silence Can Be So Loud
Literary Titan Award Winner, Wishing Well Book Award,
Book Excellence Award Winner, Independent Press Award,
Ippy Book Award Winner

THE AFRICAN BOOK SERIES

RENTED SILENCE

To Give Voice You Must First Survive
A CBC Book Award Winner

THE SICILIAN VEIL OF SHAME

Remembrance Is a Bitter Fruit

AFRICA'S UNFINISHED SYMPHONY
Indie Excellence Award Winner

A VEIL OF BLOOD HANGS OVER AFRICA

The Birthplace of Slavery

Visit www.LuciaMann.com for more information

www.ingramcontent.com/pod-product-compliance
Lightning Source LLC
Chambersburg PA
CBHW032235010726
47494CB00002B/498

* 9 7 8 0 9 8 5 6 0 3 9 7 7 *